Summer
of
Second Chances

PAT NICHOLS

Summer of Second Chances by Pat Nichols
Published by Armchair Press
ISBN: 979-8-9912411-3-7
Copyright © 2025 by Pat Nichols
Cover Design by Elaina Lee
Edited by Sherri Stewart

Available in print from your local bookstore or online.
For more information on this book or the author visit:
https://patnicholsauthor.blog
Printed in the United States of America
Summer of Second Chances is a work of fiction. Names, characters, and incidents are all products of the author's imagination or are used for fictional purposes. Any mentioned brand names, places, and trademarks remain the property of their respective owners, bear no association with the author or publisher, and are used for fictional purposes only.
Library of Congress Cataloging-in Publication Data
Nichols, Pat.
Summer of Second Chances / Pat Nichols

All rights reserved. No portion of this book may be reproduced in any form, stored in a retrieval system, or transmitted in any form by any means—electronic, photocopy, recording, or otherwise—without written permission from the publisher or author, except as permitted by U.S. copyright law.

Books by

Pat Nichols

Blue Ridge Series

Blizzard at Blue Ridge Inn
The Inheritance
The Wedding
Christmas at Hilltop Inn
The Promise
Summer of Second Chances
Whispers of Hope

Willow Falls Series

The Secret of Willow Inn
Trouble in Willow Falls
Starstruck in Willow Falls
Bridges, Books, and Bones

Butler Family LegacySeries

Big Secrets, Little Lies
Truth and Forgiveness
New Beginnings

Dedicated to my dear friend and member of my author team, Mary Tucker Fouraker, who is reading in heaven now. One day we will meet again.

Chapter 1

From the front passenger seat beside Chris, Wendy Armstrong stared unseeing at the passing scenery. She stroked the curved row of leaf-shaped diamonds encircling the pale blue stone on the ring Chris claimed matched her eyes. Her fingers glided down her right hand to the aquamarine and diamond tennis bracelet he had given her yesterday during a romantic evening at Black Sheep. The same restaurant where she and Chris had their first dinner together, four months before they exchanged wedding vows in Hilltop Inn's gazebo. That night she never could have imagined traveling to Nashville the day after celebrating their first anniversary. Yet here they were, minutes from their destination.

Chris glanced at Wendy. "You've barely spoken a word since we left Blue Ridge."

Wendy released a heavy sigh. "Kayla believes our mother can't show love she doesn't feel."

"Your half-sister is a dramatic fifteen-year-old—"

"Who has lived with Cynthia her entire life."

"I'm surprised you're still referring to your mother by her first name, especially after she told you she loved you that night at Gilmore's bar."

"She also claimed God is giving her time to become acquainted with the only grandchild she'll ever have the opportunity to love. *Her* grandchild, Chris. Not me, the daughter she abandoned nineteen years ago."

"Are you making an assumption based on who your mother was before she came back into your life?"

"Maybe. I don't know."

Chris slowed then turned into her mother's upscale neighborhood.

Wendy gripped the dashboard. "Stop!"

He pulled to the curb then shifted into park "You're having second thoughts about this visit, aren't you?"

"I've called her twice and left messages since that night at Gilmore's. She didn't respond to either."

"Your mother's dealing with a lot."

Wendy peered out the side window. A middle-aged woman walking her dog along the sidewalk smiled while passing by their car. Was she one of Cynthia's neighbors? "You do realize it was my sister who invited us to come here."

"On behalf of her parents."

"So she claimed." Wendy turned away from the window. "What if my mother told me she loves me from guilt, not based on her true feelings?"

"Does the reason matter?" Chris reached across the console and brushed a lock of blonde hair away from Wendy's cheek. "When she discovers what an amazing woman you are, she'll fall in love with you."

"You're trying to cheer me up, aren't you?"

"Yup." His smile reached all the way to his expressive brown eyes. "Am I succeeding?"

"The jury's still out." Wendy glanced over her shoulder at their son's rear-facing car seat. "I think our little guy's asleep."

Chris pressed his hand on Wendy's belly. "One of these days, we'll need to give our little gal a name."

"Choosing the perfect name requires careful consideration. Besides, we didn't name our son until the last minute." Wendy placed her hand over Chris's. "Then we named him Ryan Christopher to honor you."

"Our daughter's middle name could be Wendy."

Wendy's brow scrunched. "Wonder why Cynthia didn't give me a middle name?"

"You should ask her. For now, do you want to go back home, or are you ready for our adventure?"

Wendy blew out a long stream of air. "I promised Kayla we'd show up."

"All right, then." Chris shifted into drive and checked his sideview mirror then pulled away from the curb.

Wendy's heart beat faster with each house they drove past. Who would greet them? Her sister? Brent? Her mother? Their destination came into view. Chris turned onto the driveway. Wendy gripped the door handle. "How do you suppose Cynthia's other two children will react to the half-sister they didn't even know existed until a few weeks ago?"

Chris cut the engine. "Only one way to find out."

Breathing deeply to slow her racing pulse, Wendy pushed the door open. She hesitated a moment before stepping onto the concrete. Hot muggy air made it clear summer was days away.

Kayla rushing out the front door and racing across the yard answered at least one question. "I'm glad you're here, sis."

"Me too." Hoping her smile masked her anxiety, Wendy pulled her sister into an embrace.

Chris carried Ryan from the driver's side. "How's everything going?"

Kayla shrugged. "Okay, I guess. Can I carry Ryan inside?"

"Of course." Chris placed his son in his aunt's arms.

"Hey, little guy." Kayla blew a raspberry on Ryan's neck triggering a full-out belly laugh.

Chris grinned. "Your nephew is obviously happy to see you."

"Mom's excited to meet him."

Wendy looped her hand around her husband's muscular arm while they followed Kayla across the sidewalk and into the foyer. Cedarwood and vanilla scents hinted of burning candles. Country music drifted from the back of the house—appropriate for a family whose livelihood depended on Nashville's country music scene.

"Come on in." Kayla motioned them into the formal living room.

The contemporary décor conjured images of the Gulfport condo Wendy had shared with Kurt Peterson—the man she had believed was her first husband until she discovered his real name was Gunter Benson. Grateful her son's biological father was locked away in a Nevada prison, she settled on the white sofa adorned with an array of pink throw pillows.

Kayla lowered onto the piano bench in front of the white baby grand displaying an array of family photos. Not a single one of her oldest daughter. "Mom and Dad are on the way home from her doctor's appointment."

Chris sat beside Wendy. "How's your mom doing?"

"About the same." Kayla propped Ryan on her knee. "She doesn't talk about the C word." A young girl shuffling in stopped beside Kayla. "This is my little sister Riley."

Wendy smiled at the nine-year-old. "Hi."

The child stared at Wendy. "Mommy says you disappeared when you were five."

Disappeared? Wendy's jaw tensed. Was that how Cynthia explained abandoning her first-born child to chase a dream?

Riley sat cross-legged on the floor beside the piano bench. "Why did you run away?"

"Don't be stupid, Riley." A young teenaged boy plodded in from the foyer. "Five-year-old kids don't run away." He plopped onto a chair facing the sofa. "And if they do, their parents find them and bring them home."

"Was Wendy kidnapped by bad guys?"

"You don't get it, do you?" The boy's tone mocked. "Mom didn't want her."

Wendy cringed. Was this normal sibling squabbling or something else?

"Well now." Chris scooted to the edge of the sofa, his smile forced. "You must be Kayla's brother."

"Yeah."

He aimed his fist toward the teenager. "I'm Chris."

"I figured." The boy leaned forward to deliver a fist-bump. "Zachary. Everyone calls me Zach."

"It's a pleasure to meet you and Riley."

"Whatever." Zach's eyes shifted from Chris to Wendy. "Why did Mom throw you away?"

Kayla jerked her head toward her brother, her brows drawn together. "What's wrong with you, asking such a mean question?"

"Don't pretend like you don't want to know."

Chris slid his arm around Wendy's shoulders, his eyes trained on Zach. "Wendy's a guest in your home—"

"It's okay, darling. They deserve an answer." Resisting the urge to blurt the truth about their mother running off with the man who would one day become their father, Wendy focused on a Gilmore family photo. "Cynthia wasn't much older than Kayla when she learned she was pregnant. After I was born, she dropped out of school then did the best she could to take care of me. Working two jobs without a car took a heavy toll." Wendy's eyes met Riley's. "Your mother left me with a neighbor to pursue her lifelong dream to become a professional singer."

Riley's eyes opened wide. "Is my daddy also your daddy?"

At least she could answer that question without flinching. "No, sweetie, he isn't."

Somewhere in the back of the house a door closed, followed by footsteps. Cynthia breezed in, grinning as if returning from a party. "Wendy. Chris. Welcome to our home."

Chris stood. "It's a pleasure to meet you."

"Same here." Cynthia brushed past him with her palms pressed together while Zach bolted from his chair, headed to the foyer, and dashed up the stairs. "I've waited long enough to meet my grandson."

Wendy shot Chris her best 'see what I mean' expression as he lowered beside her.

"What a handsome boy you are." Cynthia lifted their little guy off Kayla's lap, then sat on the piano bench facing away from the keys. Ryan babbled while gripping the pink streak highlighting his grandmother's long blonde hair.

Kayla moved from the bench to the cushion beside Wendy.

After pushing off the floor, Riley sat beside her mother facing the piano, one-fingering a random series of keys.

Cynthia tapped the tip of Ryan's nose. "You favor your daddy."

Wendy pressed her lips tight. No way she'd tell her mother the truth about Ryan's biological father.

Brent Gilmore ambled in. Dark circles under his eyes hinted he'd missed more than a few hours of sleep. "Welcome to our home."

Chris stood, extending his hand. "We're looking forward to becoming better acquainted."

"Likewise." Brent accepted then released his hand. "How was your drive over?"

"Uneventful."

"If you're hungry, we brought deli sandwiches."

Riley's eyes widened. "Did you also bring some cookies?"

Her father smiled. "Your favorite kind."

"Goody." Riley lifted off the piano bench then dashed out of the room.

Cynthia peered over her shoulder. "I'll stay here with my grandson, honey, while you treat our visitors to lunch."

Visitors? Struggling to shrug off another sting of rejection, Wendy stared at the woman holding her child. If Ryan didn't exist, would Cynthia have bothered to reconnect with her? She had twenty-four hours to find the answer.

Chapter 2

After feeding Theo—the abandoned baby Erica Nelson and her daughter Abby had rescued the day he was born—she placed the four-month-old in his swing beside the round dining room table tucked in the corner of the den. Grateful he had slept through the night during her baby-duty shift, she headed to the kitchen to refresh her coffee.

In less than an hour, she and Abby would again enter the courthouse. Erica released a long sigh. Before moving to Blue Ridge, she had never stepped foot inside a courtroom. Now she needed more than ten fingers to count the number of times she'd faced a judge's bench. At least today she wouldn't sit in a jury box or be called to the witness stand.

Erica gripped her mug in both hands as she spun toward the sound of her daughter's wheelchair rolling across the den floor. Months had passed since Jimmy Barkley crashed into Abby's car. How many more would pass before her daughter's spine healed? Erica forced a smile. "Good morning, sweetheart."

Abby maneuvered into the galley kitchen with her golden retriever, Dusty, following close behind. "It will be if the judge denies Sierra's request."

"She is Theo's mother—"

"A good mother doesn't leave her newborn on a doorstep in the middle of winter."

Amanda Smith ambled in and poured coffee into her favorite mug. "Or abandon her five-year-old daughter, dooming her to be raised in a string of foster homes."

Erica scooped dog food into Dusty's bowl. "Speaking of Wendy, how do you suppose her and Chris's second day with Cynthia's family is going?"

"Good question." Amanda stirred sugar and creamer into her coffee. "Have you heard from Wendy?"

"Not a peep."

"Neither have I, which most likely means all is going well...or painfully bad."

Abby pulled a bottle of orange juice from the fridge. "If we're lucky, Sierra will go away and never come back into Theo's life."

Erica set a glass on the counter. "If she disappears, he'll will grow up imagining all sorts of reasons why his mother abandoned him."

"Not if a loving family adopts Little Pip." Abby filled the glass with orange juice. "At which point he'll no longer be an orphan, and his *Great Expectations* nickname won't apply."

Responding to a familiar sound, Erica set her mug on the counter. "Our little orphan needs attention." She returned to the den, lifted Theo from the swing, then carried him to her room. After changing his diaper, she returned to place him back in the swing.

Amanda moved beside her. "His scar is barely visible."

Abby wheeled close. "Anyone who doesn't know will never guess he was born with a cleft lip."

"Thanks to an excellent surgeon." Erica tapped her watch. "Time for Abby and me to head downtown." She nudged Amanda's arm. "Which means you're up for babysitting duty."

"Lucky me."

The infant yawned.

"Maybe he'll sleep most of the time you're gone." Amanda settled at the dining-room table and opened her laptop.

Dusty padded in then sprawled beside the swing.

Abby patted her dog's head. "Help Amanda take care of Little Pip."

"Don't worry. He's in good hands and paws." Amanda tapped her keyboard. "Maybe his canine protector will give him a giggle-worthy tongue bath while you're gone."

Dusty's tail slapped the floor in a lazy motion while Erica returned to the kitchen to grab keys from the bowl. Outside, she repositioned Abby's car from the carport to a spot beside the front sidewalk. The same routine she'd followed for the past eight months. Erica tapped the steering wheel. How much longer would it take for her daughter's spinal-cord injury to heal? A few more months? A year? Abby wheeled out the front door and onto the sidewalk—Erica's signal to open the passenger door.

As soon as her child lifted her body onto the passenger seat, Erica stowed her wheelchair in the trunk then slid behind the wheel. Fifteen minutes after leaving for town, Abby maneuvered onto the last row in the courtroom. After stowing the wheelchair behind the seat, Erica settled on the bench beside her daughter. Only three other observers had gathered, making it clear this obviously wasn't a highly publicized hearing.

The judge took her seat at the bench. Not a single juror sat in the jury box, much like the day Abby faced a judge for texting while driving and blowing through a stop sign. Strange justice how Jimmy Barkley failing to see the sign in time to respond relegated her daughter to a wheelchair.

The judge peered down from her bench. "Are both parties ready to proceed?" Following responses, she faced the defendant's table. "Who's representing Ms. Wellington?"

The woman sitting beside Sierra leaned forward. "I am, Your Honor, Legal Aid Attorney Dillard."

The judge turned toward the prosecution table. "Who's advocating for the child?"

"I'm Jillian Abernathy, Child Services Associate assigned to this case."

"We'll begin with your statement, Ms. Abernathy."

"Thank you, Your Honor." Jillian leaned forward. "Four months ago, Ms. Wellington stuffed her newborn child, with the umbilical cord stump still attached, into a gym bag before leaving him on the crisis center front doorstep." Jillian lifted a sheet of paper off the table. "This note was pinned to his blanket. *My baby's name is Theo. I love him with all my heart, but he needs more help than I'm capable of giving. Please find someone to give him the care he deserves.*" She set the note aside. "Abby Nelson, who works at the center, and her mother rescued the child. Which is why they, along with Amanda Smith, have been granted foster parent status." Jillian described Theo's birth defect, his surgery, and his current environment. "The child is thriving under the women's care."

"Thank you, Ms. Abernathy." The judge paused, appeared to read a note, then looked up. "I'm ready for your statement, Counselor."

Attorney Dillard moved her chair closer to the table. "My client wrapped her infant in a blanket before securing him safely in a gym bag. She chose to place him on the crisis center doorstep knowing full well he would be found seconds after ringing the doorbell. Two days after EMT's delivered him to the hospital for observation, Ms. Wellington checked on him—"

"Did she identify herself or enquire about his condition?"

"Not at that time, Your Honor. She viewed him through the nursery window. Seeing him, she realized she had made a hasty decision due to postpartum depression—"

"Has Ms. Wellington been diagnosed by a physician?"

"She has not."

"Continue."

"My client went to the hospital the day of her son's surgery to reveal her identity. After the surgeon provided an update, Ms. Erica Nelson invited her to lunch at her home. Subsequently, Ms. Abernathy granted Ms. Wellington permission for weekly supervised visits with her son."

"Where did those visits take place and who supervises them?"

"At the home Ms. Nelson shares with her daughter and their business partner, Ms. Amanda Smith. My client admits she made a mistake. She also believes it is in her child's best interest to be raised by his biological mother."

The judge leaned toward the prosecution table. "How old are you, Ms. Wellington?"

"Eighteen." Sierra's tone hinted of unease.

"Is your child's father in the picture?"

Sierra shook her head.

"Your attorney claims you suffered with postpartum depression. Do you know what that term means?"

Sierra glanced up at her lawyer, seemingly searching for an answer.

"I asked you, Ms. Wellington, not your attorney." The judge's voice came across as firm.

Sierra's shoulders slumped. "I um...not really."

"Tell us in your own words where you gave birth and why you left your newborn child on the crisis center doorstep."

"I live with my grandma at her house in Morganton." Sierra paused. "When I first saw my baby's face...the way his lip was all messed up...I thought how he looked had somehow been my fault for delivering him by myself."

"Why didn't you go to the hospital or at least ask your grandmother to help you?"

"I don't have insurance and Grandma's old. She's also nearly blind."

"Did she know you were pregnant?"

Sierra nodded. "That's how come I moved in with her."

"Where did you live before?"

"Um...Chattanooga...with my mother."

"Was she aware of your pregnancy?"

Sierra hesitated, as if reluctant to respond.

"Did you move in with your grandmother because your mother didn't know you were with child?"

Sierra shrugged. "Sort of."

"Is that a yes or a no?"

"Mom didn't know."

The judge appeared to refer to a note on her desk. "When did you decide you wanted to take custody of your son?"

"When...um..." Sierra exchanged another glance with her attorney, then faced the bench. "When I realized his mother should raise him."

"Do you have gainful employment, Ms. Wellington?"

"There aren't any jobs in Morganton."

"How do you propose to cover the expenses of raising a child?"

Another long pause. "My grandma gets a check every month."

"Have you told her you've given birth?"

Sierra shook her head.

The judge turned toward the prosecution table. "Based on your observation along with today's testimony, what do you recommend, Ms. Abernathy?"

Scooting to the edge of her seat, Abby crossed her arms on the back of the bench in front of her.

"In my professional opinion, Your Honor, the infant will be best served remaining in his current foster home with continued weekly visits from his biological mother."

Erica's eyes laser focused on the woman charged with determining Theo's fate.

"Thank you." The judge pivoted toward the defense table. "A number of factors impact child custody cases. The fact that you carried your child to full term indicates you care about him. I also believe you want what is best for him, Ms. Wellington." The judge paused. "Which is why I am ordering him to remain in foster care until such time as you are deemed capable of raising him." The judge peered over her glasses at the young girl. "Or until, in the opinion of this court, he should become eligible for adoption. As requested, you will continue to have supervised visiting rights."

"Thank you, Your Honor." Sierra's attorney lifted a folder off the table then escorted her client from the courtroom.

Erica leaned close to Abby. "The judge made the right decision."

"At least until she releases Theo for adoption."

Erica touched her daughter's arm. "At some point Sierra might prove to the court that she's capable of raising her son."

"Too bad finders keepers doesn't apply to babies."

Erica's brows knitted together the moment reality struck home. Abby was suffering under the illusion that Theo belonged to her. Somehow she had to correct the misconception without breaking her daughter's heart.

Chapter 3

Amanda circled the block twice before finding a parking spot on West Main Street. Showing up for a planning session in a downtown restaurant on a Friday night in peak tourist season required preplanning along with plenty of patience. After checking her image in the rearview mirror and tucking a strand of red hair behind her ear, Amanda climbed out. She waited for three cars to pass by before crossing the street. Halfway down the block she passed the driveway leading to Blue Ridge Inn's back entrance.

So much had changed since that day all those months ago when she'd checked into the inn hoping to save her marriage to Paul Sullivan. Until she discovered the name had been one of three aliases Gunter Benson used to illegally marry her, Wendy, and Erica. All at the same time. Fortunately the scumbag was locked away in a Las Vegas prison.

She strode to the end of the block, drawing in a deep breath before walking into The General Ledger Restaurant. The hostess smiled. "Are you Ms. Smith?"

"I am."

"Mr. Redding is waiting for you." The young woman led her to a table along the back wall.

Gary stood then pulled out a chair for Amanda.

"We're business partners in a political campaign. Social graces aren't required."

"I'm a born and bred Southern gentleman." He grinned while settling across from her. "My mother would disown me if I didn't treat every woman with respect."

"In that case—" Amanda hung her purse on the back of her chair. "I'll accept your gesture as a lifelong commitment to remaining a gentleman."

His smile widened. "Wise decision."

Their waiter approached. "Would you like something from the bar while you wait for Mr. Armstrong?"

"Samuel Adams for me. What about you, Amanda?"

She peered up at the waiter. "A glass of chardonnay."

Their waiter listed the options.

She chose the only label she recognized.

"Excellent choice."

Amanda's eyes drifted back to Gary. Despite his distinguished good looks, his neatly trimmed salt-and-pepper beard and muscular body made him appear more like an athlete than a bank president. "How are your fundraising efforts coming along?"

"As of this morning, we've raised eighty percent of our target. Thanks in large part to a sizeable donation from a local business owner who's had more than one run-in with the current district attorney."

"Challenging an unpopular opponent makes our job a lot easier."

Gary nodded. "Immeasurably. What's the latest with the debate arrangements?"

"DA Watson agreed to two weeks from tomorrow."

"Plenty of time for him to cook up an hour's worth of nonsense. What about a moderator?"

"Nancy Campbell. Approved by both parties."

Gary's eyes widened. "I'm surprised Watson agreed."

"Either he doesn't know about her podcast, or he believes he can outsmart her."

"If he's banking on that tactic, he's in for a big surprise."

"No kidding."

The waiter returned with their drinks

Gary tipped his bottle to Amanda's glass. "Cheers." His beverage choice proved another departure from her vision of a bank president. He unclipped his phone from his belt clip and tapped the screen. "Text from Keith. Last minute issue with a client. He wants us to proceed without him." Gary set his phone on the table. "Why don't we order first?"

"Good idea." Amanda struggled to focus on the menu. Had tonight suddenly become more of a date than a business meeting? If she had the slightest interest in pursuing a romantic relationship, Gary would be a worthy candidate. But she wasn't. Not now. Maybe never again.

"What most appeals to you?"

Amanda stared at him, and her breath hitched.

He grinned. "Your menu choice."

"I'm leaning toward a salad." Had he noticed her reaction, or had her silence prompted him to explain? Breaking eye contact, Amanda focused on the menu. Tonight, she might need a second glass of wine. Except she'd driven, so one would have to suffice. When their waiter returned, Amanda ordered a goat cheese salad. Gary chose a burger and fries. Stifling a chuckle, she pushed her menu aside. Perfect choice for a beer-drinking bank executive.

Keith's finance manager leaned back. "Linda said you moved here from New Orleans."

How much had Keith's wife told him about her? "I was born and raised in the home of Mardi Gras."

"Blue Ridge must seem dull compared to the Big Easy."

Amanda wrapped her fingers around her wineglass stem. Maybe social interaction was normal between business associates, especially those working on what would become a contentious political campaign. "Have you visited New Orleans?"

"A few years ago."

With his wife? Should she ask?

"The last trip with my ex before I found out about her affair with my assistant manager." He took a sip of his drink and set it down. "Enough about my failed marriage. Were you an executive in a Louisiana business?"

"Hardly. Before I married Preston...and after he passed...I worked as a tour guide—mostly in the French Quarter."

"I imagine you met a lot of interesting people."

"Definitely." *Including Paul Sullivan aka Gunter Benson.* "What attracted you to the banking business?"

"Fascination with numbers." He grinned. "Does my career choice peg me as a nerd?"

Amanda mirrored his smile. "Maybe a little."

"Does the fact that I played football in high school and college help offset the geek tag?"

"Along with your choice of beverage and entrée. Definitely."

"If we're comparing food and drink orders, white wine and a fancy salad indicate you're a woman with sophisticated taste."

Amanda stifled a laugh. If he had the slightest inkling about her childhood...but that was a story for another time. "Acquired taste." If they continued talking about their personal lives, would she give him the wrong impression? Except wouldn't their working relationship improve if they knew more about each other? She cleared her throat. "Do you have children?"

"A stepdaughter who lives in Florida with her father. Should have been my first clue about her mother. What about you?"

"A daughter, Morgan. She and her husband live in Atlanta. They're both engineers."

"Let me guess. They have their future all mapped out."

Amanda nodded. "Like a detailed road map."

"Typical of engineers and bankers, until unexpected events disrupt their well-laid-out plans."

Amanda broke eye contact. Such as discovering the man she believed she'd legally married had borrowed their home into foreclosure and cleaned out her bank account.

The waiter arrived with their orders. Grateful for the disruption, Amanda diverted her attention to her salad. If she hadn't married Gunter, she'd probably still be guiding tourists through the French Quarter. Maybe she owed the con man at least a smidgen of gratitude.

"How's your salad?"

"Delicious. Your burger?"

"Same."

Time to change direction. "Back to the debate. We need to set up a mock trial round to prepare Keith."

"Anyone in mind?"

"After Wendy, Erica, and I received summons to testify during the Gunter's murder trial, Keith's son, Chris, did an excellent job preparing us. Which is why I reached out to him this morning."

"And?"

"A week from today, he'll put his dad through the ringer, so to speak."

"Keeping it all in the family also saves us the expense of hiring an outsider. Good news for the campaign finance guy." Gary aimed a French fry at Amanda. "If I ever decide to run for office, I'll hire you as my manager."

"Are you admitting to political aspirations?"

"Hardly. However, if I become so inclined, you'll be the first to know."

"Hmm. Maybe I should raise my rates before I'm in demand." She chuckled. "To keep your campaign in the family, Wendy Armstrong would be a great finance manager."

"I'd never have guessed—"

"Believe me, in addition to being beauty-queen gorgeous and loaded with infectious charm, Awesam's CFO has discovered she's a whiz at handling finances."

Gary chuckled. "Another numbers expert who doesn't fit the nerd mold."

"For sure. Wendy's also creative. Case in point, she combined the first letter of our names, Amanda, Wendy, Erica, Abby, and Morgan to come up with Awesam as our company name. She added the 's' to make it easier to read."

While finishing dinner, they discussed debate media coverage along with additional fundraising events.

After paying the bill, Gary continued playing the role of a Southern gentleman by escorting Amanda to her car then opening the driver's door. "Talk about contradictions." He grinned. "You driving a pickup tops the list."

"This old truck is the last of Gunter Benson's fleet."

"What happened to the others?"

"Five were repossessed, one totaled, one sold." Amanda climbed onto the seat. "One of these days, Erica and I will replace this with two newer vehicles."

"If you need financing, you know where to come."

Amanda laughed. "It pays to have friends in the banking business."

"Even if you aren't in the market for a loan." He closed her door then returned to the sidewalk.

As Amanda backed out of the parking spot, she had to admit that Gary was fast becoming her second male friend, close behind Preston—with one huge difference. She planned to keep their relationship firmly planted in the friendship column.

Chapter 4

Breathing in mouthwatering tomato, cheese, and meat aromas, Wendy clung to her husband's arm as they entered the Gilmores' dining room. She sat between Kayla and Chris. Glasses of lemonade, two bottles of beer, along with three pizzas held center stage on a table set with formal dinnerware. Strange yet at the same time appropriate. Especially following an afternoon of idle conversation interrupted by long moments of awkward silence.

Zach, sporting wireless ear pods, appeared for the first time since storming out of the living room before lunch. Avoiding eye contact, he plopped beside Riley, across from Chris. Cynthia ambled in carrying Ryan. Moments after she settled at one end of the table, Ryan wriggled from his grandmother's arms and reached for Wendy. Cynthia seemed to hesitate, then released him to her.

Brent took his seat at the opposite end of the table from his wife. Wendy eyed the man of the house. Would he bless the meal or jump right in?

He jumped. "You're about to experience the best pizzas in Nashville."

Zach reached for a slice. Brent grabbed his son's wrist. "We serve guests first, young man." The boy yanked his arm from his father's grip. Brent shot him a stern look then faced Wendy and Chris. "You'll have to excuse my son's behavior. We haven't had dinner together since Thanksgiving."

That explained a lot. Wendy's focus shifted from Brent to her mother, then back to Brent. "I imagine coordinating busy schedules is challenging."

Cynthia nodded. "Especially with three busy children."

"At least we're together tonight. About the pizzas…" While their father described the three options, Zach scowled, Riley chewed her fingernail, Kayla tapped her phone.

Wendy wrapped her arms around Ryan. Had her mother's family always been dysfunctional or only since Cynthia had become ill?

"Which would you prefer, Wendy?"

She blinked. Unwilling to admit Brent's descriptions hadn't registered, she opted for a slice from the box closest to her. After Chris chose what appeared to be supreme pizza, Brent handed him one of the beer bottles then took the other. The rest of the family transferred slices to their plates.

Chris took a bite. "On a scale of one to ten, this is a definite ten."

Cynthia wrapped her fingers around her glass. "I hope you don't mind sleeping on the pullout in our den."

"Not at all." Wendy pinched off a piece of pizza for Ryan. Although she would have preferred a hotel room, after growing up in more than one undesirable foster home, she could handle spending one night without privacy.

Riley popped a slice of pepperoni in her mouth. "Is Ryan my cousin?"

Wendy shook her head. "He's your nephew."

"When he learns to talk, is he gonna call me Aunt Riley?"

"Would you like him to?"

"Yeah."

"Then speaking for our little guy, the answer is yes."

Riley launched into a monologue about her best friend's little brother bugging them every time she spent the night, until her mother reached across the table and tapped her arm.

"Why don't we let our guests talk for a while." She turned toward Wendy. "Have you given your daughter a name?"

Grateful her mother had upgraded them from visitors to guests, Wendy managed a smile. "We're considering several options." Not exactly the truth, but better than telling her they didn't have a clue.

"Wendy said I could visit her and Chris sometime this summer." Kayla reached for a second slice of pizza. "Is it okay if I ride back with them tomorrow?"

Wendy's gaze flicked from Kayla to her mother's raised brow. Had her sister blindsided them for shock value, or was she acting as a clueless teenager?

Cynthia caught Wendy's eye. "Kayla caught both of us off guard, didn't she?"

Yes. Her mother had just given her the perfect opportunity to turn this situation into a bonding moment without alienating her sister. "True. Although, a few weeks ago, Kayla and I talked about her visiting us. But only if you and her father approve."

Brent reached for his beer. "If timing works for Wendy and Chris, we should let Kayla go with them to save us a trip."

Chris touched Wendy's arm. "Will this week work for you?"

"As well as any other."

Kayla faced her mother. "Can I go? Please?" Her tone pleaded.

"If Wendy or Chris drives you back home so I can spend more time with my grandson."

Wendy nodded. "Deal."

"All right, you can go with your sister tomorrow."

"Thanks, Mom." Kayla bolted from her chair. After hugging Cynthia, she scooted to the other end of the table to embrace Brent. "You too, Dad."

"You're welcome, honey."

Kayla returned to her seat to scarf down another pizza slice.

Following another half hour of forced chitchat, Brent, Riley, and Kayla cleared the table. Having skillfully avoided engaging in conversation during the entire meal, Zach headed upstairs.

Eyeing Chris, Cynthia laced her fingers on the table. "Do you mind giving me a few minutes with your wife?"

"Not at all." He lifted Ryan off Wendy's lap then walked out of the dining room.

Avoiding eye contact, Wendy sipped her lemonade to quench the sudden dryness attacking her throat. She'd been five years old when she'd spent time alone with her mother—the morning Cynthia left her with the neighbor before walking out of her life.

"Come with me." Her mother lifted off her chair then headed through the foyer to the living room.

Taking measured breaths to slow her racing heart, Wendy followed. She settled on the sofa, crossing then uncrossing her legs. Should she begin a conversation or wait?

Cynthia moved to the bay window, her back turned toward Wendy. "When you showed up at my front door last year, I told you I had abandoned you to chase my childhood dream to become a famous singer. Live in a fancy house. Because I didn't want to end up old, broke, and sick like my mother, I always put my desires above those closest to me. Even though I didn't abandon Kayla, Riley, and Zach—" Cynthia turned away from the window. "I have failed as their mother."

A fist-sized lump formed in Wendy's throat.

"I don't have enough time to correct all my mistakes, at least not during however many months God grants me, but I'll do my best to try." Cynthia sat on the piano bench facing the keys. "I'm grateful for the opportunity to ensure your child's memories of his grandmother are without regret. I hope I live long enough to do so."

Struggling to deal with conflicting emotions, Wendy moved to the piano bench. "I never learned how to play an instrument."

"All those years you spent in foster homes must have taken a toll."

"I survived."

"You were such a sweet child." Cynthia pressed a key. "I'm surprised no one adopted you."

"Chris adopted Ryan." The comment tumbled off Wendy's tongue before she could swallow them.

Her mother stared wide-eyed. "What happened to his biological father?"

Wendy cringed. Now that she'd opened that door, it was too late to back out. "He's serving twenty-five to life for murder." The story spilled out beginning with how she'd met Kurt Peterson, ending with the discovery of his true identity. "Gunter hired Chris to break the news to Erica, Amanda, and me."

Cynthia fingered a melody with her left hand. "You've lived through more trauma than any young woman should have to endure."

"Despite everything that has happened in my life, I chose to reject victimhood. Now I treasure every blessing God has granted me." Wendy touched her mother's arm. "Including becoming reacquainted with you."

Cynthia placed her hand over Wendy's. "I'm glad you found me."

Fighting back tears, Wendy whispered, "So am I...Mom."

Riley bounded in. "We're gonna play Monopoly." She tilted her head. "Will you play with us this time, Mommy?"

"Absolutely. Who won the last game?"

"Zach, but he's not playing this time."

Wendy dabbed the corner of her eyes while lifting off the bench. "Would you believe I've never played Monopoly?"

Riley's eyes widened. "Really?"

"Uh-huh. Will you teach me how?"

"It's easy." Riley grabbed Wendy's hand. "Everyone starts with the same amount of money. Whoever ends up with the most at the end wins. The houses and hotels you buy also count."

"Sounds like you're an expert."

"Kind of." Riley led the way to the round table in the den. Ryan sat in his playpen surrounded by enough toys to keep him occupied. Two hours after the game started, their little guy had fallen asleep. Cynthia yawned before excusing herself. Another hour passed before the game ended with Kayla and Riley nearly tied.

After helping make the pull-out sofa, Brent escorted his daughters upstairs, leaving Wendy and Chris alone in the den. Grateful they at least had a private bathroom, Wendy changed into her pajamas then slid onto the sofa bed beside Chris. "Good night, darling."

He kissed her cheek "Sweet dreams, angel."

What seemed like hours after Chris drifted off, Wendy gave up trying to force herself to sleep. She eased off the bed, then donned her bathrobe and tiptoed to the living room bay window. Outside, the streetlamp cast a warm glow on the manicured front lawn.

"You couldn't sleep either?"

Startled, Wendy spun toward Brent. "Too much on my mind."

"Same here." He dropped onto the sofa.

Hoping he would share details about Cynthia's illness, Wendy settled on a chair facing him. "Thank you for a lovely evening."

"Tonight's the first time I played Monopoly with my girls in a long time."

"I'm glad Cynthia felt well enough to join us."

"So am I." Brent propped his ankle across his knee. "There's something you need to know about your mother and me."

Wendy eyed on his expression. Was he moments from telling her about the cancer?

Brent fingered his slipper. "My band played in a Biloxi restaurant the night I met her. Her beauty, the way she smiled while serving customers grabbed my attention. During a break, she pulled me aside to tell me she was also a singer. I invited her to sing one song with us. A week later I took her out to dinner." Brent paused for a long moment. "That night she told me she'd had a child...who'd died shortly after childbirth."

Wendy gasped. Struggling to take a breath, she pressed her hand to her throat. How many times would her mother's words stab her?

"If I had known you were alive—" Brent swallowed. "I never would have let her abandon you."

Conflicting thoughts swirling in Wendy's head threatened to throw her off-balance. She gripped the chair's arms. "I don't understand what made you decide to tell me now."

His eyes met hers. "To let you know how much she regrets her actions. It's important for you to understand the depth of your mother's remorse...and how much she loves you."

Tears pooled then tracked down Wendy's cheeks. She had forgiven her mother once. Could she do it a second time?

The aroma of freshly brewed coffee nudged Wendy's eyes open. Early dawn light shone through the window facing the backyard. She rolled over. Chris sat with Ryan in his lap drinking from a sippy cup. "How long have you been awake?"

"Half hour or so."

Wendy swung her legs over the side of the sofa bed then brushed hair away from her eyes. Last night she'd promised Brent she wouldn't tell Cynthia what he had revealed. How could she face her mother without arousing suspicion? Following a trip to the bathroom, Wendy returned to the den and sat on the chair's arm beside Chris. "Something happened last night after you fell asleep." Leaning close to his ear, she relayed her conversation with Brent. "What should I do when I see Cynthia this morning?"

"You're an extraordinary woman filled with love." Chris squeezed Wendy's knee. "Let your heart guide you."

Kayla breezed in, grinning ear to ear. "I'm all packed and ready to go with you guys."

Wendy blinked as an all-important question surfaced. Would she have the opportunity to overcome every shred of hurt to help the Gilmore family heal before time ran out?

Chapter 5

Erica sat on the edge of her bed with her laptop balanced on her thighs. She stared at the Excel spreadsheet highlighting two goals she had committed to achieving before accepting Brad Barkley's proposal. Her eyes drifted to the dresser drawer holding his engagement ring hidden beneath a layer of clothing. In a few months, she would achieve the financial goal. Even though the second seemed further away than it had two days ago, should she dismiss it as irrational, given it didn't impact her security? Except she'd made a personal commitment. Following through seemed her best move. Now all she had to do was share her idea with her partners.

Erica carried her laptop and her phone to the dining room table. Dusty sprawled on the floor between Abby's wheelchair and Theo's swing. Erica settled beside her daughter. "I'm glad you're able to join us, sweetheart."

"Lucky for me you planned this month's meeting on my day off."

Amanda ambled in from the kitchen. "As our talented vice president, you're always welcome to participate."

Abby shrugged. "This is only the third staff meeting I've attended since I began working full-time."

"Which makes today extra special." Amanda sat in front of her laptop, across from Abby.

The back door swung open followed by footsteps. "Day one of Kayla's visit." Wendy breezed in. "And she's already babysitting."

Abby leaned forward. "How'd your visit with the Gilmores go?"

"As well as could be expected, I suppose." Wendy pulled out a chair between Amanda and Erica. "At least I understand my mother better now than I did before the trip."

Amanda nudged Wendy. "Is that good or bad news?"

"More like hopeful. Kayla's staying with us for a week. Maybe longer if all goes well." Wendy nodded toward Abby. "She would enjoy meeting you."

"Why don't you bring her to the crisis center tomorrow?"

"Great idea."

The back door swung open ushering in sugar and cinnamon aromas wafting around Millie as she dashed in from the kitchen.

Abby pressed her palms together. "Do I smell snickerdoodles?"

Millie nodded. "Your favorite." The cantankerous seventy-plus-year-old neighbor who served as Hilltop Inn's chef set a plate on the table then pulled out a chair beside Abby. "Bernie and I finally followed through on our plan after meeting those fun-loving, bridge-playing ladies who stayed at the inn earlier this year."

Amanda's head tilted. "You and your assistant started a bridge club?"

"Why would we do that? Neither one of us knows how to play." Millie folded her arms on the table. "Tonight is the first meeting of our exclusive Blue Ridge Mystery Club."

"Because you plan to remain anonymous?"

Millie stared at Amanda as if she'd suddenly grown a third eye. "It's a wine and reading club."

Awesam's president leaned forward. "Are you and Bernie the only members?"

"We wouldn't have much of a club if there were only two of us, would we? Anyway, for now Bernie's neighbor Eileen, Chris's grandmother Susan, along with her friend Stanley are in the club. Our first book is Agatha Christie's, *And Then There Were None*. Her most famous. After we finish, we'll get together at my house, drink wine, and discuss the story."

Erica chuckled. "You'll definitely rival the South Carolina Bridge Gals' ability to have a good time."

"Plus, reading will keep your minds sharp. Something I learned in one of my psychology classes." Abby laced her fingers on the table. "Not that you need help in that department."

Millie nodded. "You're right on both counts."

"Hmm." Amanda tapped her chin. "Four single women and one guy. Great odds for Stanley, unless he's married."

"Doesn't matter if he is or isn't married," Millie scoffed. "Our club is about friendship and libation. Not romance."

"Tell you what." Amanda waggled her finger at their chief information officer. "If you stop hounding me about Gary Redding, I promise not to give you a hard time about Stanley."

Erica's focus shifted to Millie. How would their CFO respond, given she'd agreed to help Wendy reinforce Linda Armstrong's matchmaking ploy targeted to Amanda and Gary?

"First off—" Millie held up a finger. "Stanley's wife of seventy plus years passed away less than a year ago." Second finger. "And he's pushing ninety."

"You're not saying old men are beyond looking for love, are you?" Amanda's tone dripped of mockery.

"For any man married to the same woman for nearly seventy years, that's exactly what I'm saying. On the other hand, Gary Redding is—"

"Good grief." Amanda rolled her eyes. "You're hopeless."

Abby plucked a cookie off the tray. "This is turning into one weird board meeting."

Wendy laughed. "Presented by the Amanda and Millie show."

Erica held her hand up. "The show which I'm cancelling due to lack of interest, and I'm calling this meeting to order."

"Thanks to our peacemaker, we can finally get down to business." Amanda turned toward Wendy. "What's the latest with our finances?"

Following Wendy's report and Millie's update on Hilltop's private dining success, Amanda suggested they create a newsletter to keep guests engaged. During the discussion, Erica's mind drifted to the judge's decision about Sierra. If her partners agreed to her suggestion, she could achieve her second goal without admitting it existed. Especially since she'd never told Millie about Brad's engagement ring hidden in her dresser.

"All in favor, raise your hand."

Erica blinked. "What?"

Amanda turned toward Erica. "We're voting on me taking on the newsletter project. Where did your mind roam off to?"

"Sorry." Erica raised her hand.

"A unanimous vote. Good. I'll have a draft ready for your approval by the end of the week." Amanda closed her laptop. "Unless someone has another topic to discuss, I suggest we end our meeting to fix lunch."

"There is one more thing." All eyes focused on Erica. How should she begin? Appealing to emotion, that's how. Erica turned toward Wendy. "You grew up longing for your mother to come back into your life, didn't you?"

"Every waking moment until I finally gave up hope."

Erica glanced around the table. "You all know the judge ordered Theo to remain in foster care until Sierra proved capable of raising him or until, in the opinion of the court, he became eligible for adoption." She paused, glancing around the table. "I believe Sierra deserves the opportunity to prove she's worthy of assuming her role as Little Pip's mother."

Amanda's brows raised. "What are you suggesting?"

Erica hesitated. No more stalling. "What if she moves into our guest room, and under our guidance, she assumes full responsibility for her child's care?"

"Are you kidding me?" Amanda leaned back, her arms crossed. "You want to invite a stranger we know nothing about to live with us?"

"You, Wendy, and I were practically strangers when we moved into this house. Don't forget we invited Millie to stay in our guest room after the fire damaged her house."

Amanda glared at Erica. "The three of us were responsible adults, and Millie wasn't a stranger."

"Something else you need to consider." Millie drummed her fingers. "If Sierra spends months bonding with her son then decides taking care of a baby is too much trouble, she'd disappear all over again."

"You're right, Millie. However—" Wendy scooted her chair closer to the table. "Despite the risk, Theo deserves a chance to be raised by his mother."

Amanda's expression hardened. "Babysitting both an infant and an irresponsible teenager is beyond logical."

"I understand your hesitancy." Erica's eyes met Amanda's. "Back when we were planning what type of inn to create, you suggested a place where women who faced loss or disappointment could form friendships and heal. This is our chance to put your brilliant idea into motion."

"Using my own words against me?" Amanda snickered. "Slick move, Sherlock."

Wendy brushed a lock of hair away from her cheek. "Have you run your idea by Jillian?"

Erica shook her head. "I wanted everyone's approval before contacting Child Services." Her eyes drifted to her daughter. Why hadn't she commented on her idea? She touched Abby's arm. "Especially yours, sweetheart."

Abby stared at her half-eaten cookie.

"Are you questioning what's best for Theo?"

"All I know is we were meant to find him."

"Are you okay with me contacting Child Services, sweetheart?"

"You three are the adults, so I'll go along with whatever you decide. If you don't mind, I need to study for a test I'm taking tomorrow." Abby backed her wheelchair away from the table then spun around and wheeled through the den to the hall. Dusty padded behind her.

Erica's eyes followed Abby until she disappeared around the corner. She understood her daughter well enough to know what was bothering her.

"If you ask me—" Wendy's voice came across barely above a whisper. "Abby's worried about competition."

Erica's gaze held Wendy's. "What are you trying to tell me?"

"Think about this." Wendy laced her fingers on the table. "After you two rescued Theo, Abby convinced us to foster him. In her mind that makes him her baby. Sierra taking over would challenge her belief."

"I know that. Are you suggesting I abandon the idea?"

"Not at all. However, if Amanda crosses over to the good side—our side, we'll all need to be sensitive to Abby's feelings."

"All right, you win." Amanda uncrossed her arms. "Call Child Services to inform them that three crazy ladies are willing to jump off the deep end."

Before Amanda could change her mind, Erica grabbed her phone then pressed a number. Following a brief conversation, she set her phone down. "Jillian's meeting us here at noon the day after tomorrow."

After pushing her bedroom door closed, Abby maneuvered her wheelchair to her desk. She reached down to pet Dusty while staring at her open laptop. Why hadn't she objected to her mother's proposal? After all, she'd rescued Theo from the cold before bringing him into their home. Now, the woman who'd thrown him away wanted back into his life. Didn't anyone understand that Little Pip belonged to her, not Sierra?

Who was she kidding? Child Services would never allow a single, wheelchair-bound woman to adopt a child. Although, when Sierra failed as a mother, wouldn't she win? Abby concentrated on wiggling her big toe. If she could walk by the end of the year, she'd marry Tommy then apply for adoption.

A twinge of guilt pricked Abby's conscience. How could she summon the courage to welcome Sierra into their home and accept whatever happened? Maybe the time had come to share her deepest thoughts. Abby pulled her phone from her pocket. She hesitated for a moment then texted the person she hoped would most understand. Five minutes later, Morgan responded with a phone call.

Chapter 6

Wendy placed a plate with two eggs over easy and dry toast on the counter then poured Chris a cup of black coffee. "I'm surprised Kayla turned in so soon after dinner last night."

Chris swallowed a bite of toast. "Either Ryan wore her out or she didn't want to hang out with the old folks two nights in a row. After Dad and I discuss the best way to recruit an attorney to replace him, I'll work in our home office the rest of the afternoon."

"You're that confident he'll win?"

"Competing against Richard Watson? Without a doubt. Especially with Amanda and Gary on his team."

Wendy lifted Ryan into his high chair. "Amanda still insists she isn't interested in a personal relationship with Gary."

"So much for my mother's attempt at playing cupid."

"I hope SAGA isn't doomed to fail."

Chris raised a brow. "Is that some sort of conspiracy group?"

"I suppose 'Snag a rich guy for Amanda' could be considered a matchmaking scheme."

Chris chuckled. "Clever acronym."

"My brilliant idea, but only if it works." Wendy placed an egg muffin and banana slices on Ryan's tray. Duke sprawled beside the high chair ready to function as their little guy's cleanup crew. "I'm taking Kayla to meet Abby at the Crisis Center later this morning."

"Good way to keep her busy." Chris swallowed his last bite, then slid off his stool. "Thanks for breakfast, angel." After grabbing his briefcase from the bedroom, Chris patted Ryan's head then kissed Wendy's cheek. "You three have fun today."

"We will."

An hour after Chris left, Kayla emerged from the basement, dressed in cutoff jeans and a tee shirt featuring Gilmore's Bar and Restaurant logo. "Hey."

"Good morning," Wendy replied from the sofa where she balanced her laptop on her legs. "Are you hungry?"

"Sort of." Kayla plopped onto the sofa beside Wendy.

"In a little while, I'll take you to meet Amanda's daughter, Abby."

"Is she in high school?"

Wendy shook her head. "Abby graduated last year. Now she's studying psychology online."

"Same way you're going to school."

"Exactly. During my junior year in high school, I dreamed of going to a big university and joining a sorority."

Kayla pulled her phone from her pocket. "Going to college seems like a big waste of time. Especially since I wanna write music and play in a band like Dad."

"You have lots of time to decide your future."

"I've already decided."

Ignoring her sister's snarky tone, Wendy closed her laptop. "For now, what do you want for breakfast?"

"I dunno. Maybe a power bar and orange juice?"

Same as yesterday. At least she was predictable. "All right." Wendy carried her laptop to the kitchen then set her sister's breakfast choice on the counter.

Kayla traipsed over. In between bites, she focused on tapping her phone, making it clear she wasn't in the mood for conversation.

While her sister nibbled on her bar, Wendy packed a diaper bag then dressed Ryan in shorts and a tee shirt sporting Chris's college logo. She tapped her little guy's nose. "Are you going to follow in your daddy's footsteps to become a lawyer or choose another prestigious profession?"

Ryan babbled a response.

"You don't have to decide today." She shouldered the diaper bag, then carried him to the kitchen. "Are you ready to go?"

Kayla shrugged. "Yeah, I guess so."

"All right, then." After leading the way to the garage, Wendy secured Ryan in his car seat then climbed into the driver's seat beside her sister. "Did I tell you Abby works at a crisis center?"

Kayla shook her head. "What's a crisis center?"

"A secret place where abused women and their children find safe shelter."

"Oh." Kayla turned her attention back to her phone until they parked at the center.

"We're here." After climbing out and releasing Ryan from his car seat, Wendy strode to the front entrance then texted Abby to let her know they'd arrived.

Kayla pocketed her phone. "Why did she pick this place to work?"

"Years ago, Abby and her mother escaped to a women's shelter after Abby's father physically abused her mother."

"Lucky for us, my dad never hit Mom or any of us kids."

"Because he's a good man. Anyway, Abby has a special place in her heart for women and children who suffer from abuse."

The door clicked open. They stepped inside.

Abby peered up from her wheelchair. "Hi, Kayla. I'm Abby."

"Hi."

"Come on, I'll show you around."

Hoping spending time alone with Abby would improve her sister's sour mood, Wendy tapped Kayla's arm. "You two go ahead. I'll catch up with you in a little while." After settling on a chair with Ryan on her lap, she chose a children's book from the end table and read aloud to her little guy until the intercom buzzed.

A woman rushed into the space. She peered through the peephole, then clicked the door open.

A deputy escorted the woman and a young girl with tear-stained cheeks inside. Wendy cringed and pulled Ryan close to her chest. The bandage above the woman's eye along with the bruise on her cheek brought back memories of Child Services rescuing her from an abusive foster parent.

"Mrs. Worthington is the center's director, Ms. Carter. She'll take good care of you and your daughter." The deputy's tone came across as reassuring.

The director smiled until the deputy walked out. "You'll both be safe here with us." She leaned down facing the girl. "You can call me Ms. Pamela. What's your name, sweetheart?"

"Lucy."

"Do you like dogs?"

The child nodded.

"Well then, someone special wants to meet you. His name is Lucky." Shortly after the director escorted the battered woman down the hall, Kayla returned to the reception area. "Abby invited me to go out with her and Tommy tomorrow night. For now, a little girl who just came in needs her full attention."

Wendy laid the book down then carried Ryan to the door. "Before we head home, I'll treat you to a scrumlicious dessert—Abby's description—from the Sweet Shoppe." Following the trip downtown, they parked in the garage beside Chris's car. Kayla followed Wendy into the kitchen.

Chris sat at the dining room table, his jaw clenched. He pointed to the chair across from him. "Sit down, young lady."

Kayla hesitated, then complied.

Wendy lowered Ryan into his playpen. "What's wrong?"

His eyes laser focused on Kayla, Chris tossed a clear Ziploc bag on the table. "How do you explain this?"

Wendy gawked at what appeared to be hand-rolled cigarettes. "Is that what I think it is?"

Kayla's mouth pinched. "How'd you know?"

"Our guest room is next to our home office. Are you not aware that the distinctive smell of marijuana lingers?"

"Are you kidding me?" Wendy dropped onto the chair between her husband and sister. "You brought an illegal drug into our home?"

"It's legal in lots of places."

Wendy glared at Kayla. "Not in Georgia."

"Or Tennessee," added Chris. "This is the second time you've broken the law. The first time you drove here alone without a legal license." Chris tapped his fingers on the evidence bag. "And now this."

Kayla crossed her arms tight across her chest. "You don't understand."

Chris's mouth set in a hard line. "Understand what?"

"For the first time in my life, Mom's acting like she cares about me, Riley, and Zach."

Wendy's brow pinched. "Why is that a problem?"

"How can someone with stage-four cancer refuse chemotherapy?" Kayla's tone turned harsh. "Probably because she cares too much about how she looks to risk losing her hair."

Wendy's heart ached for her sister. "The morning before we left Nashville, Cynthia pulled me aside to explain that she had rejected treatment other than pain meds."

"Chemo would cure her, wouldn't it?"

Wendy shook her head. "The cancer has spread too far." She grasped Kayla's hand. "The most it would do is give her a few more months."

"So she's giving up?"

"She doesn't want to suffer from debilitating side effects. Instead, our mother is choosing to live her final days in this world with dignity, loving her family the best way she knows how."

Kayla unfolded her arms, her chin trembling. "I don't want Mom or Dad to know I broke the law again."

"This will remain between the three of us. However, some sort of penalty is called for." Wendy turned toward Chris. "What's appropriate from a legal perspective, darling?"

"In my professional opinion, ten hours of community service before you leave Blue Ridge."

Kayla's brows peaked. "Doing what?"

"We'll figure that out later today. In the meantime, I'll get rid of the drugs." Chris pocketed the Ziploc bag, then headed through the kitchen and out to the garage.

Tears pooled then tracked down Kayla's cheeks. "You're disappointed in me, aren't you?"

"A little." Wendy locked eyes with her sister. "You'll make up for your criminal behavior by making two promises. First, stop abusing your body with marijuana or any other drug."

"I promise." Kayla swiped her hand across her cheeks. "What's second?"

"Shower your mother with love, beginning with a phone call."

"When?"

Wendy squeezed her hand. "There's no better time than now."

"Can I text her instead?"

"No. She needs to hear your voice."

Kayla stared at her for a long moment, then pulled her hand away and removed her phone from her back pocket. She hesitated. "What if she doesn't want to talk to me?"

"Trust me. She will."

Kayla took in a discernible breath, then slowly released the air while tapping the screen. With her phone pressed to her ear, she lowered onto the den sofa. "Hey, Mom."

Understanding her sister needed privacy, Wendy lifted Ryan from the playpen and carried him to the front door. Duke followed them out to the front porch. A squirrel scrambled off the railing then raced across the driveway to the closest tree, sending their canine family member on another unsuccessful chase.

A half hour after Wendy settled on a rocking chair, Kayla walked out and dropped on the rocker beside her. "I imagine your mother was happy to hear from you."

Kayla nodded. "She reserved two rooms at Hilltop Inn for next week—one for her and Dad, plus another one for Riley and Zach. She wants our family to spend time together."

T

ears of joy pooled in Wendy's eyes. She pressed her palms together while silently thanking God for giving her and Kayla time to experience a loving relationship with each other and their mother.

Chapter 7

Abby's mind raced while Tommy stowed her wheelchair in his trunk. As soon as he climbed behind the steering wheel then backed down the ranch house driveway, her thoughts spilled out. "Something weird is going on."

He stole a quick glance at her. "What are you talking about?"

"Wendy's text. In half an hour, Chris is gonna drop Kayla off at the crisis center. Wendy says her sister wants to volunteer her time doing chores. She's sixteen. Why would she want to work during her vacation?"

"Maybe she's bored." Tommy braked at the stop sign.

"Who could possibly be bored around Wendy, and why didn't Kayla say anything the night she went to the movie with us?"

"She's a girl. How should I know what she was thinking?"

"I intend to find out." Abby sighed. "Sierra's moving into our house tomorrow. Morgan believes Mom was right to let her take care of Theo."

"She is his mother. Plus, without babysitting duty, you'll have more time to spend with me." Tommy slowed behind a slow-moving truck. "I put a deposit on a ground floor apartment that comes available in thirty days."

"Ground floor because your girlfriend's stuck in a wheelchair for a little while longer?"

"Well, yeah."

"Actually, that's kind of sweet. Are you positive you're ready to move out of your parents' house?"

"I'm twenty. Plus I have a good job and earn a decent salary, so yeah, I'm ready." The slow-moving truck turned onto a side street. "In a couple of years when I take over our family's construction business, I'll buy us a big house."

Abby glanced sideways at the man she loved with all her heart. The man she knew beyond the shadow of a doubt was her soulmate. If she couldn't walk by the end of the year, how would she find the courage to follow through on her decision to end their relationship and set Tommy free? She closed her eyes while concentrating on wiggling her big toe. Had she been imagining it moved, or did it actually happen? After flattening her hands on her thighs, she attempted to move her left big toe. She wasn't imagining it. Her eyes popped open. "Oh my gosh."

"What?"

A smile she couldn't contain spread across her face. She turned toward Tommy. "Just now, for the first time since the accident, I moved all ten toes."

"You know what that means?" He pulled off the road, shifted into park, then grasped her hand. His eyes met hers. "One day before long you'll walk again."

Abby pressed her hand to Tommy's cheek. "For us." *And for Theo.*

He kissed her fingers. "I love you so much."

"I love you more." Abby pulled her hand away from his cheek. "My toe-wiggling success is our secret until after my next therapy session."

"Got it. After I pick you up tonight, I'm taking you to dinner to celebrate."

"You're on."

He released her hand then waited for a car to pass before easing back onto the road.

By the time Tommy parked at the crisis center and removed her wheelchair from the trunk, Abby had come to one all-important decision. As soon as Sierra proved unfit as a mother, she'd reveal the secret she hadn't shared with anyone except Morgan—that she and Tommy were meant to adopt Theo.

Tommy opened the passenger door. After she lifted her body onto her wheelchair, he leaned down to kiss her cheek. "I'll pick you up at five."

"Until then." Abby maneuvered to the back entrance. Seconds after she entered a number into the keypad, the door swung open. With renewed hope, she wheeled inside and down the hall to her office. She opened the center's computer to check today's schedule. Nothing out of the ordinary. What sort of chores would suit Kayla? Cleaning? Entertaining kids? Disrupted by a knock on the door, Abby spun her chair around. "Hi."

Ms. Carter, who had arrived the day Wendy had first brought Kayla to the center, held her five-year-old daughter's hand. "Lucy wants to thank you for the gift you gave her."

Abby smiled at the child clutching the stuffed kitty to her chest. "You're welcome. Have you given your new friend a name?"

Lucy's chin dipped to her chest. "Mittens."

"Because she has white paws?"

"Uh-huh."

"You've chosen the perfect name."

The girl's mother placed her hands on her child's shoulders. "Is it okay if Lucy stays with you while I shower?"

Peering at Ms. Carter's still bandaged forehead and black eye, Abby suspected she wanted to hide other evidence of beatings from her child. "Absolutely."

"Thank you."

Ms. Carter stooped to brush a lock of hair away from her daughter's cheek. "Abby will take good care of you, sweetheart."

Seconds after the battered mother walked out, the center's director stepped inside. "Hi, Lucy." She faced Abby. "Kayla Gilmore is waiting for you."

"Thank you, Ms. Pamela." Abby's eyes remained focused on Lucy. "Would you like to ride with me to meet my friend?"

The child nodded, her eyes wide.

Abby lifted Lucy onto her lap. "Have you ever ridden in a chair with wheels?"

"Uh-uh."

"You're in for a treat." Abby maneuvered out the door and down the hall to the reception area. "Kayla, meet my new friend Lucy."

"Hi." Kayla moved close. "My little sister's favorite stuffed animal is a kitten. We don't have a real cat because my brother Zach is allergic."

"I don't have a brother."

"Know what? I love Zach, but sometimes he's as pesky as a big fat mosquito."

Lucy giggled. "You're funny."

Perfect. "I have a great idea." After motioning for Kayla to follow, Abby wheeled to a cozy room. A green and white striped sofa faced a bookcase filled with books, games, and puzzles. Painted balloons adorned two walls stretching up to the pale blue ceiling featuring fluffy white clouds. "You can stay here with Kayla and pretend she's your big sister while I finish some work."

Lucy hesitated before sauntering to the bookcase. She squatted beside the bottom shelf. After picking through the options, she carried a book to Kayla. "Will you read this one to me?"

"You picked a good one." Kayla settled on the sofa. Lucy climbed on, snuggling beside her new friend.

Pleased with assigning an important task to Kayla, Abby backed out of the room, returned to her office, and closed the door. Eager to confirm her progress, she concentrated on moving all ten toes while envisioning her and Tommy pushing Theo's stroller along Main Street. How many friends would stop to congratulate them for adopting the child she had rescued? After treating him to a cookie, they'd take him home to their new apartment on the second floor. Warmth infusing her body, Abby maneuvered to her desk. Enough daydreaming. Time to focus on work and earn her salary. Forty minutes after tapping her laptop keypad, Abby responded to a knock. "Come in."

The door swung open. Kayla ambled in. "Lucy's with her mom now." She plopped onto the love seat.

Abby turned her wheelchair toward Kayla. "Did you enjoy spending time with her?"

"She's such a sad little girl." Kayla tucked her ankle under her knee while peering around the office. "Do you sometimes get depressed working here?"

"Helping children who are victims of abuse recover emotionally as well as physically is far more than a job. It's a calling."

Kayla's head tilted. "You were abused, weren't you? Wendy told me."

"Every time my father hit Mom, I was terrified he'd kill her. Then one day we escaped to a place like this. The woman who tutored me helped me feel safe."

"I suppose being ignored is better than getting beat up."

"Both are traumatic for a child." Time to learn the real reason Chris brought Kayla to the center. "Today, you didn't come here voluntarily, did you?"

Kayla picked at a cuticle. "Did you ever smoke weed?"

"One time back in Asheville. I coughed so hard I thought my lungs would explode." Abby wheeled closer to Kayla. "Wendy caught you, didn't she?"

"Chris found my stash. He sentenced me to ten hours of community service to pay for my crime."

"Now you have nine more to go."

"Something like that." Kayla's brow pinched as if she suddenly regretted confessing. "You won't tell anyone, will you?"

"I promise not to breathe a word."

"My parents are coming to town next week. If they found out...anyway, thanks."

"You're welcome. Now, about your next assignment."

Kayla spent the rest of the day accomplishing a number of chores. Helping the ladies fix lunch. Cleaning the kitchen. Vacuuming offices. Reading to three more children. At five o'clock she ambled into Abby's office. "Even though I only have two hours left on my sentence, is it okay if I volunteer all day here tomorrow?"

"These kids are growing on you, aren't they?"

Kayla shrugged. "I guess so."

"Tell you what. Since our volunteer teacher won't be here tomorrow, you can take over classroom duty."

Kayla's eyes widened. "I won't have to teach math, will I?"

"Not your favorite subject?"

"My least."

"Mine too. Anyway, your oldest student is nine, so nothing more than basic arithmetic."

"All right then." Kayla pulled her phone from her pocket. "Chris is out front. I'll see you tomorrow." She waved over her shoulder while dashing out to the hall.

Abby shut down her computer then maneuvered out of the office. She stopped to peek into the kitchen bustling with activity. Mothers worked together to prepare supper while their children drew pictures or read books—a new type of a temporary family helping one another overcome the pain and humiliation of abuse. She released a deep, gratifying sigh while continuing to roll toward the rear entrance to wait for Tommy.

Outside, Abby donned her sunglasses while basking in the sun warming her cheeks. She smiled while focusing on her new toe-moving feat. At the moment life couldn't be better.

Chapter 8

Conflicting emotions hounded Amanda while she laid Theo in the crib beside the bed in the guest room. Although Sierra would relieve everyone of baby duties, Jillian had made it clear she and Erica would be responsible for supervising the teenage mother. Not an easy task. Especially since they had no idea about the girl's background or her true motivation.

"I've listed the household duties for our new houseguest. Jillian requiring assigned chores isn't a normal Child Services request."

Amanda spun toward Erica. "Sierra moving in with the family who are fostering her child isn't a normal situation."

"True. At least we're giving Theo the opportunity to grow up without wondering why his mother didn't want him."

"If Sierra doesn't bail, she'll need to do a lot of growing up herself before assuming the responsibility of raising a child on her own." Amanda closed the blinds. "In a way, we're fostering an infant plus a teenager."

"Except according to Sierra, she's eighteen, which means she'd already have aged out of the foster system."

"A moot point." Amanda brushed past Erica then walked out of the guest room.

Erica followed. "Abby seemed especially happy when Tommy brought her home last night." She let Dusty in from the backyard then settled on the sofa before laying the task list on the coffee table. "Maybe she's finally accepted the fact that Theo is Sierra's baby."

Amanda propped her elbows on the club chair arms. "For Abby's sake, I hope you're right."

Millie dashed in through the kitchen. "When's Jillian bringing Sierra?"

"Any minute now."

"The whole town knows about the substantial amount of money left in Theo's GoFundMe account." Millie dropped onto the other club chair. "Chances are that girl wants all that cash."

Amanda raised a brow. "Talk about cynical."

Millie waggled her finger at Amanda. "You can't tell me the money hasn't given you pause."

"At least I didn't say it out loud."

"Give it a break, you two." Erica crossed one leg over the other. "At least try to play nice."

"Not a problem." Millie huffed. "But you can both bet I'll keep a close eye on your new houseguest."

Amanda pressed her lips tight. Even the hint of a smile would reveal her gratitude for Millie's self-appointed mission. "Have either of you checked next week's reservations?"

Millie crossed her arms. "There you go changing the subject."

"I'll take your response as a no." Amanda faced Erica. "Cynthia Gilmore booked two rooms for two nights."

Erica's eyes widened. "Does Wendy know?"

"Kayla told her." Amanda turned toward Millie. "Wendy wants you to prepare a family dinner in Hilltop's dining room for their first night."

"Besides the Gilmores, who's considered family?"

"To keep our guests from being overwhelmed, just Wendy and Chris, me, Erica, Abby—"

Millie tapped her foot. "What about me?"

"If you'd let me finish, you'd know you're included."

Millie stopped tapping. "Is Sierra included?"

Amanda shook her head. "She's our houseguest, not a family member."

"I'll recruit her to help Bernie serve so I can sit at the table as a proper member of the family. Dinner for eleven will cost a bundle. Who's paying?"

"We're not charging for the rooms—family discount. Chris will pay for dinner. Wendy also wants you to bake a birthday cake for Ryan."

"His birthday isn't until a week later. Won't two parties confuse him?"

Amanda stared at Millie. "You're kidding, right?"

"Don't act so shocked. You know he's smart."

The doorbell rang.

Erica lifted off the sofa. "I'll let them in." Moments later she escorted their guests to the den then motioned toward the sofa. "Please have a seat."

Sierra hesitated before settling on the center cushion.

Jillian placed a folder on the coffee table then remained standing. "Do you have the list ready?"

"We do." Settling on the cushion beside Sierra, Erica handed the list to their caseworker.

Jillian ran her finger down the sheet of paper then passed it over to Theo's mother. "Which one of you ladies will provide me with reports?"

Erica raised her hand. "I will."

"Good." Jillian pushed the folder to Erica. "These are the weekly forms you'll need to complete. Sierra has a copy, so she understands what's expected of her."

Amanda's focus shifted to Erica the moment she opened the folder. Her hardened expression spoke volumes about the task ahead.

Jillian's eyes remained focused on Erica as well. "Any questions?"

"Everything explained." Erica laid the folder on the coffee table.

"Go ahead and show Sierra to her quarters."

Her quarters? Amanda resisted saluting the caseworker who had taken on the role of drill sergeant. She lifted off her chair. "I'll show you out."

Millie stood. "I'll come with you."

Jillian motioned for them to follow her out the front door then on to her car.

Eyeing their caseworker with suspicion, Amanda leaned against Gunter's truck. "What haven't you told us?"

"During the past week, I've spent hours grilling Sierra. She's an emotionally immature teenager who will need to accomplish some serious growing up before we'll even entertain the idea of granting her custody."

Millie snapped her fingers. "I'll put her to work in Hilltop's kitchen every Monday and Tuesday to help whip her into shape."

"While holding Sierra accountable, you ladies also need to let her know you care about her to help boost her self-esteem."

Amanda nodded. "Tough love."

"I'm glad you understand." Jillian pulled her phone from her pocket. "I need to take this. Call me if any questions come up before next week's follow-up visit." She swiped her finger across her phone then climbed into her car.

The moment Jillian backed down the driveway, Amanda faced Millie. "I appreciate your commitment to help us with Sierra. At the same time, we don't need to overwhelm her on her first day here."

Millie propped a hand on her hip. "You want me to leave her alone today, don't you?"

"I knew I could count on your keen intuition—"

"Stop with the flattery. For once, I agree with you."

"You're a wise woman." Amanda thumped Millie's arm. "You actually deserved that compliment."

"I know." She lowered her hand to her side. "I'll give you and Erica plenty of time to settle Sierra in before I bring lasagna, salad, plus dessert over."

"You're inviting yourself to dinner, aren't you?"

"What sort of impression would you give Sierra if I brought food and you didn't invite me to stay?"

Amanda snickered. "You never cease to amaze me."

"I'll take your comment as another well-deserved compliment." Millie waved over her shoulder while heading out of the carport. "I'll see you at six."

"Uh-huh." Amanda spun around then walked back inside. Overwhelming curiosity sent her straight to the open guest-room door. Erica lifted a duffle off the king-sized bed while Sierra arranged a shirt on a hanger. "How's everything going?"

"Okay, I guess." Sierra hung the shirt in the closet. "Theo's still asleep."

"His morning nap." Amanda stepped inside. "The three of us will share the bathroom across the hall. As the newest member of our household, we're counting on you to help us keep everything neat and clean."

"Erica already told me. This bedroom is a lot nicer than the one at Grandma's house." Sierra plopped onto the side of the bed. "The bed's bigger than the one in my room back in Chattanooga."

"Do your parents know you're moving in with us?"

"Doesn't matter. Lots of kids my age leave home and live on their own."

Erica exchanged a glance with Amanda then faced Sierra. "Have you ever worked at a job?"

"You mean for pay?"

"Yes."

Sierra shrugged. "Not really."

"We have good news." Erica sat beside Sierra. "Two days a week, we'll pay you to work next door with Chef Millie. Tomorrow, we'll help you open a checking account so your pay can be directly deposited to the bank."

"Why?" Sierra's brows pinched. "I mean you could just give me cash."

Amanda crossed her arms. How did Awesam's chief executive officer plan to handle that question?

"True." Erica turned toward Sierra. "The thing is, a parent needs to provide the finances required to raise a child. The cost of housing, food, clothes, medical expenses."

"That's a lot."

"Which is why our chief financial officer will help you learn how to manage your money. That's a conversation for tomorrow. For now, we'll give you time to put the rest of your belongings away." Erica stood then walked out.

Amanda closed the door then followed Erica to the den. "Good response, Ms. CEO."

"Our houseguest has a lot to learn."

"What about Wendy? Does she have a clue about what you've committed her to?"

"She will." Erica plucked her phone off the coffee table. She tapped the screen then pressed the phone to her ear. "Hey, Wendy."

At quarter to six, Abby rolled across the sidewalk to the ranch-house front porch then gripped the door handle. How long could she remain neutral while another woman cared for the baby she considered hers—even though that woman was Theo's biological mother? Releasing a heavy sigh, Abby pushed the door open then wheeled toward voices drifting from the den. Her mother and Amanda occupied chairs at the dining room table. Sierra sat on the sofa with her feet propped on the coffee table while feeding Theo a bottle. "Hey, everyone."

"Hi, sweetheart. How'd your day go?"

"Same as every other day." Abby cringed at her harsh tone. "One of our mothers along with her two kids returned home after her husband landed in jail."

Sierra peered over her shoulder. "Why did the cops arrest him?"

"Domestic violence." Abby maneuvered toward the sofa. A stabbing pain gripped her chest. Theo's tiny hand wrapped around his mother's finger—the woman who had stuffed him in a gym bag before dumping him on the crisis center front stoop. Abby moved closer. "Isn't it sweet how he wraps his hand around whatever finger is close by?"

Sierra peered at Abby. "Do you want to hold him?"

"Actually..." Abby's mother approached. "We want to give you and your baby time to bond." She placed her hands on Abby's shoulders. "Right, sweetheart?"

Struggling to swallow a snide remark, Abby forced a smile. "Of course."

The succulent aroma of tomatoes and cheese accompanied Millie who breezed in from the carport. "You ladies are in for a treat." She set a baking dish on the dining room table. "Homemade lasagna with Italian sausage and pecorino cheese."

"Yum." Sierra set Theo's bottle on the end table before lifting him to her shoulder and patting his back.

Abby spun her chair around. "Your lasagna is almost as good as your mac and cheese." She rolled toward the table while her mother moved Theo's swing between her seat and the empty chair beside Amanda. Sierra pushed off the sofa. After placing Theo in his swing, she settled on the empty chair.

Abby pressed her lips tight—understanding full well she needed to let the events play out, hopefully in her favor.

Chapter 9

Thick clouds drifting over the golf course lowered the temperature at least fifteen degrees. Grateful she'd brought a lightweight sweater, Erica pulled her phone from her pocket then tapped the weather app while Brad closed his SUV's rear hatch and climbed into the golf cart beside her. She held up her phone. "Sixty-percent chance of rain at noon."

"If the weather holds out long enough, we'll at least finish the first nine." Brad drove out of the parking lot, passed the clubhouse, then veered onto the cart path. When they arrived at the first hole, he pulled up behind their golfing buddies. Carl greeted them, then swapped Erica's clubs with his. As usual the guys rode in one cart and the gals in the other.

Gripping a club in one hand, Lauren greeted Erica with a one-arm hug. "Hopefully, we'll have a couple of hours to play while catching up." She ambled to the tee. After setting her ball, she took one practice swing before driving her ball in a perfect arc straight down the fairway. According to Brad, his deceased wife had also been an accomplished golfer.

At least Lauren's skills intimidated Erica a little less every time they played. She brushed past her friend then pressed her tee into the turf. Following a moment of hesitation, Erica gripped the club the way Brad had taught her. She took a quick glance at the green then focused on her target and swung, making sure to follow through. While landing yards short of Lauren's, at least her ball stayed in the fairway.

Always the cheerleader, Lauren high-fived Erica the moment she stepped off the tee. "Good shot."

"No matter how many times I play, I'll never catch up with you." Erica slid her club into her bag.

"You've come a long way during the past year. Especially since you never played before you met Brad." The women climbed into the golf cart. "Enough about the game. How's fostering going?"

"Theo's mother moved in with us a couple of days ago."

"At least you haven't had enough time to become too attached to him."

"That's true for Amanda and me." A cool breeze sweeping across the fairway brought a shiver. "Abby's another story."

Lauren brushed hair away from her cheek. "Your daughter needs to let go to prevent her heart from breaking."

"I know."

As soon as the guys teed off, Lauren drove away from the tee then parked halfway to the green. She and Erica climbed out and strode onto the fairway. After taking their second strokes, they returned to the cart to continue riding along the path. "After all these years, Carl and I are still in contact with our foster child and her mother. Since Theo's mother is living with you, if she's granted custody, chances are she'll allow Abby to stay in his life. Speaking of Abby, how's her therapy going?"

"About the same. She has another session tomorrow." After the men returned to their cart, Erica took her third shot before they continued on to the green. The flag flapped in the breeze as she ambled to her ball and lined up her putter. *Nice and easy.* Her stroke stopped two feet short of the target. She stepped up and swung again, ending the first hole with a bogey. Erica retrieved her ball before stepping off the green.

Brad leaned on his putter. "One stroke over par. Good job."

"Better than last week's double bogey, but not as impressive as your birdie."

"A little luck plus enough wind blowing in the right direction." Since the night Brad vowed to limit their time together to golf outings with the Lowes, he'd acted more like her coach than the man who had proposed to her. Had Lauren noticed the change in his demeanor? If she did, would she comment?

After Carl sank his putt, he placed the flag into the cup. They returned to their carts to drive to the second tee.

Before they had time to finish the eighth hole, the light drizzle threatening to give way to serious rain forced their return to the clubhouse.

Inside the pro shop, Lauren linked arms with Erica and Brad. "Given the weather has thrown a curve into our plans, why don't you two come to our house? We'll throw some burgers on the grill and spend a lazy afternoon chilling on our screened porch."

Erica hesitated. They had planned to spend the entire day with their friends, so why not accept. Besides, she had wanted to visit their home since the day Lauren described the view. "Sounds like fun."

"We'll have a ball." Lauren released Erica's arm then grabbed her golf bag before heading toward the exit.

Avoiding eye contact with Brad, Erica shouldered her bag. "You don't mind, do you?"

"Spending time at their home isn't much different than hanging out at the clubhouse after playing eighteen holes." His tone lacked even a hint of enthusiasm.

"I suppose you're right," she murmured as they approached the exit.

They scurried across the parking lot, stashed their clubs, and climbed into the SUV's front seat moments before the drizzle gave way to a downpour. Wiper blades swept wide arcs across the windshield as they headed out of the parking lot. Erica glanced sideways at Brad's clenched jaw. Was he concentrating on driving, or regretting accepting Lauren's invitation? Maybe she should have waited for him to respond. "I'll understand if you'd rather skip going to the Lowes'—"

"If I had any qualms about spending the afternoon with our friends, don't you think I would have begged off?"

Erica winced. Why hadn't she left well enough alone? "I just..."

"What?"

Lightning flashed, followed by a distant thunderclap. "I wanted to make sure you're okay."

"Trust me. I'll let you know when I'm not." Brad's harsh tone stood in stark contrast to his words.

Rain pummeling the roof drowned out the uncomfortable silence that ensued. Erica laced her fingers across her stomach while focusing on the road ahead. By the time they parked in the Lowes' driveway, a fist-sized knot gripped her stomach.

Brad cut the engine. "Do you need an umbrella?"

"It's only a couple of feet." Erica jumped out then dashed into the open garage. Brad caught up with her as they headed inside and climbed up to the three-story home's main level.

Lauren met them at the top of the stairs. "We're delighted you're joining us." She escorted them into their great room anchored on one end by the kitchen and on the other end by a massive brick fireplace.

Erica eyed the cozy yet sophisticated décor. "Your home is gorgeous."

"Wait until you see the view." While Brad joined Carl in the kitchen, Lauren led Erica out the French doors to a wide screened deck. An outdoor U-shaped sectional sofa with a firepit functioning as a coffee table faced the heavily wooded backyard.

"Do you spend a lot of time out here?"

"Mostly during weekends plus when we have friends over."

Carl opened the door. "Do you ladies prefer beer or chardonnay?"

"Wine for me. What about you, Erica?"

"The same."

"Coming right up."

Erica moved close to the screen. She peered down at the steep terrain leading to a railroad track. "I see what you mean about the view. You're on Blue Ridge Railroad's scenic route, aren't you?"

"Twice a day, ten months a year, a trainload of tourists passes by."

"Here you go, ladies." Carl stepped onto the deck. He handed Lauren the wine along with two glasses while Brad set a tray on a round glass-top table before opening two beers.

Lauren filled the wine glasses, handing one to Erica. "How about a tour before our guys play chef?" Without waiting for an answer, she stood. "Come on." Lauren looped her arm around Erica's elbow steering her through the den to the front foyer. Bookcases covered one wall in the sitting room on the right.

"Given you teach English plus creative writing, I assume you're the reader."

"Carl and I both enjoy reading."

Erica pulled away from Lauren then stepped into the room. "Have you ever considered writing a book?"

"Funny you should ask. Becoming an author is one of the top five items on my bucket list. I'm leaning toward romantic suspense. Speaking of romance—" Lauren moved beside Erica. "I hope you don't think I'm prying, but it's obvious something's going on between you and Brad."

Erica's back stiffened. "What do you mean?"

"Jan and Brad were our closest friends, so I know how much he loved her. I also know how he looks at you the same way he did her—with pure joy and adoration. At least he did until a couple of months ago. Now you both treat each other as if you're casual acquaintances instead of two people madly in love."

Breaking eye contact, Erica faced the window. So Lauren *had* noticed. "We're taking things slow."

"Slow is one thing. You two seemed to have slammed on the brakes."

During the past year, Lauren had become a close friend. Maybe the time had come to trust her with the truth. "Several months ago Brad sort of proposed."

Lauren's brow pinched together. "How does a man 'sort of' propose?"

Erica explained, leaving out details about her goals. "I haven't told Brad, but a few days ago I opened the box."

"Considering your left ring finger is still unadorned, you obviously haven't accepted his proposal."

"I wasn't quite ready."

Lauren ran her finger around her wineglass rim. "Are you still in love with Brad?"

"Deeply."

"He's not only a dear friend; he's also my boss. So please understand when I tell you there's a limit to his patience, and Brad's is running dangerously low."

Erica stared at the golden liquid in her wineglass. Lauren had verbalized what she had known in her heart but couldn't bring herself to admit. Sierra assuming responsibility for Theo at least set her on the course toward achieving her second goal. If she continued waiting for her next two paychecks to accomplish her first, would she risk damaging her relationship with Brad? Erica set her wineglass on an end table. "Do you mind if I borrow your car for half an hour?"

Her friend's eyes met hers. She seemed to understand.

"Come with me." Lauren led the way to the kitchen then removed her keys from her purse and placed them in Erica's hand. "The red car's mine. I'll cover for you."

"Thank you for being a good friend." Erica embraced Lauren, then headed straight to the garage. Ten minutes later she parked on the ranch house driveway. At the same time she stepped onto the pavement, Amanda crossed the side yard from the inn.

Awesam's president ran her hand along the hood. "Did you ditch your golf game to buy a car?"

"Borrowed it from Lauren." Erica's eyes met Amanda's. "A few minutes ago, she helped me accept reality."

Amanda's face lit with a smile. "You're ready, aren't you?"

"Let's just say my priorities have shifted a little." After rushing inside and heading straight to her room, Erica returned to Lauren's car then backed down the driveway. Events from the past year played in her mind until she pulled into the Lowes' garage. What had Lauren told the guys about her absence? Erica hesitated a moment. Had she made the right decision? She clutched an item off the passenger seat then climbed out and headed straight to the main level. At the top of the stairs, she paused to dismiss the last thread of doubt before walking out to the deck. Lauren sat on the sofa's center section with her feet propped on the firepit coffee table. Carl sat on one end of the U, Brad on the other.

Lauren lowered her feet to the floor. "The guys turned off the grill to wait for you."

Brad stood, his brow pinched. "Are you okay?"

Their eyes met. Erica's heart pounded in her chest. "The night you surprised me with a proposal I was reeling from painful childhood memories plus two failed marriages. I told you I needed more time. In reality I needed to ensure I could accept your proposal for all the right reasons. I set a goal to save a substantial amount of money for my own financial security. As of today I'm three grand short."

Brad lifted Erica's left hand. "Is that why you're not wearing my ring?"

"Not exactly." She held up the ring box. "Right here, in the presence of two people who have accepted me as their friend from the moment I first met them, I want the man I love with all my heart to propose to me a second time."

Brad's eyes met hers. "Finding one perfect soulmate is rare. Discovering a second is nothing short of a miracle." Time stood still as he lifted the box from her hand then dropped to one knee. His lips curved into a heartwarming smile the moment he opened the lid. "Erica Nelson, will you marry me and make my life complete?"

Tears of joy pooled then tracked down Erica's cheeks. "Yes, Brad Barkley, I will marry you and make my life complete."

Their friends cheered the second Brad lifted off his knee to kiss his now official fiancée. When their lips parted, Erica pressed her hand to her chest. "For the first time in my life, my heart and my mind are perfectly synchronized."

Lauren rushed toward them, wiping her fingers across her cheeks. "I'm thrilled for both of you."

Carl clapped his hand on Brad's shoulder. "I'm counting on being your best man again."

Brad's eyes remained locked on Erica's. "What do you think, my love? Should we allow this character to be part of our wedding?"

"Along with Lauren, absolutely."

Chapter 10

The first hint of dawn invaded the inky black sky when Brad parked his Corvette on the ranch house driveway behind Abby's car. Erica leaned across the console to stroke his cheek. "If you walk me to the door, you'll end up late to school."

Grasping Erica's hand, Brad kissed her fingers. "Because I couldn't resist kissing you?"

A delicious tingling sensation raced through Erica's limbs. "I feel like a teenager sneaking home eight hours past curfew."

Brad grinned. "The principal might be forced to call you to his office."

Resisting the urge to wrap her arms around his neck, Erica pulled her hand away. "Call me after school."

"Better yet, I'll pick you up at five to take you out to dinner."

The first time in weeks. "I'll count the hours." Erica climbed out then hastened through the carport and into the kitchen.

"Good morning, Future Mrs. Barkley." Amanda handed Erica a coffee mug. "If Millie still lived in our guest room, she'd grill you until you spilled every single detail about last night."

"Hopefully she didn't see Brad's car."

The kitchen door swung open followed by Millie charging in. "An all-nighter can only mean one thing."

Sensing her cheeks were seconds from turning bright pink, Erica cleared her throat. "How—"

"I saw Brad turn onto your driveway." Millie grabbed Erica's left hand. "Gorgeous ring. When's the wedding?"

"We haven't set a date."

"At least you've taken our high school principal off the market." Millie thumped Amanda's arm. "If you're smart, you'll do the same with Gary."

Amanda huffed. "Isn't today one of your days off?"

"What's your point?"

"Why were you outside before the crack of dawn?"

"I enjoy drinking a cup of coffee while watching the sunrise from my front porch."

Amanda raised a brow. "Perfect spot to snoop on your neighbors?"

"Hmph." Millie strode out, pulling the door closed behind her.

Erica set her mug on the counter. "Maybe Millie's right about Gary."

"Don't you start—"

"I'm just saying it wouldn't hurt to give him a second look."

Amanda folded her arms tight across her chest. "Don't you have something important to do, such as sharing the good news with your daughter?"

"I'm on my way." Erica waved over her shoulder while walking out of the kitchen toward the hall. The light shining under Abby's door made it clear she'd awakened. Erica knocked.

"Is that you, Mom?"

She stepped inside, leaving the door open. "Good morning."

Dusty yawned then stretched while Abby maneuvered her wheelchair out of her bathroom. "Not nearly as good as yours." She moved closer. "I want to see your ring."

Erica stared at her daughter. "How'd you know?"

"You're wearing the same golf outfit you wore when you left yesterday."

"So much for subtlety." Erica smiled while holding up her left hand, her fingers splayed.

"Oh my gosh, Mom, what a gorgeous ring. Mr. Barkley has great taste."

"Given he'll soon become your stepfather, maybe it's time to refer to him as Brad."

"Hmm. Do you suppose either he or Jimmy would mind if I called him Dad? After the wedding, of course."

"Why don't you ask them?"

"I will. By the way, Tommy's taking me to my therapy session this afternoon."

"I'll look forward to an update."

Theo's cry perked Dusty's ears while sending Abby wheeling toward the door.

Sensing her daughter's motive, Erica gripped the chair handles. "Neither of us needs to respond, sweetheart. His mother's in charge now."

Abby peered over her shoulder, her brows pinched. "I'm just gonna let Dusty out."

"Okay." Erica released the chair then followed her daughter out to the hall.

Sierra stepped out from the guest room carrying Theo. "Do babies always wake up this early?"

Abby nodded. "You can forget sleeping late, at least until Theo's old enough to start school."

Avoiding eye contact, Sierra headed straight to the kitchen.

"She still doesn't have a clue." Abby's tone hinted she hadn't accepted Sierra's role as Theo's mother.

"Give her time, sweetheart. She'll learn."

"If she doesn't give up and abandon Theo a second time."

Erica's eyes followed Abby as she wheeled out of sight. Did her daughter possess the maturity to avoid an all-out rivalry with Sierra? Erica grabbed a change of clothes from her room before heading across the hall to the bathroom. After turning on the shower, Erica peeled out of the outfit that had thwarted her stealth return then stepped into the tub. Luxuriating in the warm water cascading down her body clarified one remarkable fact. The love she shared with Brad exceeded far beyond what she had believed possible. In her heart, she hoped Amanda would summon the courage to fall in love again.

Three hours after showering, Erica ambled to Hilltop's three-car garage converted to a spa. Based on Wendy's suggestion, the reception area now included a state-of-the-art treadmill, adding one more option for guests. She checked the bathrooms to ensure fresh towels were ready for guests using the sauna then unlocked the massage room. Erica strode into her office and opened her laptop. One appointment scheduled for today.

With ten minutes to spare, she returned to the work area. After spreading sheets on the massage table, she ambled to the waist-high cabinet anchored to the dark blue accent wall. Erica switched on the subtle overhead lights before lighting a candle. Breathing in the fresh scent, she opened the cabinet then turned on her CD player. Soft background music drifting from the wall-mounted speakers added to the relaxing environment.

"Are you ready for me?"

Erica turned toward the middle-aged woman standing in the open doorway. "I am. Please come in. I hope you and Mr. Jones are enjoying your stay at Hilltop."

"Immensely."

Short answer. Maybe she's not the chatty type. "When did you last have a massage?"

"About six weeks ago."

"Perfect time for another. I'll wait in my office. Call out when you're ready." Erica walked into her office, leaving the door ajar. She placed her engagement ring on the desk before selecting massage oil.

"I'm ready."

Erica returned to her work area, ready to treat her client to a Swedish massage. Pleased the woman remained silent, she concentrated on deep circular motions intermingled with long flowing strokes. At the end of the hour, Erica gently tapped the woman's arm. "How are you feeling?"

Mrs. Jones opened her eyes. "Refreshed."

"Excellent. I'll step out while you dress." Erica returned to her office. After cleaning oil off her hands, she slid her ring back on and held her hand up to the window. The diamond sparkled in the sunlight like tiny fireworks.

"What a gorgeous ring."

Erica spun around. "Thank you."

"Based on your smile, I'm guessing you're newly engaged."

Erica nodded. "Since yesterday."

"Congratulations. My husband and I are celebrating our twenty-fifth anniversary tonight."

"Congratulations to you as well. We're honored you've chosen Hilltop as your home away from home."

"Your inn came highly recommended." She handed Erica a generous tip.

"Thank you. I hope you have a wonderful evening."

"And I hope you have a beautiful wedding followed by many years of happiness."

As soon as her client left, Erica pocketed the cash and her phone before locking her office. Stepping out to the warm sunshine, she turned away from the ranch house and headed to the stone walkway bordering Millie's masterpiece, Hilltop's English country garden. She paused beside the brass plaque dedicating the garden to Eleanor Harrington, the property's original owner. Smiling, Erica strolled up the center path. She settled on one of the curved wrought-iron benches facing the five-foot-tall bronze fountain. Chirping birds added delightful musical notes to water cascading down the fountain's three tiers and splashing into the circular pool. A gentle breeze rustled the leaves in the woods beyond the backyard fence.

Erica's eyes drifted to the gazebo featuring white wrought-iron panels between the pillars. Wendy and Chris had stood beneath the chandelier suspended from the cone-shaped roof to exchange their wedding vows.

Amanda ambled over and sat beside Erica. "Today's arrivals are all checked in. You and Brad should have your wedding and reception here at Hilltop, to continue an Awesam tradition."

"Two weddings in the gazebo is a pattern." Erica nudged Amanda. "Three and it becomes a tradition."

"If Abby and Tommy end up marrying—"

"You know what I meant."

"Which is why I'm ignoring you. How'd the massage go?"

Erica pulled two bills from her pocket. "You tell me."

"Another satisfied client." Amanda crossed one leg over the other. "I assume the ring on your finger means you reached your financial goal."

"Not yet." Erica pocketed the cash. "But I will before our wedding."

"Other than Wendy and me, I doubt anyone could understand your motivation."

"Don't forget Millie's comment about banking all her paychecks in case she gets a hankering to invite a lonely old codger to share her bed." Erica removed her phone from her pocket. "Abby's home from therapy." She responded to the text before lifting off the bench. "Hopefully, she has good news."

They left the garden, entered the house, and headed into the den. Abby was on the sofa with Tommy balanced on the sofa arm beside her. Sierra curled up on a club chair beside Theo's swing.

"How'd therapy go—" Erica stared at Abby's feet propped on the coffee table, her toenails painted pink. "Oh my gosh, you got a pedicure."

Her daughter smiled. "To celebrate today's special occasions."

Sierra's head tilted. "What's special about today?"

Abby held up a finger. "First Mom is engaged. Second…" Abby pointed to her feet. "Watch closely." With what appeared to take minimal effort, she moved all ten toes.

Her hand pressed to her chest, Erica settled beside Abby. "Does this mean—"

"That I'm making progress? Oh yeah."

"Abby's therapist says her chance to walk again has improved big time," added Tommy.

"I still have a long way to go." Abby leaned close to Erica.

"At least you're well on your way, sweetheart."

From behind the sofa, Amanda tapped her hands on Abby's shoulders. "News this important calls for a celebration."

"We've got that covered." Tommy headed to the dining room table then returned carrying a Sweet Shoppe box. "A half dozen cupcakes."

Abby smiled. "Awesam's favorite way to celebrate."

The doorbell rang. Erica glanced at her watch. "Brad's here to take me to dinner."

"I'll let him in." Amanda headed to the foyer, returning with Erica's fiancé.

Settling beside Erica, Brad leaned forward. "I hear congratulations are in order for one of my favorite former students."

"We're celebrating your engagement plus my toe-wiggling feat." Abby giggled. "Good pun, huh."

The doorbell rang again, followed by footsteps. Millie rushed in. "Am I missing some sort of party?"

Amanda leaned against the sofa. "Don't tell me you were still sitting on your front porch from this morning."

"I was taking a walk."

"Actually—" Abby peered over her shoulder. "I'm glad you're here." She demonstrated her toe-wiggling accomplishments.

"Talk about a celebration." Millie pressed her palms together. "You're going to dance at your mom and Brad's wedding, then one day at your own."

"I have an idea." Brad pulled his phone from his pocket. "Instead of Erica and me going out to dinner, I'll have a meal delivered here for all of us. You choose the restaurant, Abby."

"Hmm." Abby tapped her finger to her chin. "How about a couple of pizzas and maybe an Italian salad?"

"Great idea."

While Brad placed the order, Erica envisioned a future filled with promise for her daughter and the young man who remained steadfast by her side.

Chapter 11

Friday, a half hour before Hilltop's check-in time, Wendy carried Ryan from the ranch house carport, passed through the kitchen, and entered the den where Amanda was sitting on the couch with Sierra. "I appreciate you watching Ryan while I greet our new arrivals."

Amanda lifted him into her arms. "I love spending time with my honorary grandson."

Sierra looked up from her magazine, her brows raised. "What do you mean by honorary?"

"Wendy and I are only related by circumstance, which means I don't qualify for official grandmother status."

Sierra scratched her head. "What circumstances?"

"One of these days I'll explain it to you."

Struggling to wriggle from Amanda's arms, Ryan pointed to Dusty. "Dogie."

Amanda laughed. "Upstaged by a four-legged family member." She placed Ryan on the floor, smiling as their little guy winced from Dusty's tongue bath before squealing with delight.

"Now that Ryan has been properly welcomed, I need to join Kayla." Wendy set the diaper bag and purse on the coffee table. "She's next door in the event her family shows up early."

"Are you ready for tonight's blended family dinner?"

"I will be by six o'clock." Wendy kissed her son's cheek. "Be sweet for Nana."

Ryan responded by grasping a lock of his grandmother's hair.

Wendy chuckled. "He's obviously fascinated by red hair. See you later." She waved over her shoulder while heading to the kitchen. After grabbing an inn key, Wendy headed straight to the inn's front porch. Kayla sat on the steps holding the black cat that claimed the space as his daytime hangout when Millie began setting out food. "I see you've met our guest critter."

"Does he have a name?"

"Millie calls him Inky. Isn't your brother allergic to cats?"

"When he gets close to them. He'll stay far enough away from me to avoid a sneezing fit." Inky sprang off Kayla's lap. "You and Chris aren't gonna tell my parents about my crime, are you?"

Wendy glanced sideways at her sister. Had she forgotten what they had told her, or didn't Kayla trust them to keep their word? "We haven't changed our minds."

"Dad warned all us kids about the danger of taking drugs or pills from anyone except a doctor."

"Your father is a wise man."

"Yeah, I know." Kayla picked cat hairs off her shirt. "I think Mom's sorry she didn't keep you after she met Dad."

Wendy stared wide-eyed at her sister.

"I sort of figured out the timeline."

"Impressive for someone who doesn't like math."

Kayla plucked a leaf off the step. "Are you still angry at Mom?"

For abandoning her, no. Wendy's jaw tensed. *For telling the man she'd met at a bar that her daughter had died shortly after childbirth...*

"How come you're not answering?"

Wendy blinked. No way could she tell the truth. "I'm working on it. After your parents arrive, do you want to stay here with them until time to come to our house?"

"I don't know. Maybe." Kayla pulled her phone from her pocket. Her thumbs tapped the keypad, making it clear she didn't want to answer any more questions.

Wendy leaned back, rested her elbows on the step behind her, and closed her eyes. If Brent hadn't told her about her mother's deception, she wouldn't have faced forgiving her a second time. The sun warming her cheeks summoned memories. Moving to Gulfport after aging out of the foster system. Walking barefoot on the beach. On the other hand, if her mother hadn't abandoned her, she wouldn't have given birth to Ryan or met Chris.

Kayla nudged her. "They're here."

Opening her eyes, Wendy pushed to her feet. The family she had only known for a few months climbed out of Brent's SUV. Everyone except Cynthia pulled a suitcase across the driveway and onto the sidewalk. Wendy climbed up to the top step while Kayla pocketed her phone. Time to fill her role as one of Awesam's gracious innkeepers. Summoning her best smile, Wendy climbed onto the porch. "Welcome to Hilltop Inn."

"We're happy to be here." Brent gripped his wife's elbow as they climbed onto the porch.

Kayla hauled her suitcase up the stairs. Riley followed and piped up, "Do I have to sleep in a room with Zach?"

Her brother scoffed. "Yup. Mom and Dad don't want you staying with them, so you're stuck with me."

Brent ruffled Riley's hair. "You'll survive two nights with your brother."

"Your dad's right, Riley." Wendy unlocked the front door then held it open. "Especially since your room has twin beds."

Zach followed his parents and Riley into the foyer. "Any other kids staying here?"

"Not at the moment." Wendy motioned toward the desk. "We'd like you all to sign our guest book."

Brent ambled over. "I noticed you aren't charging us for the rooms."

Wendy nodded. "Our family discount."

"That's quite generous." He signed then handed the pen to his wife while Riley ambled into the living room. "This is a fancy hotel."

Zach scoffed. "It's a B and B, not a hotel."

Wendy resisted rolling her eyes. Were all thirteen-year-old boys this cantankerous? "Actually, a bed and breakfast is a type of hotel, just smaller and more personal."

Riley planted her hands on her hips. "See?"

"Whatever." Zach yanked his phone from his back pocket before trudging to the staircase and dropping onto the second step.

Millie rushed in from the den wearing an apron featuring the inn's logo. "Welcome to Hilltop. I'm Chef Millie as well as a family member."

Cynthia laid the pen on the desk. "Nice to meet you, Millie."

"I've heard a lot about you."

Hoping to quash any inappropriate comments, Wendy stepped between Cynthia and Millie. "Hilltop is fortunate to have an award-winning chef on staff."

Millie's chest puffed. "I'm preparing one of my signature dinners for tonight's family gathering, plus a birthday cake for your grandson."

Brent moved to his wife's side. "We look forward to becoming better acquainted."

"We need to give everyone time to settle in." Wendy lifted a key off the desk while Riley and Kayla wandered into the turret room off the foyer. After sharing the well-rehearsed spiel about Hilltop, she escorted Cynthia and Brent to the den. "You're staying downstairs in the Rainbow Suite." She unlocked the door to the left of the hearth. "This also served as the Harringtons' master bedroom. They were the original owners."

Cynthia stepped inside. "Whoever decorated is a real pro."

"Our CEO deserves the credit. You'll meet Erica tonight during a private family dinner we're planning for you in the inn's dining room."

"Is she a relative?"

"In a sense."

Cynthia ambled to the French doors leading to the back patio while Brent set both suitcases on luggage stands. "Gorgeous view."

"Designed by our chef to honor Eleanor Harrington." Wendy handed Brent the key. "Tonight you're all invited to dinner in Hilltop's dining room. In the meantime, I'll let you two settle in." She pulled the door closed. Time to deal with squabbling siblings. Wendy returned to the foyer. "Are you kids ready to see your room?"

Riley bounded from the turret room. "Is it round like this one?"

Wendy shook her head. "Different guests are in that room. You and your brother are sharing the Bluebell Suite."

Zach pushed off the step. "Talk about lame."

"Despite its name, Bluebell is our most masculine suite." Wendy grabbed the key off the desk. "Come on, I'll show you." All three siblings followed her to the second-story hall stretching from the front of the inn to the back. She unlocked the door.

After pulling her suitcase inside, Riley bounced on the bed closest to the window. "This one's mine."

Scowling, Zach headed straight to a chair to resume doing whatever he'd been doing on his phone.

Wendy laid the key on the dresser. "The door locks when you close it, so be sure to take the key with you when you leave." She turned toward Kayla. "What'd you decide?"

"I think I'll hang out here."

"All right. I'll see y'all at six." After closing the door, Wendy returned to the first floor. A couple walked in from the front porch carrying shopping bags from a number of different stores. "I see you've found some Blue Ridge treasures."

"Boosting the local economy is one of my wife's favorite pastimes."

"Don't let him fool you." The woman grinned while holding up a bag from Mountain City Apparel. "My hubby did his share of economy boosting."

"Our locals appreciate you both. Do you have dinner reservations?"

The husband nodded. "Six at Grace Prime Steakhouse."

"Excellent choice." Moments after the guests headed upstairs, Wendy returned to the ranch house. "How's our little guy?"

"He has a new friend." Amanda pointed to Ryan sitting on the floor beside Sierra holding Theo on her lap. "Good training before he meets his little sister for the first time." She lifted her grandson into her arms. "Everything okay next door?"

"The Gilmores are all checked in. Kayla's staying with her siblings until dinner. Do you mind if Ryan stays with you while I drive home to wait for Chris?"

Amanda cocked her head. "What do you think?"

"Silly me for asking." Wendy plucked her purse off the coffee table. Smiling, she waved over her shoulder while heading to the kitchen. "I'll see you in a couple of hours."

Fifteen minutes before six, Wendy slid the Hilltop Inn's dining room doors open. A floral arrangement and candles graced the table set for eleven, plus a high chair for Ryan. Pleased with the formal setting, she walked into the kitchen. "The table looks amazing, ladies."

Bernie nodded toward Sierra sitting at the island beside Theo's swing. "The three of us are working well as a team."

Millie placed the last beef Wellington on a baking pan. "Until I join the party. Then you're in charge." She rattled off baking instructions to Bernie before pointing her finger at Sierra. "I'm counting on you to help serve our guests as if this wasn't your first time waitressing."

"Bernie's a good coach. I won't forget what she taught me."

Wendy spun toward her sister's voice drifting into the kitchen. "Time to greet my first guests." She returned to the dining room. "The young people are the first to arrive."

Zach shrugged. "Kayla's idea, not mine."

Riley thumped her brother's arm. "She also made you leave your phone in our room."

"Good for Kayla." Brent escorted his wife in from the living room.

Cynthia gripped a gift bag. "Thank you for arranging this event, Wendy."

Riley peered up at Wendy. "What's for supper?"

"You can bet we're not having pizza," Zach muttered.

Brent slid his arm around his son's shoulders. "Tomorrow after our hike, we'll find the best pizza joint in Blue Ridge."

"Speaking of tomorrow, while Zach and his father traipse through the woods, I want to spend the day shopping with my three daughters."

Riley hugged her mother. "Can I buy a new stuffed animal?"

"Of course." Cynthia's eyes met Wendy's, her brows raised. "You don't have other plans, do you?"

If she'd already had plans, she'd break them. "I'm available."

"Wonderful. Why don't you and Kayla pick Riley and me up at ten tomorrow morning and bring my grandson along."

"It's a date." Wendy swallowed the lump rising in her throat. No matter what motivated the invitation, for the first time in her life, she would shop with her mother.

Millie breezed in from the kitchen without her apron. "I'm joining you as a family member while my staff serves us."

Her staff? Wendy stifled a giggle. "Hilltop's chef—"

Millie held up a finger. "And chief financial officer."

"Our multi-talented neighbor is also our little guy's honorary Grammy Millie."

Millie's chest puffed as the rest of the Awesam family ambled in.

After introducing Amanda, Erica, and Abby, Wendy directed her guests to their seats. Following Chris's heartwarming blessing, Bernie and Sierra served spinach salad and fresh-baked rolls. Wendy enjoyed her meal while marveling at the lively conversation and laughter around the table. A stranger would never guess this was the first time all twelve spent time together as a family. Thanks to Chris engaging him, even Zach acted as if he enjoyed the evening. By the time everyone had finished the main course, Wendy came one step closer to forgiving her mother a second time.

As soon as Bernie and Sierra cleared the plates, Millie stood. "Tonight we're celebrating Ryan's first birthday a week early, especially for the Gilmore family." She stepped into the kitchen then returned and set a decorated cake in front of Wendy. "One cake for the adults—"

Bernie followed with a miniature version. "Plus one for our birthday boy."

Following a rousing version of "Happy Birthday," Bernie placed Ryan's cake on the high-chair tray. Cynthia, Amanda, and Chris snapped photos of their little guy's delight over his first taste of sugar-laced cake and icing.

Wendy swallowed the lump rising in her throat the moment Cynthia handed Ryan what would likely be the first and last birthday gift from his maternal grandmother.

Chapter 12

The aroma of freshly brewed coffee nudged Wendy's eyes open. "Aww." She sat up and leaned back against their headboard. "You're the best husband on the planet."

"Married to the most amazing wife." Chris handed her a coffee mug. "Decaf prepared exactly the way you like it."

"Perfect." She sipped, delighting in the sweet vanilla flavor. "What time is it?"

"Eight-thirty."

"Oh my gosh, is Ryan awake?"

"Awake, fed, and dressed. Kayla's entertaining him, so you have time to shower while I fix us breakfast." Chris leaned down to kiss her cheek before walking out of their bedroom.

Wendy smiled while peering around the cozy space, which other than a few feminine touches hadn't changed since Chris's bachelor days. A testimony to his sense of style. She swung her legs over the side of the bed then padded into the bathroom, set down her mug, and turned on the shower.

The moment steam fogged the glass, Wendy stepped under the rain head while summoning memories from last night's dinner. Millie behaving herself. Abby and Kayla chatting as if they'd known each other for years. Cynthia and Amanda fawning over their grandson. Wendy ran her fingers over her growing baby bulge, praying her mother survived long enough to meet her second grandchild.

Twenty minutes after stepping into the shower, Wendy had finished drying her hair, applying makeup, and dressing. Eager to begin her day, she hurried into the great room. "Oh my gosh." Breathing in the mouth-watering cinnamon, bacon, and cheese aromas, she headed to the kitchen. "Cinnamon rolls and an omelet?"

Chris nodded. "With mushrooms and spinach."

"My favorite." Wendy patted Chris's cheek. "If you decide to give up law, you could apply for a job as a chef."

"Given my lack of kitchen skills, I think I'll keep my day job." Chris divided then plated the omelet, handing Wendy the center piece.

Kayla placed her nephew in his high chair then joined Wendy and Chris at the table. "The only time Mom ever took us kids shopping was when we needed new clothes." She pinched off a piece of cinnamon roll for Ryan. "Today's different. We're gonna shop for fun before Dad takes us all to dinner."

In between bites, Kayla relayed snippets from her work with Abby. "If I wasn't going back to Nashville with my parents tomorrow, I'd read more books to Lucy and the other kids."

Wendy swallowed a bite of omelet. "Maybe next summer you can come back and split your time between volunteering at the crisis center and babysitting for Ryan and his baby sister."

"Even better." Chris aimed his fork at Kayla. "If you stay a few weeks, you could also earn money working for me."

Kayla's eyes widened. "Doing lawyer stuff?"

"Helping around the office, answering the phone—stuff like that."

"I'll have my driver's license by then. Maybe Mom will let me drive her car." Kayla blinked, her lips drawn into a straight line. "What if Riley wants to come with me? Especially if...you know."

Wendy's heart ached for her sister. She reached across the table and curled her fingers around Kayla's hand. "You're both welcome to come and stay as long as you want, honey."

"Now that we have next summer figured out—" Chris pushed away from the table. "You two head on over to Hilltop Inn while I clean up."

Wendy smiled. "Thank you, darling."

"Glad to help." Chris lifted off his chair then stacked the plates and carried them to the kitchen sink.

"I'll brush my teeth and meet you back here in five." Wendy released Kayla's hand then hastened to the master bathroom as reality hit home. Her role as big sister had taken on a whole new dimension. She gripped the vanity while peering at her image. Somehow she had to help Kayla and Riley, maybe even Zach, face the future without their mother. But how? Everything hinged on her relationship with the Gilmore family. Wendy peeled her fingers off the vanity. Hopefully her mission would begin today.

After brushing her teeth and reapplying a touch of lipstick, Wendy returned to the great room carrying the full weight of the responsibility on her shoulders. "I'm ready for a fun day, I think."

"Me too." Kayla glanced up at her then pocketed her phone.

Twenty-five minutes after backing out of the garage, Wendy parked beside the train track across from Southern Charm restaurant.

Riley climbed out after her mother. "Where's the train?"

"Taking tourists to a town a few miles away." Wendy removed the stroller from the back. "Tell you what. Next time you visit, we'll take that ride."

Riley bent down then straightened and held up a penny.

Kayla moved Ryan from his car seat to his stroller. "My sister has a jarful of pennies she's picked up off the ground."

"Some of them are shiny like this one." Riley pocketed her treasure. "Can I push Ryan?"

"Sure." Wendy shouldered her purse while leading the way toward Depot Street. They turned right and walked across the railroad track. At the next corner, they crossed the street to the sidewalk to join the throng of tourists strolling along East Main.

After roaming through the first shop and returning to the sidewalk, Riley relinquished stroller-pushing duty to Kayla. As they passed by the next store, a couple also staying at Hilltop Inn walked out of Sweet Shoppe.

"Fancy meeting you folks here."

Riley pointed to the sign suspended over the sidewalk. "What do they sell?"

The woman smiled. "Delicious cupcakes and cookies."

Riley tugged on Cynthia's arm. "Can we go in, Mommy? Please."

"Let's wait until after lunch and come back for dessert."

"Okay." Riley skipped ahead.

Two doors down, they walked into Owl's Nest. Jennifer, the owner, who had become close friends with the Awesam partners, greeted them. Her focus shifted from Wendy to Cynthia. "You two look enough alike to be related."

"For good reason. I'm Cynthia Gilmore." Her face beamed while she looped her arm around Wendy's elbow. "This beautiful young woman is my daughter. So are Kayla and Riley."

"You have a lovely family, Wendy."

A warm sensation radiated through Wendy. "Thank you."

"I'm proud of my daughters." Cynthia glanced around. "Which is why I want to buy the four of us matching bracelets to celebrate our time together."

"We have wonderful options for you to choose from."

While Jennifer led them to a display, Wendy exchanged a knowing glance with Kayla. Her sister's pinched expression made it clear they both understood the significance of their mother's gesture. Swallowing the lump rising in her throat, Wendy pushed the stroller beside the counter. After viewing an array of chain bracelets, they opted for Riley's favorite. As soon as Cynthia paid, they each donned the keepsake which would serve as a lasting memory of what would likely be the first and last summer the four of them would spend together.

Relieved she'd kept tears at bay, Wendy pushed the stroller out to the sidewalk. Moments after entering the next store, Wendy pulled Kayla aside for more relationship building. "Remember how I told you I'm a recovering shopaholic?"

"Uh-huh. The day we bought matching cowgirl hats at Gaylord."

Wendy nodded. "The morning I first met Amanda and Erica at the Blue Ridge Inn, we came into this store. Even though I'd already bought an expensive coat and gloves the day before, my shopping addiction kicked in. I couldn't decide between two sweaters, so I decided to buy both. When the saleslady ran my credit card, it was denied."

Kayla's eyes widened. "What'd you do?"

"I told her my husband would pay for the sweaters the next day."

"Did she believe you?"

"I doubt it. Anyway, out of necessity, that day turned out to be the beginning of the end of my wasteful shopping habit."

Cynthia strode over with a white, waist-length jean jacket draped over her arm. "Try this on, honey." She handed Kayla the jacket.

Kayla moved to a mirror then slipped into the jacket.

Her mother straightened the collar. "Perfect fit. It's yours if you like it."

"I love it. Thanks, Mom."

"The first of your back-to-school wardrobe."

Riley rushed over carrying a pink tee shirt. "I don't think this one's too big for me."

Cynthia patted her daughter's head. "Even if it is, you'll grow into it in no time."

Following another hour of shopping, they carried their bags back to the SUV before crossing the street and waiting for a table at Southern Charm. Wendy leaned close to Kayla. "This is the restaurant where Erica, Amanda, and I enjoyed lunch following my credit card fiasco."

"Really?"

Wendy nodded. "Amanda treated us."

Visibly tired, Cynthia settled on a bench beside the front porch. Wendy sat beside her. "How are you holding up?"

"Well enough."

"Spending the day together has been fun."

Cynthia fingered her new bracelet. "I want to leave my family with more good memories than bad." She touched Wendy's hand, her voice barely above a whisper. "I believe God brought you into my life, knowing how much Kayla and Riley would need an older sister."

Fearing she was seconds from erupting in tears, Wendy nodded while patting her mother's hand.

Kayla rushed over, her phone in her hand. "Do you mind if I spend tonight with Abby instead of you and Chris? She says it's okay with her."

Wendy peered up at her sister. "Spending time with Abby is a wonderful idea." Especially since she'd be one more family member who could help comfort Kayla when the time came.

Chapter 13

Covering for Bernie while she took care of personal business, Amanda carried the last breakfast dishes from Hilltop's dining room to the kitchen sink. "Another full house."

Millie rinsed the plates. "Tourists flocking to Blue Ridge used to irritate the dickens out of me. All the traffic. No place to park downtown. Then you hired me as the inn's chef, and some of those same flocks helped me pad my bank account."

"Speaking of bank accounts—" Amanda climbed onto an island stool. "Have you saved enough money to reel in some unexpecting old geezer?"

"Honey, culinary talent and infectious charm are all I need to attract a man."

"If you ask me, your definition of charm is obviously a lot different than mine."

"I didn't ask, but since you brought up the subject of men—" Millie spun toward Amanda. "How about we bet that I land a man to keep me warm at night before you do?"

"Know what?" Amanda slapped her hand on the island. "I'll take that bet. What's the big reward?"

A mischievous grin curled Millie's lips. "The loser buys the winner a sexy but tasteful nightie. By the way, blue is my favorite color."

"I'm curious." Amanda tilted her head. "Doesn't your mystery club meet for the first time tonight?"

"You already know the answer, so what's your point?"

"Did you already tag the only male member of your mystery club as a prime candidate before you challenged me to a wager?"

Millie huffed. "I already told you Stanley's pushing ninety."

"Is that a yes or a no?"

"Let me put it this way." Millie waggled her finger at Amanda. "How much older is Gary than you?"

"I have no idea."

"Then I'll tell you. He's forty-eight, so four years."

"How do you know, and what is your point?"

"Gary and my son graduated high school the same year. My point is, if I win this bet, it'll be because I attracted an old codger who's young enough to keep up with me."

Amanda laughed. "You've set a high bar."

"So have you." Millie turned back toward the sink then moved plates to the dishwasher. "On the other hand, if you ditch your stubborn streak—"

"I have a question." Amanda drummed her fingers. "Who did you irritate the dickens out of before you met me?"

"In case you haven't noticed, you give me as hard a time as I give you."

"Self-preservation."

"Baloney. I'm your frustration outlet, which you wouldn't need if you had a good-looking, successful man like Gary in your life." Millie snapped her fingers. "Score one for Hilltop's award-winning chef."

Stifling a laugh, Amanda slid off her stool. "I wonder if Walmart sells sexy yet tasteful nighties."

"Forget Walmart. I want my reward to come from Victoria's Secret."

"Whatever strikes your fancy." Amanda waved over her shoulder while heading straight to the door. "Although I doubt Victoria sells flannel nightgowns. Score one for Awesam's president."

She escaped to the den before her number-one antagonist had a chance to respond. Outside on the back patio, Amanda breathed in the sweet scent of Millie's rose bushes adorning her English country garden. Out of nowhere, Gary popped into her mind. Dismissing the thought as an irrational response to Millie's ridiculous challenge, she donned her sunglasses and traipsed back to the ranch house.

Five minutes before her guests were due to arrive, Millie arranged gourmet snacks on the dining room table. Satisfied with her spread, she uncorked her favorite red wine then set it beside an ice bucket chilling a bottle of chardonnay and two beers. Years had passed since she last helped Eleanor prepare one of her fancy dinner parties. How long had it been since she'd thought about those days when Hilltop had been a private home? Weeks? Months? Despite missing her best friend, her life became far more meaningful after the Awesam team converted the Harrington home to the Hilltop Inn. Now she needed both hands to count the number of people she counted as close friends.

Responding to the doorbell, Millie rushed to open the front door. All four guests stood on the porch while a car backed down the driveway. "Who's behind the wheel?"

Susan Armstrong smiled while crossing the threshold. "My son has taken on the role as our private driver to protect us and his reputation. After all, how would it look if our future district attorney's mother or any of her friends were arrested for a DUI?" She looped her hand around her friend's arm. "Millie, meet Stanley, an old family friend."

"Old is an appropriate description." Stanley's eyes met Millie's. "Thanks for including me."

"You're welcome. Especially since a man's perspective is important."

The elderly gentleman leaned on his cane. "I'll hang in there, unless you change from a mystery to a romance reading club."

"Not a chance."

"I'd welcome a mystery with a little romance." An attractive silver-haired woman followed Bernie into the foyer. "I'm Bernie's neighbor, Eileen. You picked a doozy of a book for our first discussion."

Stanley nodded. "The quintessential murder mystery."

"With one heck of a shock ending." Millie led her guests to the dining room. "Make yourselves at home."

Eileen lifted a plate off the table. "Bernie says you're one of the best chefs in Blue Ridge."

Millie's chest puffed. "On my days off, Bernie holds her own in Hilltop's kitchen."

"My cinnamon buns aren't quite as good as Millie's, but close."

After everyone filled their plates and chose their libation, Millie escorted her guests to the living room. The three females sat on the sofa while Stanley opted for an easy chair. Millie settled on her recliner.

Eileen set her wine glass and plate on the coffee table. "First question I have about *And Then There Were None* is what would compel ten strangers to respond to a mysterious invitation and travel to a private island in the middle of nowhere?"

"Curiosity?" Susan plucked a canape off her plate. "Besides, the world was safer back in 1939 than it is today."

Stanley wrapped his fingers around his beer. "I wouldn't call the beginning of World War two safe."

Eileen nodded. "Good point. My second question, would any of us have accepted the invitation?"

"Definitely." Stanley tilted his beer toward Eileen. "But not unarmed."

Susan grinned. "Millie and I are both pistol-packing mamas. You can bet neither one of us would have shown up without our guns."

Bernie swallowed a sip of chardonnay. "Millie takes her gun to Hilltop every morning and stashes it in a kitchen drawer. Not that she'll ever need to use it."

Eileen's eyes shifted to Millie. "Have you ever pulled the trigger?"

Millie stared at her. "Why would I own a gun if I didn't know how to use it?"

Eileen shrugged. "My husband's gun is still hidden in his dresser drawer. I've never shot it."

"Maybe it's time you learned." Millie lifted her wine glass off the end table. "Back to the book. That creepy 'Ten Little Soldiers' poem was a smart way to introduce the plot."

Susan nodded. "Which is why Agatha Christie is a brilliant storyteller."

"Hmm." Bernie tapped her steepled fingers to her lips. "I wonder if this book inspired someone to create Clue. You know—the board game?"

"Back in the eighties, that game was made into a movie." Stanley popped a cheeseball into his mouth. "Delicious. Did you make or buy these?"

Millie raised a brow. "I'm a chef. What do you think?"

He grinned. "Your husband was a lucky man."

"Smart answer." *If he were five years younger*... Who was she kidding? The challenge with Amanda was a ploy to push her into a relationship with Gary, not to win a silly bet. Millie took a long sip of wine. Besides, how would she find a suitable man at her age, and a sexy nightie was definitely out of the question.

Bernie tasted a cheeseball. "We should add this to our private dinner appetizer menu."

Millie nodded. "Great idea."

"Speaking of private dinners—" Susan crossed one leg over the other. "After the characters ate and gathered in the parlor for drinks, that voice accusing them of murder gave me the chills."

Bernie leaned forward to peer around Eileen at Susan. "Did any of the men in your family ever defend someone arrested for murder?"

Susan hesitated for a long moment. "Years ago there was this eighteen-year-old who claimed self-defense after he stabbed a man. My husband struggled with that case, mostly because the boy had been a troublemaker." She seemed to stare into space. "Because he was obligated to provide the best possible defense, he defeated the district attorney."

Stanley grabbed another cheeseball. "Your husband was a darn good lawyer."

"Yes, he was. Except…despite the fact that his client came from a well-respected family, he never knew for certain whether or not he had released a killer back into society. On the other side of the equation, what bothers my son most about running for DA is the possibility of one day convicting an innocent person."

Eileen's head tilted. "Then why is he running?"

"Out of a sense of duty. Especially after our current DA tried to railroad Jimmy Barkley." Susan faced Millie. "How's Abby coming along?"

"We're hoping she'll ditch her wheelchair before the new year." The calico sprang onto Millie's lap. "If we had found ourselves in the same situation as Agatha's characters and one of us ended up dead, would we have turned on each other?"

"No." Bernie leaned back. "Because we're not strangers."

"I disagree." Stanley set his beer down. "We all have regrets we keep to ourselves. If we believed we'd be the next victim, those regrets would rouse our suspicions about everyone, even our closest friends."

"Agatha's characters were all haunted by dark truths..."

Millie tuned the conversation out while peering over Stanley's head to her bookcase. Eleanor's journals displayed on a middle shelf revealed her biggest regret. How would her friends react if they discovered she'd had a love affair with a man who traveled to Blue Ridge for business? Or that after discovering he had a wife, she'd married Rupert on the rebound while secretly waiting for her lover to return. Her focus drifted from one guest to the other. What regrets hounded Bernie? What about Stanley or Eileen?

Susan lifted her wine glass. "One more reason *And Then There Were None* is the perfect psychological thriller."

Three hours, two bottles of wine, and two beers after Millie tuned back in, everyone accepted Eileen's suggestion for their next reading project. After Susan called Keith, everyone helped carry plates and glasses to the kitchen. Stanley set the ice bucket on the kitchen table. "Do you ladies mind if I bring my friend Gordon Davenport to our next meeting?"

Bernie nodded. "Fine with me."

"Same here," added Susan.

Millie tilted her head. "Why does that name sound familiar?"

"He lived in Blue Ridge until the late sixties. Three months ago, he moved back to town and bought the house next door to mine."

"All right then, bring him along." The doorbell rang. "Your driver has arrived." After escorting her guests to the foyer and bidding them goodbye, Millie headed straight to her bedroom, her curiosity raised. She removed her high school yearbooks from a box stashed in her closet. Leafing through her freshman book, she found Gordon Davenport's photo among the juniors. He graduated the same year as Rupert. Memories about the handsome classmate began to bubble up. Gordon played football and dated one of the cheerleaders. During his last year, he served as class president. Like a lot of young people who grew up in small towns, he didn't return to Blue Ridge after college. Why had he returned after being gone so many years? Maybe she'd find out during the next mystery club party.

Chapter 14

Monday morning, Millie's ringtone startled Erica awake. Her heart pounding in her chest, she grabbed her phone from the nightstand and swiped her finger across the screen. "What's wrong?"

"I'll tell you what's wrong. This is Sierra's first official morning to cover for Bernie. It's half past six, she isn't here, and she's not answering her phone. If she doesn't show up by seven, either you or Amanda need to come in her place."

Erica switched on the bedside lamp. "I'll handle this."

"You'd better, because I'm not about to put up with her nonsense." Millie ended the call.

Releasing a heavy sigh, Erica climbed out of bed. Amanda's comment about fostering an infant and a teenager resonated as she strode to the guest bedroom. She knocked once, then walked inside and turned on the overhead light. "Wake up, Sierra."

"Huh?" The young woman who had never officially held a job rubbed her eyes. "What's going on?"

"Today's Monday." Responding to Theo's whimper, Erica lifted him from his crib. "Showing up for work on time is a sign of maturity and responsibility. Why didn't you answer your phone?"

"Ringer's turned off." Sierra swung her feet to the floor. "Am I in trouble?"

"Let's just say your boss isn't pleased."

Abby appeared in the doorway. "You didn't set your alarm, did you?"

Sierra shrugged. "Guess I forgot."

"Millie won't tolerate irresponsibility." Abby maneuvered her wheelchair into the room with Dusty padding beside her. "You need to go to work before she fires you."

"What about feeding Theo?"

"You don't need to worry, I'll take care of Little Pip."

"His name's Theo." Sierra ambled to the closet. "Besides, don't you have to go to work?"

"I'll make time." Abby's tone hinted of disgust.

Sensing a battle brewing between her daughter and Theo's mother, Erica carried the infant across the room. "You have twenty minutes to get ready, before I walk you next door."

"Why do you need to go with me?"

Abby snickered. "You obviously haven't faced Millie when she's ticked off."

"I'm just a little late." Sierra opened a dresser drawer. "What's the big deal?"

Abby pivoted her wheelchair toward Sierra. "Are you kidding me?"

"We don't have time to argue, ladies." Erica placed Theo in Abby's arms. "Meet me in the kitchen when you're ready, Sierra." She grabbed a diaper off the dresser then pushed Abby to her bedroom and tossed the diaper on the bed. "I'll let Dusty out and prepare Theo's bottle."

Abby laid Theo on her bed then stroked his cheek. "You can count on me to take care of you."

"Come on, Dusty." Erica turned away from her daughter and headed to the den. After letting their canine family member out to the backyard, she continued on to the kitchen. Her jaw clenched while she measured formula into a bottle. The more Sierra failed, the more Abby would believe Theo belonged to her. Maybe allowing the teenager to live in their home had been a huge mistake. Although who better to help her become the mother Theo deserved, than the Awesam family? No matter how challenging, they had to give Sierra time to grow up.

Erica returned to Abby's room and handed her the bottle.

"Sierra doesn't have a clue."

"We need to exercise a little patience—"

"Because she's totally irresponsible?"

"Sierra has a lot to learn, sweetheart. Which is why you're the perfect role model."

"Why didn't her mother teach her what she needs to know? Unless she's as unreliable as her daughter."

Amanda traipsed in from across the hall. "What's all the commotion?"

Abby peered over her shoulder. "Sierra didn't show up for work on time."

"What a shocker." Amanda brushed hair away from her cheek. "I imagine Millie is bent so far out of shape she can barely stand up straight."

Erica plucked the discarded diaper off the floor. "Which is why I'm not letting Sierra go to the inn alone."

Amanda headed toward Abby's private bathroom. "If you don't coddle her, maybe dealing with our chef's wrath will help straighten her out."

"Amanda's right, Mom."

"The next time Sierra's late to work—if there is a next time—I'll let her go alone. Today, she needs a friend." Erica touched her daughter's shoulder. "Thank you for helping take care of her child."

"He's still our responsibility, Mom."

"Only when we need to step in. I'll come back before Tommy picks you up." Erica pulled her hand away. After returning to her room to dress, she let Dusty back inside, then strode to the kitchen.

Amanda joined her. "Your role as Awesam's peacemaker has taken on a whole new dimension."

Erica filled a mug with coffee. "Raising an only child didn't prepare me to deal with teenaged rivalry. Especially over a baby."

"Transforming a rundown mansion into an inn was a piece of cake compared to preparing a juvenile for motherhood."

"No kidding." Erica stirred creamer and sugar into the mug while Amanda scooped dog food into Dusty's bowl. "Abby's question about Sierra's mother made sense. I wonder if her father was in the picture or if she had siblings?"

Amanda removed her coffee mug from the cabinet. "Her silence about anyone in her family other than her grandmother speaks volumes."

"I suppose that's the reason Jillian advised us not to probe until Sierra has time to settle in."

"If you ask me, she's occupied our guest room long enough to answer a few basic questions."

"I suppose you're right."

"No supposing about it."

Sierra meandered in, yawning. "I'm ready to go now."

"All right." Erica set her mug on the counter while Sierra slid her phone into her back pocket. She plucked a key off the counter then led the way out to the carport. Time to try a little probing. "I'm curious. Before you moved in with your grandmother, did you live with your mother and father?"

"No!" Her defiant tone made it clear she wasn't in the mood to reveal any information.

They crossed the driveway to the inn's front sidewalk. "No matter how Millie responds, you need to apologize."

"Whatever."

Time for some parental discipline. "Hold on, young lady." Erica halted while grabbing Sierra's arm. "Showing up to work with attitude, especially on your first day, won't sit well with your boss or with me."

Sierra's chin dropped to her chest. "I'm sorry."

Erica released her arm. "Okay, now you're ready." She led the way onto the porch, unlocked the front door, and stepped into the foyer. Grateful no guests were in sight, Erica escorted Sierra through the den.

The second they stepped into the kitchen, Millie spun away from the counter—her eyes narrowed, her finger pointing to a baby swing. "Do you see that? I bought it with my own money so you wouldn't have to lug Theo's swing all the way over here, and you couldn't bother to show up on time?"

"I'm sorry—"

"Sorry won't cut it, unless you take responsibility. Don't you know how to set your phone alarm?"

"I guess I never had to use it."

"Teenagers." Millie scowled while thrusting her open palm toward Sierra. "Give it to me."

She hesitated, then placed her phone in Millie's hand.

"What's your password?"

"Umm..."

Millie tapped her foot. "Do you or don't you want to keep your job?"

"It's May twenty-five."

"Your birthday?"

Sierra nodded.

"You need a better password." Millie's foot stilled. "How much time do you need to get ready for work?"

"I dunno." She shrugged. "Maybe an hour?"

"Lesson number one." Millie tapped the phone's screen. "Your alarm is set to go off at five every Monday and Tuesday morning. So, no more excuses for showing up late." She returned the phone. "The plates are on the sideboard. Now go set the dining room table for fourteen guests."

"Yes, ma'am." Sierra scrambled to the dining room.

Millie closed the door then faced Erica. "If you think I was too harsh—"

"I don't."

"Good, because that girl needs some serious discipline." Millie cracked eggs into a bowl. "You can go back home. I promise not to shoot her."

"Thank you—"

"For not shooting her or not firing her?"

"Both. Call if you need me to come back over." Erica walked out. Back at the ranch house, she refreshed her coffee before ambling to the den.

Amanda stopped tapping her laptop keyboard and looked up. "How much steam blew out of Millie's ears?"

"Enough to keep Sierra from showing up late again. I asked one question about her family."

"And?"

"She's nowhere near ready to confide in us."

Amanda leaned back from the dining room table. "I believe that's partially our fault."

"How so?"

"In Sierra's eyes, you, Abby, and I are successful, hard-working women who don't know what it means to struggle."

Erica snapped her fingers. "Because she has no idea how much we've overcome."

"Exactly."

"When she returns from the inn, we need to enlighten her. Until then, I'll relieve Abby of baby duty." Erica headed straight to her daughter's bedroom. "Thanks to Sergeant Millie, Sierra won't have any more excuses for not showing up to work on time."

"He's such a sweet baby." Abby stroked Theo's healed lip.

Her child's reaction confirmed one heartbreaking fact. Abby wanted Sierra to fail as a mother. Erica drew in a deep breath. "Thank you for stepping up, sweetheart. I'll take over now to give you time to shower and dress." She lifted the infant from Abby's arms and carried him from the room before Abby had a chance to object.

Chapter 15

Four hours after assuming babysitting duty, Erica secured Theo in his swing beside the dining room table then stepped into the kitchen. "What if Sierra's not in the mood to listen to us?"

"Doesn't matter what mood she's in." The timer went off, and Amanda removed bacon from the microwave. "We're not backing out."

"You sound like Sergeant Millie."

"The sooner we learn about Sierra's past, the sooner we'll be able to help her."

"I suppose you're right." Erica removed a pitcher of lemonade from the fridge while Amanda finished preparing BLTs.

A blast of warm air followed the kitchen door swinging open. Sierra stepped inside.

Erica handed her the pitcher. "How'd your morning go?"

"Okay, I guess."

"We have lunch ready for you." Erica and Amanda carried the plates to the table.

Sierra followed. She set down the pitcher then plopped onto a chair and glanced at her son. "Did someone change his diaper?"

Erica nodded. "Twice since you left." After saying the blessing, she filled three glasses with lemonade. Given Sierra's short attention span and habit of gobbling down her food as if she didn't know where her next meal would come from, Erica and Amanda had agreed to jump right into the conversation. "You might be under the delusion that our lives have been easy. Nothing is further from the truth." *Here goes.* "Actually, I grew up in a three-room apartment with a single mother who was addicted to drugs and alcohol. I sat beside my sixteen-year-old brother on our building's front stoop the day he died in a drive-by shooting. If the bullets hadn't missed me by inches, I wouldn't be sitting here."

Sierra's eyes widened. "Really?"

"There's more. Not long after my mother died of an overdose, I married a policeman." Erica paused. "Jack used me as his punching bag until Abby and I escaped to a women's shelter."

Amanda pushed her sandwich aside. "Like Erica, I also grew up without a father. My mother did the best she could to raise me, until she was diagnosed with cancer. I dropped out of high school to take care of her. After she passed away, I went back to school. Not long after graduating, I met my soulmate. Preston and I were married fourteen wonderful years before a drunk driver took his life."

Erica remained glued on Sierra's pained expression. "Every time you see Wendy, she seems happy. However, soon after her fifth birthday, her mother abandoned her. Until she turned eighteen, Wendy grew up in a string of foster homes. A few months ago, she reunited with her mother, only to discover she's dying of cancer." Erica reached across the table to touch Sierra's arm. "We're sharing our stories with you so you'll know you're safe to tell us about your past whenever you're ready."

Sierra broke eye contact. "This is the nicest house I've ever lived in." She pulled her arm away from Erica's grasp. "My mother, three sisters, me and my little brother lived in an old trailer that was too hot in the summer and too cold in the winter." Sierra's body seemed to curl in on itself. "Mom doesn't have a job. Instead she gets a check every month she says is from Uncle Sam."

Did Sierra understand what she meant? Amanda wrapped her fingers around her glass. "How often do you see your dad?"

"I've never seen him." Sierra picked at her cuticle. "I don't think any of us kids had the same father."

Erica inched her chair closer to Sierra. "Chances are neither did my brother and I."

The teenaged mother remained silent for a long moment. "Mom told me and my sisters if any of us got pregnant, we'd be on our own 'cause the last thing she needed was another kid to feed."

Amanda swallowed a sip of lemonade. "Does anyone back in Chattanooga know about Theo?"

"I haven't talked to Mom since I left Tennessee." Sierra paused. "His father knows, sort of."

"Meaning what?"

"When I found out I was pregnant, he told me to…you know. I couldn't do it. That's how come I hitched a ride to Grandma's house."

"A wise choice. About Theo's father." Amanda folded her arms on the table. "Have you been in touch with him?"

"I texted him."

"Since you moved in with us?"

"Yeah. He didn't text back."

Erica studied Sierra's pinched expression. How many more strikes did she have against her? An idea that could solve two problems began to take root until the words poured out. "What's the last year of school you attended, honey?"

"Tenth grade."

Perfect. "The fact that you're here proves you want to provide a good life for Theo, right?"

Sierra nodded.

"Which is why you need to earn a high school diploma equivalency, and Abby is the perfect person to help you."

"Really? I'd like that," the teen whispered.

"Great idea." Amanda pulled her plate close. "Now that we have a plan, how about we eat these yummy BLTs?"

Grateful for Amanda's suggestion, Erica took a bite of sandwich. Now all she had to do was figure out how to break the news to her daughter. A tall task at best.

Moments after Sierra swallowed her last bite, she responded to her baby's whimper. "Time for Theo's lunch." She scurried to the kitchen to prepare his bottle, then pulled him into her arms and carried him to her room.

Amanda scooted her chair away from the table. "Promising Abby's tutoring services is risky as well as brilliant."

"Which is why I need you to help me break the news tonight."

"I have a better idea. Instead of you and me ganging up on Abby, Brad should partner with you. After all, who better to help sell the idea than an education professional who is also your daughter's future stepfather?"

Erica stared at Amanda. "Actually, your suggestion makes sense."

Amanda grinned. "What else would you expect from Awesam's president?"

"A little more humility?"

"Why waste the energy?"

"Good point." Erica grabbed her phone. Five minutes after texting her fiancé, he called. She carried the phone to the kitchen. "Thank you for responding so quickly. Are you available tonight?" She explained. He responded. After the call ended, Erica returned to the den.

Amanda peered up at her. "What's the verdict?"

"Brad's coming over at five with sandwiches and shakes for four in case Tommy plans to stay for supper."

"He obviously agrees with me. To give you guys privacy, I'll take Sierra and Theo out to dinner." Amanda carried the plates to the kitchen. "Besides, spending a few hours alone with our teenaged mother will give me the chance to ask more questions."

Erica followed with the pitcher and glasses. "If you ask the right questions, you might learn something about Theo's father."

"That's my plan, Sherlock."

Erica glanced at her watch. "In the meantime, I have a two o'clock massage."

"You go ahead, I'll finish cleaning up."

"Thanks."

Amanda thumped Erica's arm. "We're family; we help each other."

"Always."

Erica pocketed her phone then grabbed her key and headed out the back door, hoping for a quiet client.

Following a long afternoon of volleying between anticipation and anxiety, Erica rushed to open the front door to greet Brad. "I'm glad you're here."

"So am I." He kissed her cheek before carrying Bob's Eatery containers to the dining room table. "Abby's a smart young woman." He wrapped his arms around Erica and pulled her close. "Which is why I suggest telling her what's going on soon after she arrives."

Erica breathed in the lingering scent of his woody aftershave. "We're totally in sync." Dusty barked from the backyard while pawing the sliding glass door. "Our trusty canine is announcing Abby's arrival."

Brad released her. "Dusty's better than a doorbell."

"Definitely." Erica slid open the glass door.

Dusty bounded to the foyer moments before Abby wheeled into the den with Tommy walking beside her. "Hey, Mom, Mr. Barkley...I mean Brad. You don't mind if I call you by your first name, do you?"

Brad chuckled. "Considering I'm your future stepfather, any name other than Mr. Barkley works for me. By the way, I brought sandwiches and shakes for the four of us." He seated Erica.

Abby maneuvered onto the chair Tommy pulled out for her. "Is tonight some sort of special occasion?"

How should I respond? Erica caught her daughter's eye while Tommy moved her wheelchair away from the table. "More like a meeting of the minds."

Abby's eyes shifted from her mother to Brad, then back to her mother. What weren't they saying? She waited for Brad to bless their meal and pass out the food and drinks before pouncing on her mom. "After what happened this morning, you want to talk about Sierra, don't you?"

"We do." Her mother unwrapped her sandwich. "Sierra opened up to Amanda and me during lunch. To begin..."

Abby focused on her mother's expression while listening to details about the conversation. Not surprising news. Anyone who knew Theo's mother had dumped him on a doorstep would have guessed she'd come from a dysfunctional family. Abby's eyes shifted to her former high school principal. Brad had obviously shown up for a reason.

Her mother paused. "Sadly, Sierra never finished school."

Brad swallowed a bite of sandwich. "Statistically speaking, most adults without a high school diploma end up on welfare or behind bars."

Tommy plunged a straw into his milkshake. "Are you saying Sierra should go back to school?"

"Given her responsibilities, not in the traditional sense. She's an excellent candidate to earn a GED, which will help her secure a better future for Theo."

"We believe you're the perfect person to tutor her, sweetheart."

Abby pursed her lips. Smart move bringing in reinforcements. With her former principal and future stepfather staring at her, she needed a good excuse to beg off. "With my work schedule plus my own studies, I don't see how I could possibly take on another responsibility."

Tommy nudged her arm. "I'll help you."

Abby stared at him. Whose side was he on?

"I can handle the math and science stuff, while you help her learn the rest."

Brad snapped his fingers. "Good idea, Tommy. You two working together will help Sierra mature into a competent young woman."

Abby fingered her sandwich. If she resisted and Sierra failed, would everyone blame her? Better to go along with the plan. That way, when Sierra proved unfit to raise Little Pip, she'd be ready to step in. "Okay, I'll do it."

Her mother reached across the table and squeezed Abby's hand. "I'm proud of you, sweetheart. You too, Tommy."

A momentary stab of guilt pricked Abby's conscience, until she dismissed it as misplaced emotion.

The sun had dipped toward the horizon by the time Amanda received an all-clear and returned home. After parking beside Abby's car, she carried Theo, who was asleep in his car seat, to the guest room and moved him to his crib. "Sleep tight, Little Pip," she whispered.

Sierra followed. After tossing three shopping bags on the bed, she wrapped her arms around Amanda then quickly released her. "Thank you."

"You're welcome. Tell you what." Amanda brushed a lock of hair away from Sierra's cheek. "When you pass tests to earn your GED, I'll take you shopping again."

Sierra's eyes widened. "Really?"

"Absolutely. Tomorrow we'll talk more about your next steps. In the meantime, get a good night's rest." Amanda left Sierra alone with her son. Returning to the den, she spotted Erica and Millie out on the patio. Eager to compare notes despite their neighbor's intrusion, she stepped outside and sat beside Erica, across from Millie. "What brought you here past your bedtime?"

"Curiosity."

Erica cleared her throat. "Seems our chief information officer noticed Brad and Tommy's cars parked in our driveway."

Amanda rolled her eyes. "Why am I not surprised."

Millie huffed. "At least I waited until they left to come over. By the way, Abby accepted the tutoring challenge."

"Reluctantly," added Erica. "Thanks to Tommy volunteering to help her and Brad's encouragement. Letting go of the illusion that Theo belongs to her will take more time, plus a little heartache. Anyway, Brad will create a curriculum for Sierra, so she can begin studying in the next couple of days. Hopefully, she'll take this seriously."

"Given what I promised a few minutes ago, I'm confident she'll do whatever it takes to pass the test."

"Good." Erica folded her arms on the table. "I'm dying to find out what you learned during the past couple of hours."

Amanda hesitated.

Millie folded her arms across her chest. "Are y'all seriously clamming up because I'm sitting here?"

"I suppose you'd wheedle the news out of one of us." Amanda focused on the setting sun painting pink and orange swaths across the sky. "Would you believe tonight was the first time anyone has ever treated Sierra to a shopping spree? Watching her face light up was worth every dollar I spent."

Erica nodded. "Sounds as if you won her over."

"Enough to learn about Theo's father. His name's Dereck Hackett. He's a twenty-something-year-old who lives with two older brothers four trailers away from Sierra's mother. Based on Sierra's comments, I'm guessing he's not what we'd consider a good candidate for fatherhood."

Millie bolted to her feet as if a firecracker had exploded under her chair. "I have an important matter to tend to." She dashed to the gate and disappeared around the corner.

Erica unfolded her arms. "What do you suppose she's up to now?"

Amanda flicked at a gnat. "Something mischievous, no doubt."

"That much I know."

Chapter 16

Following a morning preparing for today's meeting, Amanda parked in the Armstrongs' driveway behind Gary's car. In a couple of minutes, she would see him for the first time since they enjoyed dinner at The General Ledger. Would he treat her differently than he had before that night? Dismissing the question as ridiculous, she shouldered her purse then plucked her folder off the passenger seat and headed straight to the front porch.

Responding to the bell, Linda pulled the door open and greeted Amanda with a brief hug. "The guys just finished a game of pool. This time my husband earned bragging rights. Gary might have let him win to help lighten the mood before we put Keith through the wringer."

Amanda nodded. "Gary's more than an effective campaign finance manager."

"In addition to being a good friend, he's handsome, smart, and charming." Linda grinned. "Which I imagine you discovered when Keith stood you two up for dinner."

Something clicked in Amanda's brain, rendering her speechless. The little hints. Millie's incessant nagging. Erica and Wendy's subtle comments. Linda and Keith had unleashed a coordinated matchmaking scheme! Did Gary have a clue, or was he also an innocent victim?

"Anyway, the guys are glad you're here." Linda led the way downstairs to the high-ceiling paneled room. The men sat across from each other at the round pedestal table. Gary faced a window overlooking the patio beneath the deck. Linda linked arms with Amanda while steering her toward the table. "Are you guys ready for a stimulating afternoon with two of the smartest women in Blue Ridge?"

Amanda resisted rolling her eyes. Could she be any more obvious?

Keith scowled. "Watson's up to something."

"Why am I not surprised?" Linda released Amanda's arm then moved to the table.

After hanging her purse on the high-backed leather chair, Amanda settled across from Linda. "What's going on?"

"Our opponent's campaign manager called." Gary leaned back, his jaw clenched. "His client requested a change from a moderated debate to a town hall-style question-and-answer event a week from Saturday."

Linda's eyes shifted from Gary to Keith. "I assume you accepted the challenge."

"Rejecting would have screamed weakness."

Gary crossed his arms tight across his chest. "There's no doubt they'll pack the audience with troublemakers."

Amanda tossed her folder on the table. "So much for the practice questions we prepared."

Keith faced Amanda. "We need to find out if Nancy Campbell is still willing to moderate."

"I'm on it." Amanda yanked her phone from her purse. She punched the podcaster's number then pressed her phone to her ear. Nancy answered. Following a brief conversation, Amanda ended the call. "She's still on board."

"Good." Keith planted his forearms on the table. "We need to spend the rest of the afternoon anticipating every possible question Watson's conspirators might throw at us."

"First." Gary uncrossed his arms then mirrored Keith's position. "Is there anything in your family's past that we haven't talked about that could undermine your campaign?"

Keith and Linda exchanged a glance that spoke volumes. "There was one incident." Keith broke eye contact with his wife. "Nearly forty years ago." He relayed the details.

When he finished explaining, Gary's eyes remained laser focused on his friend. "The record's sealed—"

"Doesn't matter. When politics are involved, nothing is a hundred-percent safe from arm twisting to well-placed bribes. Especially if a crooked politician is willing to do anything to win."

"In that case, we need to come up with a response in the event Watson or one of his minions dig it up."

"Gary's right, darling." Linda touched her husband's arm. "Besides, your otherwise sterling reputation will override any fallout."

Keith took a deep breath. "I hope you're right."

Buckling down, the team spent the next four hours crafting responses to every possible question that might come up. By five o'clock, exhaustion compounded by hunger sent the crew upstairs to the kitchen. Amanda set her purse on the counter while Keith popped the cap off two beers.

Linda removed a bottle of chenin blanc from the undercounter chiller. After pulling the cork, she filled two glasses, handing one to Amanda. "To our brilliant campaign and finance managers. We couldn't do this without you two on our team."

"I'm just the money guy." Gary smiled at Amanda. "You're the brains."

She blinked. Was he flirting?

Linda opened the fridge. "I hope you guys don't mind ham and cheese sandwiches and a salad."

"Sounds good to me." Gary clasped Keith's shoulder. "Followed by a bragging-rights rematch."

"You're on."

Amanda swirled her wine glass while watching Gary tease Keith about his lack of pool skills. If he'd known about Linda's matchmaking ploy, wouldn't he have invited her on a date by now? Following their dinner, he'd called her twice—both times to ask questions about the campaign.

Gary's eyes met Amanda's and lingered. Sensing her cheeks were seconds from turning bright pink, she blinked then turned away. No matter what Linda, Keith, or anyone else had in mind, she and Gary were nothing more than friends and business partners. Weren't they?

"Supper's ready." Linda set plates on the kitchen island before orchestrating the seating arrangement.

Amanda ended up sitting between the men. With her shoulder inches from Gary, she struggled to focus on her food. What was it about the bank president that stirred her emotions? His good looks? His easygoing manner? The subtle scent of masculine cologne? Amanda struggled to focus on her salad bowl while stabbing a cucumber slice. Her reaction was nothing more than the power of suggestion. By the time they finished eating, she had half convinced herself the Armstrongs weren't playing matchmakers. Until the guys headed to the basement while Amanda stayed to help Linda clear the dishes. "Thank you for dinner."

"You're welcome." Linda set plates in the dishwasher. "The four of us should go out to dinner for fun sometime. Maybe take in a movie."

So much for dismissing the matchmaking conspiracy theory. Should she confront Linda? Not in the middle of a critical political campaign. Better to change the subject. "How's everything going with your daughter and son-in-law?"

"Would you believe Allison and Mark are already talking about having another baby?"

"Maybe they're trying to keep up with Wendy and Chris."

"The more grandchildren the better." Linda closed the dishwasher. "Why don't we go down and cheerlead our guys?"

Our guys? She was definitely playing cupid. Amanda faked a yawn before grabbing her purse off the counter. "I'd best head home while I'm still alert enough to drive without falling asleep at the wheel."

"I understand."

Did she?

Linda walked Amanda to the front door. "I'll tell the guys goodbye for you."

"Thanks." Following a friendly embrace, Amanda walked out and headed straight to Gunter's truck. By the time she pulled into the carport and parked beside Abby's car, her exasperation had escalated to the boiling point.

Erica spun toward the kitchen door swinging open. "How'd your meeting go?"

Amanda slammed the keys on the counter. "You need to come outside with me."

"Why?" Erica raised a brow. "Did you wreck the truck?"

"We need to talk." Amanda glared at her. "Privately."

"All right." Erica followed her to the carport. "I'm listening."

Amanda leaned back against the truck's hood, her arms folded tight across her chest. "I know what's going on."

Erica raised a brow. "What are you talking about?"

"The real reason the Armstrongs recruited Gary." Amanda shook her finger at Erica. "Don't pretend you don't know."

Erica hesitated. Denying would only add to the drama. Besides, Amanda knew her well enough to recognize a false denial. "Did Linda tell you?"

"I figured it out on my own. How many people are in on the scam?"

"I would hardly call what's going on a scam."

Amanda tapped her foot. "Does Wendy know?"

"She figured it out on her own."

"What about Millie?"

Erica breathed deeply, then slowly released the air. "Wendy and Millie named the mission SAGA—Snag a Guy for Amanda."

Amanda glared at Erica. "Are you kidding me?"

"You have to admit that's clever in a convoluted sort of way. Look—" She touched Amanda's arm. "Even though I understand your reaction, are you open to a suggestion from our little family's resident peacemaker?"

Amanda puffed her cheeks then blew a long stream of air. "You'll tell me no matter how I respond, so you might as well go ahead."

"Now that you've blown off steam, literally and figuratively, keep your discovery between the two of us. That way you'll maintain control and have a little fun with Millie."

"Actually—" Amanda stared at her for a long moment. "That's a clever move."

"As well as calculated."

"All right. No one other than you and maybe Wendy needs to know that I'm on to SAGA." Amanda lowered her hands to her sides then brushed past her.

Erica stifled a smile. Whether or not Amanda would admit reality, her reaction proved one undeniable fact. Awesam's president was falling hard for Gary Redding.

Chapter 17

After scooping cat food into a dish on Hilltop's front porch and refilling Inky's water bowl, Millie scurried back to the kitchen. "Our resident kitty is all fed. Now we have twenty minutes before the rest of our club shows up."

Bernie finished wiping down the counters. "What makes you think everyone will go along with your wild idea?"

"We're the Blue Ridge Mystery Club—"

"We read books—"

Millie scoffed. "Is the word book in our name?"

"No—"

"Which means we're not limited to *reading* mysteries."

Bernie stashed a bottle of cleaner under the sink. "Do Erica or Amanda have any idea what you're up to?"

"Doesn't matter either way." Millie grabbed a foil-wrapped plate of freshly baked oatmeal raisin cookies off the island. "As Awesam's chief information officer, I'm responsible for knowing everything that goes on around here. Especially who's who and what's what." She spun around then rushed through the den and foyer.

Bernie followed close behind as they left the inn and scurried across the lawn to Millie's front porch. Stopping to catch her breath, she motioned toward the calico perched on the windowsill. "Is your guard cat always on duty?"

"He's old and curious, same as our club members." Millie rushed inside. "Should I serve herbal tea or decaf coffee?"

"I don't know." Bernie shrugged. "Maybe tea?"

Millie set the cookies on the living room coffee table before hustling to the kitchen. Ten minutes later, she placed a tray of mismatched cups and saucers beside the plate before peeling off the foil. "We're all set." Responding to the bell, Millie hastened to the door. She peered beyond Eileen to a second car pulling onto her driveway. "Go on in. Bernie's waiting in the living room."

Susan climbed out of her late-model sports car then ambled up the sidewalk. "You didn't arrange this get together to discuss books, did you?"

"Good assumption."

Susan stepped onto the porch. "I can't wait to hear what you're up to."

"You'll find out soon enough."

"Such anticipation." Susan chuckled while brushing past Millie to go into the foyer.

Ignoring the comment, Millie stared wide-eyed at a three-wheeled, open-top vehicle turning onto the driveway and parking behind Susan's car.

Stanley climbed from the passenger side and removed his helmet while another man slid from behind the wheel. After dropping their helmets onto the seats, they made their way to the porch. "Millie, meet my friend Gordon Davenport."

Her eyes remained glued to the bright red vehicle parked in her driveway. "What in the Sam Hill is that contraption?"

Gordon fingered his thick white moustache. "A brand-new Polaris Slingshot. Cost me a pretty penny."

Millie stared up at the white-haired gentleman whose deeply lined face hinted he'd spent a lot of time outdoors. "Are you suffering from a late-in-life crisis, or are you some sort of wannabe daredevil?"

Gordon burst out laughing. "You're right, Stanley. Your mystery club leader has plenty of gumption."

"What you call gumption, I call good old-fashioned horse sense." Millie led the men into the living room where the three women had settled on the sofa. "A three-wheeled motorcycle rider's joining us." She moved a seat from the dining room beside the easy chair while Stanley introduced his guest. Unwilling to give up her seat to the newcomer, Millie pointed to the side-by-side chairs. "You guys sit there. Pass the cookies, Bernie, while I fix another cup of tea."

"No need." Stanley lowered onto the dining room chair. "Gordon's welcome to mine."

"Tea and cookies instead of canapes and adult beverages?" Susan grinned while passing the plate to Stanley. "At least we didn't need a designated driver for today's event."

Irritation mingling with curiosity about Gordon, Millie settled on her recliner. Could she trust the new guy with her plan, especially since she barely knew Stanley? Although Susan had known him for years. Besides, Millie needed answers sooner rather than later.

Gordon propped his ankle across his knee. "What's the big mystery?"

Millie stared at the newcomer. How much had Stanley told him about their club? "What sort of books do you read?"

"Mostly thrillers. James Patterson. John Grisham. Which is the main reason Stanley invited me to join the club."

What other reasons did he have? Millie blinked. Another question for another day.

"We all know we're not here to discuss books." Bernie eyed Millie while crossing one leg over the other. "So, you might as well stop stalling and get to the point."

Millie huffed. "All right." She spent the next twenty minutes explaining everything that had happened from the time Abby and Erica found Theo on the crisis center stoop until the day before yesterday.

When she finished, Stanley drummed his fingers on his chair's arm. "What does all this have to do with us?"

Millie leaned forward. "As chief information officer, I'm obligated to protect my partners from potential threats."

Stanley stopped drumming, his brows pinched. "What sort of threat does a teenager and an infant pose?"

"Not them." Millie huffed as if he didn't have a clue. "Theo's father."

Susan set her teacup on the coffee table. "I didn't think he was in the picture."

"He isn't. At least not yet. Sierra contacted him, so chances are he'll show up." Millie leaned back. "His name's Dereck Hackett. I need your help to find out more about him and figure out what sort of problems he might cause."

Eileen swallowed a bite of cookie. "We're mystery book club readers, not private investigators."

Bernie nudged her neighbor. "The word 'book' isn't in our title, which somehow gave Millie the wild notion that we're up to solving a real-life mystery."

Stanley nodded. "An intriguing idea."

Eileen stared at Stanley as if he'd lost his mind. "Intriguing is a far cry from logical." She faced Susan. "What's your opinion?"

"I understand where our leader's coming from." Susan's focus shifted to Millie. "Where does this Dereck character live?"

"Chattanooga."

"Which makes this crazy idea even more illogical." Eileen lifted her teacup off the coffee table. "How could we learn anything meaningful about a stranger who lives in another state?"

Susan shrugged. "We can search for him on the internet."

"I agree with Susan." Stanley reached for a cookie. "Besides, what's the harm in trying?"

While the debate continued with Bernie and Millie on one side and Susan and Stanley on the other, Millie kept a close eye on Gordon's bemused expression. Surely an old guy who drove a wild three-wheeler would cotton to the idea. She waited for a lull in the debate, then pounced. "It's time for you to stop sitting there all smug and tell us what you're thinking."

Gordon fingered his soft-soled shoe. "What you're proposing is best handled by professionals—"

"You're a newbie." Millie waggled her finger. "Your opinion doesn't count."

Gordon's eyes remained locked on hers. "I suggest you holster your trigger finger and listen to the second half of my answer."

Stanley nodded. "Believe me, you're going to want to hear what he has to say."

Shocked the stranger's retort hadn't made her blood boil, Millie withdrew her trigger finger. "You have thirty seconds to explain."

"Just so happens I'm a retired cop and my son's an FBI agent." His grin returned. "Which means we have connections to dig up details about your target—all legal, mind you."

Eileen's brows raised. "Without involving the rest of us?"

"Every successful investigation requires a good team."

Susan's eyes shifted from Gordon to Millie. "You want your mission to succeed, right?"

"Why else would I involve all of you?"

"Exactly. Which is why I suggest we let our professional take the lead and assign tasks to the rest of us."

Millie drummed her fingers on her recliner's arm. Why should she give up control to a craggy ex-cop she hadn't invited? Although he did have connections. How would he respond to a compromise? Only one way to find out. Her eyes locked on her competition. "I'll only agree to dual leadership, meaning no decisions without my approval."

"That goes two ways."

He obviously wasn't a pushover. Millie squared her shoulders. "Agreed. Do we or don't we have a deal?"

Gordon lowered his foot to the floor. "We have a deal."

"In that case, we need to get down to business." Two hours after Millie and her new partner launched a heated discussion, every team member had their marching orders. Confident she had successfully stood her ground with a tough ex-cop, Millie scooted to the edge of her recliner. "Now that we have a plan in place, we need to put our next book discussion on hold. Instead we'll devote our next meeting to comparing notes."

Stanley cocked a brow. "A week doesn't give us much time."

"Your friend claims he's a pro, which means seven days should be plenty of time."

"Millie's right." Gordon thumped Stanley's arm. "We can accomplish a lot in a week."

"All right." Stanley stood and stretched. "Replace tea and cookies with beer and snacks, and I'm all in."

"You're on."

After Millie thanked her guests and bid them goodbye, Bernie lingered. "Never once since you hired me as your assistant did I expect tonight to happen."

"A professional investigation?"

Bernie shook her head. "Chef Millie Cunningham has finally met her match."

Chapter 18

After placing Ryan in the crib for his afternoon nap, Wendy headed out the front door with Duke padding beside her. A squirrel skittering across the driveway sent him on another unsuccessful chase.

At the sound of Wendy's whistle, their lovable black lab scurried back to her side, his wagging tail stirring up a breeze. "What would you do if you actually caught a critter?" With a muffled bark, Duke fell in step beside her down the winding driveway to the mailbox. When they reached the road, Wendy waved at a neighbor driving by before removing the stack of mail.

Inside the house, she grabbed a letter opener then ambled to the leather sofa while Duke sprawled on the floor in front of the French doors leading to the back deck. Wendy set the opener on the cushion beside her then sorted through the mail. Junk. An envelope addressed to Chris. A credit card statement. More junk until...

Cold sweat popped out on the back of her neck the second she uncovered the last envelope.

A Las Vegas postmark. Months had passed since she'd received a letter from Ryan's biological father. Obviously the warning Chris mailed as her attorney didn't stop him. Should she rip the unopened envelope to shreds and toss it in the trash? Unless—what if the letter wasn't from Gunter but from a guard or another prisoner with news about him?

Duke padded over, sat on his haunches, and plopped his head on the cushion beside her as if sensing her anxiety. "You're right, I need to find out what's inside." She grabbed the opener. After slicing the envelope open, she pulled out a single sheet of lined paper folded into thirds. Lifting the first third, the handwriting told her everything she needed to know about the sender. Wendy unfolded the letter. Breathing deeply to slow her racing pulse, she forced her eyes to focus.

Dearest Wendy,

Spending hours alone in a prison cell with nothing to do but self-reflect has had a profound impact on me. I realize now that my gambling addiction combined with my desire to have a loving family clouded my judgement. You must believe that had I met you before I met Amanda and Erica, you and I would be legally married, we would still be living in Gulfport, and I would be raising my son.

I want you to know how sorry I am for all the anguish and suffering I've caused you, and that I am a changed man. If you can find it in your heart to extend me mercy, please respond so I'll know life is treating you and our child well. If you're reluctant to send his picture, at least will you kindly tell me everything you can about him? Knowing he's thriving will help me endure the pain of losing you both.

Warmest regards,

Gunter

Wendy caught her lower lip between her teeth. Had the man she'd known as Kurt Peterson changed, or was he playing on her emotions to pull another con? After reading the letter a second and a third time, she carefully examined every word. He seemed sincere.

Wendy set the letter on the coffee table then strode to Ryan's room as if he were in danger. Gazing at him sleeping peacefully tugged at her heartstrings. She couldn't imagine being separated from her child for a couple of days, much less for years. What would it hurt to at least tell Gunter the child he had fathered was thriving? Wendy slipped out to the hall then headed downstairs to the newly finished basement.

Inside the office she shared with Chris, she removed a sheet of stationery from her top desk drawer. She hesitated, staring at the blank page. Would a handwritten letter come across as too personal? Wendy pushed the sheet aside then booted her laptop. After typing, deleting, and retyping for twenty agonizing minutes, she pressed print. Satisfied she had created a neutral response, she plucked the single sheet from the printer.

Gunter,

I am writing for no other reason than to inform you that Ryan Christopher Armstrong is a happy, thriving one-year-old. He speaks several words and pulls himself to a standing position. Chris and I expect him to take his first steps any day now.

Praying you stay safe and continue to become a better person than you were before you were convicted.

Regards,

Wendy

Satisfied, she folded the letter. Wendy addressed and stamped an envelope then slid the letter inside and carried it upstairs to the den. Staring at the letters lying side-by-side on the coffee table gave her pause. How could she convince Chris she'd taken the appropriate step? Maybe she could begin by preparing one of his favorite dinners.

Startled by Cynthia's ringtone, Wendy scrambled to the kitchen counter and pressed FaceTime. "Hi."

"Did I catch you at a good time?"

"Your timing's perfect." Wendy climbed onto a stool. "I just finished a little office work. How are you feeling?"

"Decent enough, considering. How's my grandson?" Other than looking a little tired, her mother seemed okay.

"He's as sweet as ever."

"Has he taken his first step?"

"Close but not yet. Are my sisters and brother enjoying their summer?"

"Zach has a part-time job at a fast food restaurant. Kayla's babysitting five days a week for a neighbor until school starts. Riley's going to a church camp with her best friend in a couple of days, which is why I'm calling." Cynthia paused. "Do you mind if I drive over next week and spend a couple of days with you—to help make up for lost time?"

Wendy pressed her palm to her chest. "Not at all. In fact, you're welcome to stay here with me and Chris. That way you'll have more time to spend with Ryan."

"I'd love to. Thank you." After chatting for a few more minutes, Cynthia ended the call.

Convinced the timing of her mother's call confirmed she'd responded appropriately to Gunter, Wendy ambled to the fridge to begin preparing her Win-Chris-Over dinner.

Hours later, the mouthwatering aromas of tomato, rosemary, and garlic wafted through the great room. The garage door opening sent Wendy to the kitchen window. Dismissing the tinge of apprehension, she joined Duke at the back door to greet Chris. "Welcome home, darling."

He pulled her into his arms. "Spaghetti and a hug from the most beautiful woman on the planet. Lucky me." Chris kissed her cheek then patted Duke's head before heading to the playpen. He lifted his son into his arms, delighting him with a raspberry on his neck.

Smiling from ear to ear, Wendy removed garlic bread from the oven before plating the spaghetti and cutting bite-sized pieces for Ryan. While dining Italian style and sharing news about Cynthia's upcoming visit, second thoughts about sharing the letters with Chris crept into Wendy's conscience. By the time they finished dessert and cleaned up the kitchen, regardless of the outcome, she knew what she had to do. "I have something important to share with you." She carried Ryan to his play mat before settling on the sofa.

Chris sat beside her. "Good news or bad?"

"That depends." She handed him the envelope from Las Vegas.

After reading the letter, he tossed it on the coffee table and grabbed the other envelope. "You wrote to him?"

Wendy shrugged. "I kind of feel sorry for him."

Chris glared at her. "Are you serious?"

"People can change, you know."

"Not psychotic narcissists." Chris retrieved Gunter's letter. His jaw clenched while he ran his finger down the page. "Do you realize that in two short paragraphs, he referred to himself sixteen times?"

Wendy crossed one leg over the other. "How else could he explain?"

"What don't you understand about letting your attorney handle correspondence from a criminal?"

"I'm not afraid of him."

"Maybe you should be." Chris pulled her response from the envelope, then read it aloud.

Wendy pumped her foot. "I took a lot of time figuring out exactly how to respond."

"I'm questioning your logic, not the letter's contents."

Wendy's foot pumped faster. "Gunter is Ryan's father." Instantly regretting the comment, she placed her hand on Chris's thigh.

"No, Wendy, he's not." Chris brushed her hand away.

"What I meant was—"

"I know exactly what you meant." Chris bolted off the sofa then lifted Ryan into his arms. "My son and I are going out on the deck."

Conflicting emotions rattled Wendy's brain. Chris needed time alone. She slid her letter into the envelope, leaving the flap unsealed. After all, didn't the decision on how to respond to the man whose bed she had shared for three years belong to her? Especially if Gunter had changed?

Wendy ambled to the room they were transforming into a nursery for their daughter. Pressing her hand to her baby bulge, she eyed the paint swatches taped to the wall. Chris understood more than anyone that Gunter's deception had led her to Blue Ridge and into his life. Couldn't he at least show a little compassion?

"As your attorney, I'm advising you not to send that letter."

Wendy spun toward Chris standing in the doorway, holding their boy. "What about as my husband?"

"In my professional opinion, sending your letter would be a huge mistake." His lips drew into a hard, thin line. "At the same time, the decision is yours to make, not mine." Turning away from her, Chris carried their little guy across the hall to his room, closing the door behind him.

Wendy drew in a deep breath. Even though Chris was angry or disappointed, he was right. The final decision belonged to her. She returned to the great room and plucked her letter off the coffee table. After hesitating for a brief moment, she slipped it back into the envelope. Tomorrow she would rely on her feminine charm to overcome the first big disagreement with her husband.

Chapter 19

After changing into a casual outfit for tonight's date, Erica spritzed perfume on her neck before stealing one last glance in her dresser mirror. As a thirty-eight-year-old, she could still pass as her daughter's older sister. Erica plucked her purse off the dresser then headed to the den. Abby, Tommy, and Sierra sat around the dining room table while Theo slept in his baby swing. "Do the three of you need anything before I leave?"

"No thanks. Tommy ordered us a pizza and a salad." Abby opened a textbook to begin their second tutoring session.

Pleased her daughter had taken on the task, Erica shouldered her purse and headed to Awesam's office off the foyer. Their choice of study food summoned memories of Abby and her friends gathering in their Asheville den to tackle homework assignments—those same friends who abandoned her after news of their home's foreclosure became public. During the past eighteen months, her daughter had enrolled in a new high school halfway through her senior year, abandoned her dream to go away to college, and been injured in a serious accident. How much more trauma could she endure?

When Brad's Corvette eased up the driveway, Erica headed out to the front sidewalk to join her fiancé. "Top's down tonight."

He climbed out and kissed her cheek. "I'll put it up if you want me to."

"No need. I came prepared." Erica followed Brad to the passenger side, smiling as he opened the door for her. She lowered onto the leather seat. While he skirted the front of the red sports car, Erica dug a hair tie from her purse then pulled her long dark hair into a ponytail.

Brad climbed in beside her. "Before dinner, I need to do a favor for a friend."

"What sort of favor?"

He buckled his seatbelt. "You'll see." After backing down to the street and driving the short distance to the corner, he turned away from town.

"Does your friend live in McCaysville?"

Brad shook his head. "Blue Ridge. How's Sierra's tutoring going?"

Erica released a sigh. "Seems her reading comprehension and math skills fall way short of what Abby and Tommy expected from a high school student. One more strike against her."

"Troubled home lives often negatively impact students' motivation to learn."

Erica ran her fingers along her seat belt. "After all the trauma Abby's had to deal with, I don't know how she'll cope if Sierra proves capable of raising Theo."

"My future stepdaughter is a strong young woman. She'll survive, especially with Tommy supporting her."

"I admit Abby and Tommy are good for each other. Speaking of stepchildren, how's Jimmy enjoying his new fire-fighting career?"

"Seems he's found his calling. Rescuing people helps ease his guilt over putting Abby in a wheelchair."

Erica brushed a stray hair away from her cheek. "The trial proved the accident was unavoidable."

"Doesn't matter. Jimmy still feels responsible. At least Ashley's helping him cope."

"Are they thinking about marriage?"

"Not as far as I know." Brad turned onto a familiar road.

"We're going to Lauren and Carl's, aren't we?"

He glanced at her. "Not tonight."

"How many of your friends live on this street?"

"Just two."

Erica shifted her focus from Brad's profile to the wooded lots they drove past. Four houses beyond the Lowes', Brad pulled onto a paved driveway leading to a log cabin-style house on a wooded lot. "Are we dropping in on strangers?"

"Sounds like fun, but not tonight." Brad parked in front of the double car garage below the main level before circling to open her door.

Erica swung her legs to the pavement. "Why are we here?"

"The property's been on the market for a while." Brad helped Erica to her feet. "The real estate agent is a long-time friend—"

"So are half the people in Blue Ridge."

"True. Anyway, she wants my opinion."

Erica raised a brow. "You're a high school principal and a former football coach. What do you know about real estate?"

"Nothing, which is why I brought you." Brad looped his hand around her elbow while they made their way to the backyard then onto a covered deck spanning the full length of the house. An outdoor fireplace anchored one end, a large grill the other. He released Erica's elbow before moving to the railing overlooking the wooded backyard.

Erica ambled beside him. "Who lived here and why are they selling?"

"A retired couple. To move closer to their grandchildren."

"Given the number of tourists Blue Ridge attracts, I wonder why they didn't keep the property as a rental?"

"Maybe they didn't want the hassle. Do you want to help me check out the inside?"

"Might as well."

Brad strode across the deck to open the French doors.

Erica stepped into the massive great room and peered at the smooth walls which stood in stark contrast to the paneled ceiling. A stone fireplace flanked by built-in shelves stood on one end. She pointed to the scratched wood floors. "They had at least one big dog."

"Two German shepherds."

Erica strode to the dated kitchen with dark cabinets anchoring the other end of the great room. She ran her fingers along the island's white tile countertop. "The layout looks a lot like Lauren and Carl's place, except smaller. How long has the house been on the market?"

"Little more than five months."

"Probably because it needs some work."

"Which is why the owners lowered the price. Let's check out the bedrooms."

"Lead the way." Erica followed Brad upstairs and into the main bedroom. "The carpet's outdated and worn." She opened the French doors and walked out to the upper deck half the size of the one downstairs. "At least this is a perfect spot to enjoy a morning cup of coffee."

Brad nodded. "Or a full moon."

"True." Erica stepped back inside then moved on to the ensuite bathroom. "Butterfly wallpaper isn't a strong selling point." She peeked into the large walk-in closet. "Lots of storage space."

After viewing the two remaining bedrooms and bathroom, they headed back to the main floor then down to the finished basement. "This would make a good hangout for kids."

"Or a media room with a giant television screen. For movies or football."

"That too." Erica peeked into the half bath before walking out to the patio.

Brad held her hand while they climbed up to the main deck. He released her hand before lowering onto the outdoor sofa—other than two barstools at the kitchen island the only furniture the owners left behind. "Now that you've seen the entire house, what opinion should I give my friend?"

Erica sat beside her fiancé. "The house has good bones and plenty of potential, especially if the kitchen and main bathroom are remodeled. The wood floors need to be refinished and all the carpet replaced. Out here, everything's perfect." She swept her arm in a wide circle. "All this wood wraps around us like a warm summer day."

Brad grinned. "I didn't know you had a poetic streak."

"I'm a bit of an interior decorating expert."

"Among many other talents. Next question." Brad slid his arm around her shoulders. "If all the changes you suggested were done, could you imagine living here?"

Erica blinked as the light suddenly dawned. Her imagination took flight, and she leaned into him. "This isn't about your friend wanting your opinion, is it?"

He squeezed her shoulder. "The day you officially became my fiancée and spent the night at my house, I knew."

Surprised yet pleased he had recognized her discomfort, she placed her hand on his thigh. "I honestly thought I could adapt, until we walked into the bedroom you shared with your first love. Playing with Jan's golf clubs is a far cry from living in the home where you raised your boys."

"Nothing is more important than making you happy."

"One more amazing quality I love about you." A warm sensation radiated through Erica. "To answer your question, yes, I can imagine making this *our* home."

He pulled his arm off her shoulders. "I'll be back in a sec." Brad dashed down the stairs and around the corner of the garage. He returned with his cell phone pressed to his ear.

Listening to half of the conversation sent a warm sensation radiating through Erica. When the call ended, her eyes locked on his. "You were talking to your real-estate friend, weren't you?"

He ran his finger along her cheek, releasing a delicious tingling sensation. "She's on the way over with dinner, a bottle of wine, and a contract."

Erica tilted her head. "What would you have done if my response had been different?"

A smile spread across his face. "Today isn't the first time I've been here."

"You already knew my answer, didn't you?"

"I was ninety-percent certain and hopeful for the other ten." His fingers laced with hers. "I want this home to be exclusively ours."

"Meaning?"

"You choose the colors as well as the kitchen and bathroom designs. Everything, including all new furniture."

"There are a few pieces from your house I'd like to keep."

"Whatever you want, my love."

Erica gazed deep into his eyes. "You and I will grow old together in this beautiful home while spending countless hours out here."

Brad kissed her fingers. "Yes, we will."

Chapter 20

An hour before her mother's scheduled arrival, Wendy unlatched the baby gate leading to the basement. "Time to make sure everything's ready for your Nashville grandmother." Ordering Duke to stay, she gripped the handrail while backing down ahead of her little guy's crawling feet first to the landing. The moment he reached the bottom, she whistled. Duke padded down and followed Ryan into the play area separating the office from the guest room. "Have fun, you two."

Wendy waved over her shoulder then entered the room where her mother would sleep tonight. The pale blue walls, matching Scandinavian-style end tables, and an overstuffed club chair created a cozy setting. A television screen anchored to the wall opposite the bed gave their guests an entertainment option.

After rearranging the decorative pillows adorning the bed and ensuring the ensuite bathroom was spotless, Wendy moved to the French doors. She peered beyond the patio beneath the deck to the backyard sloping down to a creek. How much would she learn about her mother during the next couple of days? Would Cynthia admit what she'd told Brent about her?

Startled by her father's wife's ringtone, Wendy pulled her phone from her pocket. "Hi, Donna."

"I hope you're well."

"Couldn't be better. What about you?"

"My boys left for camp yesterday, and well…" Her tone hinted of anxiety. "I need to talk to someone I can trust."

"I'm listening."

"Not over the phone. In person." She paused. "I'm on my way to Blue Ridge. Also, I booked a room in town for tonight, so I won't need to stay with you. I should arrive at your house by one-thirty. Unless you have other plans."

Rejecting her stepmother wasn't an option. "I look forward to seeing you. Except…I won't be alone. My mother is on her way from Nashville."

Silence.

Wendy turned away from the French doors, her chest tight. "If you're uncomfortable—"

"The fact that we're both on our way to your house can only mean one thing. Your mother and I are meant to become acquainted."

The tension gripping Wendy's chest eased. "The three of us will have the afternoon to ourselves before Chris comes home."

"I appreciate you for accommodating me, Wendy."

"You're always welcome in our home." As soon as the call ended, Wendy texted Chris. "Bring four steaks. Donna's joining us for dinner." Wendy pocketed her phone then carried Ryan upstairs closing the baby gate behind her. "Now all I have to do is figure out how to break the news to your other grandmother." Ryan's babbled response as if he understood made Wendy smile. "You're one smart little guy."

Two hours after Donna called and a half hour before her arrival, Duke's bark sent Wendy rushing out the front door. Duke followed, his wagging tail confirming he approved of the new arrival.

Wendy greeted Cynthia on the driveway, welcoming her with an embrace. Although her mother's face appeared paler than the last time she'd come to town, she didn't seem to have lost weight. Hopefully, a good sign. "Ryan will be happy to see you when he wakes up from his nap."

"I can't wait to give him a big grandmother hug." She opened the rear hatch then circled behind the vehicle and pulled out a stuffed puppy. "This was one of Riley's favorite baby toys, which she's lovingly passing on to her nephew."

"He'll love it." Wendy lowered the carry-on bag to the pavement then released the handle while Cynthia closed the hatch. "Our guest room is all ready for you." She pulled the bag inside then over to the stairs.

"Hold on." Cynthia grabbed Wendy's arm. "You're pregnant, so I'm not letting you haul my suitcase down there."

"I don't mind—"

"Sorry, mother knows best. Either let me carry it or leave it here until Chris comes home."

"We'll wait for Chris. In the meantime, would you like something to drink?"

"A big glass of ice water after I freshen up a bit."

"Your suite is downstairs to the left."

"Thanks."

The moment Cynthia reached the bottom step, Wendy headed to the kitchen. After filling two glasses with ice and water, she glanced at the microwave clock. Eighteen minutes before Donna's arrival. How would her mother react to meeting the woman married to her daughter's biological father? Should she call Donna and tell her not to come over until later or maybe tomorrow morning? Another glance at the clock. Seventeen minutes.

"Now I understand why Kayla enjoyed staying with you."

Wendy spun toward her mother.

"She had her own private suite." Cynthia climbed onto a stool. "Did you catch her smoking weed while she stayed with you?"

"What?" Wendy stared at her mother.

"She doesn't know that I smelled marijuana on her shirt the day before she drove here."

Rattled by conflicting emotions, Wendy slid a glass of water across the counter. Should she lie to her mother or break her promise to Kayla?

Cynthia downed half the water. Her eyes remained focused on Wendy until she set the glass back on the counter. "You caught her, didn't you?"

Wendy's lips tightened.

"Back in the day, Brent and I smoked our share of grass, but I wasn't coping with a cancer-ridden mother. Besides, I knew you and Chris would set her straight if she lit up in your house."

No point denying what she knew. "Chris destroyed her stash and sentenced her to ten hours of community service at the crisis center."

"Good for him."

"Kayla promised she wouldn't smoke again."

Cynthia broke eye contact. "I hope she respects you enough to keep her promise."

"Chris's stern lecture about the law helped." Wendy glanced sideways at the microwave. Five minutes. "I need to tell you something."

"About Kayla?"

Wendy shook her head. "A couple of hours ago, my stepmother called." She paused. "Donna's minutes away from turning onto our driveway."

"You were afraid to tell me, weren't you?"

"I had no idea how you'd react."

"How could you?" Cynthia shrugged. "You barely know me."

"I could meet her out front and tell her to come back tomorrow."

"Nonsense. In a strange sort of way, she's family. Showing up on the same day means we were meant to meet."

"Same thing Donna said."

Cynthia grinned. "I like her already."

"Good." Wendy nodded toward Duke racing to the window. "Because she's here." Despite her mother's comment, Wendy's shoulders tensed as she hastened to the door. How would the women react the moment they came face-to-face? "Hey."

Donna embraced her. "Thank you for agreeing to let me come."

Cynthia ambled over.

Douglas Hewitt's wife extended her hand. "There's no mistaking you're Wendy's mother. I'm Donna Hewitt."

"Cynthia Gilmore." She sandwiched Donna's hand. "Welcome to my daughter's home."

Wendy led the way onto the porch, then inside and over to the great room sofa. "Would you like something to drink?"

"I know it's a bit early." Donna set her purse on the end table before settling on the sofa. "But if you don't mind, I'd love a glass of white wine."

"Make it two." Cynthia sat on the other end. "We could both use a little liquid courage."

Donna smiled. "We met two minutes ago and already understand each other."

Cynthia nodded. "So it seems."

The tension gripping Wendy's shoulders eased a bit as she headed to the kitchen. She removed a bottle of chardonnay from the under-cabinet wine chiller and poured two glasses. After delivering the drinks and placing a bowl of mixed nuts on the coffee table, Wendy lowered onto a chair across from the sofa and set her water glass on the end table.

Glass in hand, Donna turned toward Cynthia. "I hope you don't mind me telling you Wendy has become the daughter I've always longed for."

"Not at all."

"Good, because I want to hear everything you remember about her when she was a little girl."

Cynthia raised a brow and stared at her for a long minute. "Do you know about my history with my daughter?"

Wendy nodded. "She knows."

"All right then." Cynthia tucked her ankle under her knee. "Wendy was a sweet little girl, always smiling. She loved milkshakes and playing with her stuffed animals in the tent we made out of sheets."

Snippets from Wendy's first five years seemed to roll off her mother's tongue, which played havoc with Wendy's emotions. If she'd been half as delighted being a mother as her tone suggested, she wouldn't have abandoned her only child. Was she putting on a show, or was she reacting to the wine?

Duke nudged Wendy's arm and scurried toward the hall signaling her little guy had awakened. She slipped away, returning five minutes later. Cynthia stopped talking mid-sentence the moment Wendy lowered her son onto his play mat with Duke sprawled beside him. "Ryan's always a little shy when he wakes up from a nap."

"So were you." Cynthia swirled her wine. "I wish I had never told Brent what I told him about my first-born child."

Wendy stared at her mother. If they were alone, would she admit telling him she'd died, or was this the closest she'd come to a confession?

"I've talked a blue streak." Cynthia grabbed a handful of nuts. "Tell me about your family, Donna."

"I have two wonderful boys—" Donna scowled. "Whose father is a serial adulterer."

Cynthia's eyes widened. "The same man who fathered Wendy?"

"She's fortunate Douglas was never part of her life." Donna downed the last drop of wine then aimed her empty glass toward Wendy. "Do you mind if I have a little more?"

"Not at all." Recognizing her stepmother needed another glass of courage, Wendy rushed to refill both glasses.

After swallowing a sip, Donna swirled her wine. "Two days ago, I did something I should have done years ago."

Cynthia aimed her glass at Donna. "Did you kick the bum out or shoot him?"

The hint of a smile softened Donna's features. "Even better. I shocked him with divorce papers."

Images of her father's smug expression the day she and Chris confronted him at his home played in Wendy's mind. "How'd he react?"

"As my attorney had predicted, Douglas threatened me with legal action. That's when I told him if he didn't move out, I'd tell his sons the truth about him. For the first time in our marriage, I actually saw defeat in his eyes. In a way I felt sorry for him, but not enough to back down. Yesterday, after our boys left for camp, Douglas packed a bag and moved out." Donna paused. "My husband and his family are well-connected, which is why I haven't told anyone other than you two."

"You can trust Wendy and me with your secret."

Donna smiled at Cynthia. "I know."

Ryan crawled to Wendy then pulled up to his feet. "I believe our little guy is ready for his grandmothers to love on him." She carried him to the sofa, placing him on the center cushion. "The time has come for you both to decide what you want your grandchildren to call you." For the remainder of the afternoon, Wendy's mother and stepmother mulled over names while showering their grandson with love. By the time Chris returned home, the two women had finished the bottle of wine and forged a friendship.

Chris set the steaks on the kitchen counter then strode over. "How's everything going?"

Wendy greeted her husband with a hug. "Starting today, Ryan will know Donna as Mimi and Cynthia as Glamma."

"Perfect names." After kissing Wendy's cheek, Chris dropped to one knee and stretched his arms toward his son. Grinning from ear to ear, Ryan released his grip on the coffee table. "Dada." He took his first steps straight into his father's arms.

Cynthia pressed her hand to her heart as tears filled her eyes. "Seeing my grandson walk for the first time is a miraculous gift from God."

Adequate words failed to express the joy filling her heart. Wendy reached for her mother's hand. As their fingers intertwined, she understood deep in her soul that she would treasure this moment for the rest of her life.

Chapter 21

Since Bernie had a medical appointment, Amanda had offered to cover for her. Now she carried the last breakfast plates from Hilltop's dining room to the kitchen sink. "Your frittata was a big hit."

Millie finished wiping down the island. "What else would you expect from an award-winning chef?"

"I don't know. Perhaps a little humility, or at least a thank you for the compliment?"

"Thank you, Madame President, for acknowledging that hiring me as Hilltop's chef was a brilliant move."

"Humility-Mildred Cunningham style." Amanda rolled her eyes. "How's your mystery club going?"

"Our second meeting's an hour from now."

"Noon? A little early for libations, don't you think?"

Millie shot a questioning glance at Amanda. "Depends on how late we meet."

Amanda's brows furrowed. "Why do I have the impression there's more going on than a book review?"

"Just because my friends and I are senior citizens doesn't mean we don't have other plans after dark." Millie propped her hands on her hips. "I suggest you stop with the misplaced suspicion and tell me what's going on with the political campaign."

Time for a little fun. "You mean the saga?"

Millie's jaw dropped, her eyes wide. "Did Erica tell you?"

Feigning ignorance, Amanda raised a brow. "Tell me what?"

A blush crept up Millie's neck turning her cheeks bright pink. "I don't have time to answer your ridiculous questions." She tossed her towel on the island then spun around and dashed out of the kitchen.

Amanda patted herself on the back while swallowing a laugh. After finishing breakfast duty, she returned to the ranch house. She grabbed a bottle of water from the fridge before heading to the den and sitting across from Erica.

"How'd breakfast go?"

"Your suggestion not to tell our chef that I know about the snag-a-guy-for-Amanda ploy was brilliant." She twisted the cap off her bottle while relaying her interaction with Millie.

"I can't believe she actually blushed."

Amanda grinned. "Her pink cheeks were a sight to behold."

"Maybe now Millie will stop hounding you about Gary."

"She won't be able to help herself. At least until she figures out what's going on. In the meantime, I'll continue having fun at her expense." Amanda took a long sip of water. "Where's Sierra?"

"In the backyard with Dusty. She's studying while Theo's napping."

"Good for her." Amanda recapped her water bottle. "Have you and Brad decided on a wedding date?"

Erica shook her head. "Brad understands my commitment to help foster Theo and help Sierra grow up. Besides, we'll need time to finish updating our house."

"Another interior design project for you to tackle."

"Day after tomorrow, we're meeting with a contractor to plan kitchen and main bathroom remodels." Erica pushed her laptop aside. "Jimmy and

Ashley want to buy his parents' house when his apartment lease is up, so there's no rush for Brad to move."

Amanda peered over her shoulder at Sierra rushing straight from the backyard to her room. The young mother carried a textbook in one hand and a baby monitor in the other. "Theo must be awake."

"So it seems." Erica stood and stretched. "Time for me to head to the spa and prepare for back-to-back massages. Thanks for covering check in for me."

"Glad to help." Eager to spend an hour relaxing before check-in time, Amanda escaped to her bedroom and closed the door. Forty minutes after settling on her chair and opening a book, the doorbell rang. So much for an entire afternoon alone. She bookmarked the page then headed to the foyer and peered through the peephole. Two young men with scruffy beards, one wearing a ballcap backwards, stood on the stoop looking around. Amanda pressed the speaker button. "May I help you?"

The guy wearing the cap moved closer. "Does Sierra Wellington live here?"

Amanda raised a brow. "Who's asking?"

"Dereck Hacket, and this here's my brother Jay. We drove over from Chattanooga."

"It's okay to let them in."

Amanda spun toward Sierra who held her child in her arms. "Which one of these guys is Theo's father?"

"Dereck."

"Are you sure you want to talk to him?"

"Why not? I invited him to come."

"All right, but I'm staying with you." Amanda pulled the door open. The guys shuffled across the threshold, their hands shoved in their jean pockets. Tattoos covered every inch of skin below their tee shirt sleeves.

"I'm Amanda Smith, Miss Wellington's guardian and her son's foster parent." Keeping a close eye on the strangers, she escorted them to the den sofa while Sierra settled on a club chair. "What can we do for you?"

Dereck exchanged a glance with his brother. "I didn't know Sierra had a baby 'til a couple months ago."

Jay's chin jutted out. "Now he wants to do what's right."

Amanda eyes shifted from one brother to the other. "Meaning what?"

Jay gawked at Amanda as if she'd asked a ridiculous question. "Taking care of Sierra and the kid, what do you think?"

That you're up to no good. "I see." Amanda crossed one leg over the other. "Do you have gainful employment, Dereck?"

"Me and Jay got a business."

"What sort of business?"

"Doing odd jobs. Stuff like that."

Amanda raised a brow. "Do you have any idea how much it costs to take care of a family and raise a child?"

"The government will help out. The guy living in our third bedroom moved out, so there's a place for the kid."

"His name's Theo." Amanda pumped her foot. "Are you talking about marriage or a live-in arrangement?"

Dereck shot another questioning glance at his brother.

Which one of these guys is calling the shots, and what do they really want? "Who's older, you or Jay?"

"Me." Jay eyed Amanda." You don't gotta have a big house or wear fancy clothes to raise a kid, especially a boy."

"You're right. However, a child needs a stable environment and preferably married parents who love and respect each other."

"Look." Jay leaned forward, his arms crossed on his knees. "Me and my brother got some deals cooking that'll make us good money so's we can move to a nice neighborhood."

Amanda's eyes remained fixed on Dereck's big brother. "What sort of deals?"

Jay hesitated, as if conjuring up some sort of acceptable explanation. "What you'd call a business franchise. It's confidential 'til it's a done deal."

Hilltop Inn's ringtone sent Amanda dashing to the kitchen. After responding, she returned to the den. "Are you boys driving back to Tennessee today?"

They exchanged glances. Again, Jay took the lead. "Nah. We're staying in town."

"For now, we have our own business to take care of." Amanda motioned for them to follow her. "I'll show you to the door."

Jay stood first. "What time can we come back tomorrow so's Dereck can talk to his baby's mama?"

Now what? Take control of the situation. "One o'clock."

"We'll be here." They followed her through the foyer and out the front door.

Amanda waited for them to climb into their pickup and back down the driveway before returning to the den. "After I check our guests in, we'll talk. In the meantime, if the doorbell rings, don't answer."

Sierra peered up from the club chair, her jaw set. "They're not bad guys."

"Until I know more about them, I don't want either one of them here without me or Erica present. Do you understand?"

"I guess."

"Not good enough."

Sierra huffed. "Yeah, I understand."

"A bit better. I'll be back shortly." Amanda rushed outside then across the side yard to the inn's front sidewalk. She stopped to shift into innkeeper mode, then she climbed onto the porch. "Welcome to Hilltop Inn." After escorting the young couple into the foyer and signing them in, she repeated the well-rehearsed spiel about Hilltop's amenities before leading the way up to the Butterfly Suite. "Please let us know if there's anything we can do to make your stay extraordinary."

Relieved they were the day's only check-ins, Amanda rushed back to the ranch house den. No sign of Sierra. She knocked on the guest-room door. No response. Amanda knocked again, then turned the knob. Locked. "We need to talk." She waited.

The door inched open. Amanda stepped inside.

Sierra plopped onto the chair beside Theo's crib. "You didn't need to send them away."

How could she not understand? "I'm responsible for your and Theo's safety." Amanda sat on the edge of the bed. "How did you end up with a guy like Dereck?"

Sierra shrugged. "He treated me nice. Like I was special."

If Theo's biological father thought so much of her, why had he told her to get rid of his baby? Better to wait and ask that question later. Amanda summoned her warmest smile. "You are special, but not because Dereck says you are."

"I'm an adult, so I can do whatever I want." Sierra's tone screamed of juvenile defiance.

Was she thinking about running away with Dereck? Amanda blinked. "Yes, you can. However, until you're granted legal custody, you aren't allowed to take Theo away from our home."

"You don't have to tell me. I know." Sierra crossed her arms, her foot tapping at a fast speed. "You can leave now."

"We'll talk again tonight." Alarmed by Sierra's response, Amanda walked out, closing the door behind her. She dropped onto the den sofa, kicked off her shoes, and propped her feet on the coffee table. Somehow the Awesam partners had to convince Sierra to stay put—if for no other reason than to protect Theo.

An hour after Amanda left Sierra alone, Millie stormed in from the kitchen. "Whose truck was parked in the driveway earlier?"

Amanda peered over her shoulder. "Don't you ever knock before barging in?"

"I demand an answer." Millie stood across the coffee table, her arms folded tight across her chest. "Now."

"Dereck Hackett and his older brother."

"Exactly what I thought. I'm calling an emergency meeting tonight. Make sure Sierra joins us."

"Why?"

"I have information about Dereck she needs to hear."

Amanda stared at Awesam's chief information officer. "Is that what your mystery club meeting was all about?"

Millie jabbed her finger toward the dining room table. "Right. Six o'clock sharp."

Ten minutes before six, Erica pulled a chair away from the table to make room for her daughter's wheelchair. "Everyone except Wendy will be here."

Abby maneuvered into position. "Did Millie give you any sort of clue about this meeting?"

Amanda sat across from Abby. "Only that she had important information about Theo's father."

Abby's head tilted. "Good news or bad?"

"Given Millie's demeanor, I'd say the latter."

"Is everyone here?" Millie as she rushed in from the back door. She set a plate of cookies and stapled sheets of paper on the table before settling between Awesam's president and CEO. "Where's Sierra?"

Erica aimed her thumb over her shoulder. "In her room."

"One of you needs to get her out here."

"I'll go." Erica hurried to her door, knocked once, then stepped into the guest room. "We're ready for you to join us."

Releasing a heavy sigh, Sierra lifted Theo from his crib then trudged to the den. While Erica returned to her seat, Sierra secured her baby in his swing beside the table before dropping onto a chair between Abby and Amanda.

Millie scooted her chair closer to the table. "A week ago our mystery club agreed to tackle a real-life mystery. Today we met to share everything we've learned about Dereck Hackett and his brother."

"So what?" Sierra folded her arms tight across her chest. "I already know all about him."

"You might think you know, but thanks to Gordon Davenport—"

Amanda nudged Millie's arm. "Who's Gordon and how do you know him?"

"He's our newest club member. Fortunately for us, he's also a retired cop. Even better, his son's an FBI agent."

Abby laced her fingers on the table. "This Gordon guy did some serious detective work, didn't he?"

"You bet he did." Millie tapped her fingers on the paper she'd brought. "First off, Dereck and his brother were raised by a single mother—"

"Big deal." Sierra's eyes narrowed. "So was I."

"With one important difference." Millie's tone hinted of irritation. "Their mother has been behind bars the past three years for armed robbery and dealing drugs."

Sierra huffed. "Everyone in the trailer park knows about her."

"Do they also know her sons spent time in juvenile correctional facilities for following in their mother's footsteps?"

Sierra shrugged.

Millie eyes remained trained on Sierra. "Two months ago their roommate was arrested for dealing drugs. By the time the cops showed up to search their trailer, the Hackett boys had destroyed every trace of evidence implicating them as accomplices."

"Maybe 'cause they weren't guilty."

"If that's the case, how do you explain the fact that neither brother has had any sort of a job, yet they have money to buy food, pay rent, and lease a truck from a shady dealer?"

Sierra thrust her chin out. "People can change, you know."

"You're right. Some people wake up and take charge of their lives. On the other hand—" Millie tapped her finger on the papers. "Everything our mystery club uncovered about the Hackett brothers tells us those boys are headed for jail or an early grave."

"I don't like how you're talking about Theo's father." Sierra bolted from her chair sending it crashing to the floor. "And I don't like you!" She raced to her room, slamming the door behind her.

Erica's shoulders pulled forward. "Should one of us go talk to her?"

Amanda shook her head. "Sierra needs time alone to come to terms with reality."

Millie reached for a cookie. "Thanks to me and my band of detectives, she knows the truth."

Amanda leaned forward. "I have to admit this time you're right."

The corners of their chef's lips curved into a grin. "You had a hard time letting that comment roll off your tongue, didn't you?"

"Yeah, but I'll get over it."

Abby fingered a cookie. "Even if Sierra earns a diploma, she can't be trusted to do what's best for Theo."

Erica leaned toward her daughter. "With our help she'll learn, sweetheart."

Chapter 22

Erica checked her watch for the second time in five minutes. Quarter after one and no sign of the Hackett boys. She dropped onto a club chair across from Amanda. "Maybe they changed their minds and decided to hightail it back to Chattanooga."

"Dereck maybe, but not Jay."

Millie stopped pacing. "I'm telling you those two are up to no good." She hauled a chair from the dining room table to a position between the club chairs before dropping onto the sofa. "Bums like them don't show up on time. Unless they're doing something illegal such as closing a drug deal."

Erica raised a brow. "What's with the chair?"

"My position of authority." Millie peered over her shoulder. "Where's Sierra, and why isn't she out here with us?"

Erica shrugged. "The only time either Amanda or I have seen her since last night was when she prepared a bottle for Theo."

"Did she say anything about the Hackett brothers?"

"Not a peep."

"Hmm." Millie's lips pursed. "Maybe she's finally accepted reality."

Amanda scoffed. "More likely she's confused and refuses to talk to us."

Responding to a ping, Erica plucked her phone off the end table. "A text from Abby, asking if the guys are here." She responded, then set her phone back down.

"Did either you or Amanda contact Child Services to tell Jillian what's going on?"

Erica exchanged a glance with Amanda before eyeing Millie. "We decided to wait until we talk to Dereck and Jay today."

Millie huffed. "If you ask me, you should've already called her." Dusty padded over and sniffed her pant legs. She patted his head, triggering a tail wag. "You smell my cats, don't you?"

"While we're waiting—" Amanda tilted her head. "Why don't you tell us more about the new guy in your mystery club?"

"Not much to tell." Millie shrugged. "I barely know him."

"Is he good-looking?"

"He's old and wrinkled like the rest of us. What do you think?"

Amanda's eyes remained focused on Millie. "What kind of car does he drive?"

"He doesn't—"

"Drive?"

"A car." Millie crossed her arms. "He gets around on a Polaris Slingshot."

Amanda raised a brow. "What in the heck is a slingshot?"

Erica chuckled. "It's a three-wheeled motorcycle."

Amanda stared at her. "How do you know?"

"One of our Asheville neighbors drove one."

"News flash." A grin played on Amanda's face. "Our chef's boyfriend rides a motorcycle that won't tip over."

Millie huffed. "Gordon's not my boyfriend."

"Are you sure?" Amanda's tone hinted of amusement. "Maybe he's looking for a little romance with a fascinating widow."

"In case you've forgotten, Susan and Bernie are also widows—"

"Yeah, but you're the only member of your club who's an award-winning chef."

Millie waggled her finger at Amanda. "I know what you're doing—"

"Besides killing time?"

"For your information, the only reason Stanley invited Gordon is because he enjoys reading mysteries."

Amanda's grin widened. "Uh-huh."

"Hmph."

Erica chuckled. "The Amanda and Millie sitcom is alive and well."

The doorbell rang.

"They're here." Millie scurried to the dining room chair facing the sofa as if she'd taken on the role of judge. "One of you needs to let them in."

Erica's focus shifted from Millie to Amanda. "Should we ask Sierra to join us?"

Amanda stood. "Better to wait. She'll come out if she wants to face these guys." She headed to the foyer.

Erica breathed deeply to slow her racing pulse.

Amanda returned. She directed the Hackett brothers to the sofa before returning to her chair.

Dereck glanced around the room. "Where's Sierra?"

Millie folded her hands on her lap. "Taking care of *her* baby."

Jay's eyes narrowed to a slit. "Who are you?"

Millie mirrored his narrow-eyed expression. "I'm your worst nightmare."

Erica broke into a spasm of coughing.

Amanda cleared her throat. "Ms. Cunningham is our company's chief information officer."

Jay smirked. "Sounds like a made-up name."

Millie's jaw clenched. "You have no idea—"

"I'll handle this," Amanda interrupted.

Responding to Amanda's sharp tone, Millie clamped her mouth shut.

Amanda scooted to the edge of her chair. "Ms. Cunningham's position grants her the authority to keep us informed about everything impacting our business and our family."

Jay shrugged. "Whatever."

"With that in mind, one of you needs to tell us the real reason you're in Blue Ridge."

Jay exchanged a glance with his brother. "Me and Dereck got everything figured out. First we'll take Sierra and the kid back to Chattanooga with us—"

"Stop right there." Amanda aimed her palm toward Jay. "The kid—whose name is Theo—is our foster child. Which means no one can legally take him anywhere without our or the court's permission."

"Sierra won't leave Blue Ridge without Theo," added Erica. "So you might as well forget about her going anywhere with you."

Jay propped his ankle across his knee, his eyes locked on Erica. "How long you gonna foster Theo?"

"Until Sierra's granted parental custody."

He fingered his expensive-looking sneaker. "After that she can do what she wants, right?"

"Technically."

"Okay, here's what me and Dereck are gonna do." Jay's tone reeked of arrogance. "Go back home and make a nice place for his kid. All we need is some cash."

"Well now, the truth finally comes out." Amanda leaned back. "You're here to con us out of money, aren't you?"

"Not you personally." Jay's chin lifted higher. "My brother has rights as the kid's old man. What kind of lame name is Theo, anyway?"

"The name means 'God's gift.'" Erica's posture stiffened. "You're mistaken if you believe Sierra has money."

"Don't matter. I'm talking about the ten grand in the kid's GoFundMe account."

A knot gripped Erica's stomach. Of course, they'd know about the fund.

Jay yanked his phone from his pocket while staring at Erica as if she didn't have a brain in her head. "Everything's out there. All you gotta do is know how to find it."

Amanda leaned back, crossing one leg over the other. "You boys think you're real smart, don't you?" Her foot pumped. "People donated money to help Theo, not to line your pockets."

"So then Me and Dereck are gonna get us a lawyer."

"Legal representation costs a bundle—"

Millie grabbed Amanda's arm. "You need to let me handle this."

Erica's eyes shifted between Awesam's president and chief information officer. Who'd win this battle?

Amanda hesitated for a brief moment. Her foot stilled. "You have the floor."

Millie's focus shifted from Amanda to her targets. "You boys are going to need a good lawyer if you don't march your butts out of here right now and leave Sierra alone."

Jay tilted his head toward Dereck. "Get a load of the old lady."

Erica gripped her chair's arms, hoping Millie hadn't stashed her gun in her pocket.

"With age comes wisdom, young man." Millie lifted off her chair. "How old are you, Dereck?"

"He's twenty-two going on twenty-three."

"At least you're smart enough to do simple math." Millie took one step forward. "Do you always let your brother talk for you, or do you have the brains to speak for yourself?"

Dereck's eyebrows drew together. "No, ma'am. I mean yes, ma'am."

"Good. Are you aware of your state's consensual consent laws?"

"He don't—"

Millie raised her hand, then jabbed a finger toward Jay. "I don't want to hear another peep out of you until I say it's okay for you to talk. Do you understand?"

Jay's chin dipped an inch. "Whatever."

"All right." Millie lowered her hand. "Now, do I need to repeat the question?"

Dereck shook his head. "I don't know nothing about that law."

"In that case, let me be the first to inform you that Sierra was a minor when you slept with her." Millie took a step closer. "You're five years older than her, which means you broke Tennessee's statutory rape law regarding sex with a minor. Do you know what that means?"

Leaning close to his brother, Jay whispered in his ear. "We wanna know what makes you an expert on the law?"

"Smart question." Millie moved closer to the coffee table. "I'm the ranking member of an organization supported by a police officer and an FBI agent."

Erica struggled to stifle a laugh.

"Yeah, right." Jay's tone mocked.

"How else would I know about your mother serving a sentence for armed robbery? Or that your roommate was arrested for dealing drugs? Or that you and Dereck spent time in juvenile correction?" Millie planted her fists on her hips. "How is it you have a source of income without working? Unless you're engaged in illegal activity."

Dereck sneered. "You don't know what you're talking about, lady."

"Yes, she does." Sierra strode in from the hall, stopping beside Millie. "Lots of neighbors suspected you were up to no good."

"Oh, yeah?" Dereck planted both feet on the floor. "Then how come no one called the cops?"

"Maybe people don't wanna get involved."

Amanda and Erica stood then moved into position flanking the two women. Erica nudged Sierra's arm. "What do you want these boys to do?"

Sierra drew in a deep breath. "If they don't go back to Chattanooga and leave me and my baby alone, I'll file charges against Dereck."

Jay bolted to his feet. "Let's get the heck out of here."

Dereck stood, his eyes focused on Sierra. "I didn't mean you no harm."

"Forget her. She and the kid ain't worth the effort." Jay grabbed his brother's arm and pulled him toward the foyer. The front door opened then slammed shut.

Millie brushed her hands together as if wiping away grit. "Good riddance to those two bums."

Amanda thumped Millie's arm. "Kudos to you, Ms. CFO, for standing up to the Hackett brothers."

"You can bet those punks will never admit they were outwitted by an old lady." Millie's chest puffed. "I would've made a doggone good attorney, but I'll settle for being the brilliant creator of Blue Ridge's first authentic mystery club."

Amanda laughed. "Too bad you're so modest."

"False humility is a colossal waste of time." Millie turned to face Sierra. "You're way too good a person for a guy like Dereck."

"Jay's the bad one. Dereck goes along with whatever his brother does because he's weak." Sierra wrapped a lock of hair around her finger. "When

Jay asked for money that belongs to my son, I realized there's no way I'd let Theo end up like either one of those guys."

The tension gripping Erica's muscles eased as she wrapped her arm around Sierra's shoulders. "Today you've taken one giant step toward earning custody of Theo."

"Do you think I can be a good mother?"

Erica squeezed her shoulder. "Yes, I do."

Amanda nodded. "We all believe in you, right, Millie?"

"I didn't until you marched in here and sent Dereck and his brother scurrying away like a couple of sewer rats." Millie faced Sierra. "Erica and Amanda are excellent examples of good mothers. So, watch and learn."

"You can also learn a thing or two from Millie." Responding to a ping, Erica pulled her arm away from Sierra's shoulders then grabbed her phone and read Abby's text. Should she respond with a text or a phone call? Better to hear her daughter's reaction. "I'll be back in a few." Erica headed to her room while pressing Abby's number.

Abby grabbed her phone off her desk and swiped her finger across the screen. "Are they there now?"

"Dereck and Jay left a few minutes ago."

"With or without Sierra?"

"Without."

Listening to her mother's recap, Abby teetered between relief for Little Pip's safety and disappointment that Sierra hadn't gone back to Chattanooga with the Hackett brothers. "What are the chances they'll come back?"

"Considering Sierra threatened legal action against Dereck, I'd say zero." Her mother paused. "Today, perhaps for the first time, Sierra understands who the Hackett brothers really are. She's growing up fast."

When the call ended, Abby lifted a framed photo of her cradling Theo before his surgery. Peering up at the ceiling, she whispered, "Tommy and I are meant to adopt Little Pip so he'll have two parents raising him, aren't we?"

An unexpected heavy sensation pressed down on Abby. Lowering her chin, she pressed the photo to her chest. If Sierra abandoned Theo, would he grow up with a hole in his heart only his birth mother could heal? Confusion rocked her brain as Abby squeezed her eyes closed. *Show me what you want for Theo...then give me the courage to accept your will.*

Chapter 23

Thirty minutes before the town hall event's scheduled start time, Amanda entered the Hampton Inn meeting room. Bedecked in a royal blue suit and three-inch heels, she stood behind the last row gripping a chair back while scanning the room. Would a hundred seats be enough, or would they face a standing-room-only situation? How many people would step up to the microphone to ask questions?

Nancy Campbell strode in. "Do you have any idea how many people will show up?"

"We don't have a clue." Amanda released her grip. "Although we're confident our opponent invited coconspirators."

"To be expected in a political campaign, I suppose." Nancy walked up the center aisle, stopping to test a microphone secured to a stand. She moved on to test three cordless mikes lying on a small round table set up between two tall stools. After testing all three, she spun around. "Sound system works. The room is a good size."

Amanda joined her at the front of the room. "We appreciate you moderating."

"A couple of years ago, I invited two candidates running for city council to my podcast. Two totally different personalities. The one who was most likable won the election, proving nice still plays well in small towns."

"That speaks well for my candidate."

"Hopefully, a lot of his supporters will show up." Nancy nodded toward the back. "The man of the hour has arrived."

Amanda spun around.

Keith and Gary, looking handsome as well as distinguished in suits and ties, headed up the aisle. "A crowd is already gathering in the hall."

Amanda's eyes shifted from Gary to Keith. "Anyone you know?"

"Quite a few, including two of our neighbors and several clients. The hotel manager is standing guard until we're ready to open the doors." Keith approached Nancy. "Good to see you again."

"Likewise." She motioned to the stools. "As the first candidate to arrive, you have the privilege of selecting your side."

Keith turned to Amanda. "What do you think, left or right?"

"Considering you're the right candidate for the job." She pointed. "That one."

Gary moved beside Amanda. "Good choice."

"Thanks." The brush of Gary's shoulder against hers sent a tingle surging through her limbs. Had he noticed? Blaming the sensation on nerves, she inched away. "This is the first time I've seen you dressed up since we began working on Keith's campaign."

He leaned close to her, smiling. "First time I've seen you wearing a skirt and high heels."

Was he flirting? *Ridiculous.* A simple response in kind.

The door swung open and Richard Watson marched in. A middle-aged woman wearing a tan pantsuit trailed behind him.

"Is she Watson's campaign manager?" whispered Amanda.

Gary nodded. "Shirley Dickerson, one of his former law partners."

Keith extended his hand as his opponent headed up the center aisle. "I'm looking forward to a productive session."

The smile playing on Watson's lips failed to reach his eyes as he accepted Keith's welcoming gesture. "Productive and well worth our time." His over-the-top Southern accent was on full display.

Keith released his hand.

"Now that you're both here—" Nancy stepped forward. "You'll be seated on the left, Mr. Watson, Mr. Armstrong on the right. About the process—"

Amanda kept a close eye on Watson's smug expression while Nancy reviewed the terms both campaigns had agreed to earlier in the week. How soon after the hour-long session began would someone ask a question meant to destroy Keith? Ten minutes? Thirty?

Nancy paused. "Any questions?"

Keith shook his head. "We're good to go."

"Same here." Watson buttoned his jacket.

"All right." Nancy glanced at her watch then motioned toward the accordion-style temporary wall behind her. "Mr. Redding, Ms. Dickerson, please escort Mr. Armstrong and Mr. Watson to the other side of the wall behind us." Moments after they complied, she called the hotel manager, then joined Amanda at the back of the room beside the window.

Fifteen minutes after the door opened, only a half dozen seats remained empty. Chris and Linda Armstrong entered, slipping into the last row. Amanda remained standing, scanning the audience while Nancy strode to the front. She lifted a microphone off the table then faced the audience and began explaining what to expect during the hour-long event.

Gary ambled in behind Shirley. She remained close to the door. He moved beside Amanda.

After requesting the audience applaud only at the beginning and the end of the event, Nancy stretched her arm toward the opening in the temporary wall. "Ladies and gentlemen, please welcome our candidates, District Attorney Richard Watson and Counselor Keith Armstrong."

The men walked out amid applause. They shook hands, then lifted microphones off the table and moved into position. After each made a brief opening statement, half a dozen residents scrambled to line up in the center aisle.

Nancy held her mike close to her mouth. "Please state your name before asking your question."

The first questioner had been one of the guests during Hilltop Inn's grand opening. His question, as well as the next six, related to the district attorney's role and the candidates' experiences. Forty five minutes later one woman and one man stood in the aisle. With fewer than fifteen minutes remaining, Amanda held out hope they'd been wrong about their opponent's potential underhanded attack.

Until the man stepped up to the mike.

Nancy gave him the go-ahead.

"Thank you. I'm Gerald Corbin."

Gary's brow pinched.

"Do you know him?" whispered Amanda.

"Name sounds familiar."

"My question is for Mr. Armstrong." Corbin paused. "Do you condone using your position as an attorney to cover up a crime, sir?"

Amanda cringed knowing full well what was about to happen.

Keith squared his shoulders. "I do not."

"But your father, who founded the Armstrong law firm, didn't hold the same opinion, did he?"

"My father was an honorable man."

"That's debatable, considering he used his friendship with the sheriff and a judge to cover up a crime."

Having anticipated the question, Keith lifted off his stool. "My father took steps he believed were necessary to protect three minors—"

"Who smoked while drinking themselves into a stupor and started a fire. Burning down that barn was no accident, sir."

Nancy stepped forward. "This isn't a courtroom—"

Corbin jabbed his finger toward Keith. "You were one of those minors, weren't you?"

"Please take your seat, Mr. Corbin, and allow Mr. Armstrong to respond." Nancy's tone hinted of anger.

Amanda glared at Watson's smug expression while his conspirator spun away from the microphone and lumbered back to his seat.

Chris stood. "I'd like to comment." He headed straight up the aisle then lifted the mike off the stand and faced the audience. "Before my father answers, you folks need to know that Mr. Corbin is a member of Mr. Watson's former law firm. The incident he's referring to is a sealed record which means the information is unavailable to the public. That same information is meant to remain sealed unless the persons named are involved in future illegal activity. Given my father and the other two minors have not been accused of any crimes, the means by which Mr. Corbin obtained the information is highly suspect."

Chris paused, glancing around. "Having worked with my father since graduating law school, I assure you he has never abused his role as an attorney. Furthermore, had I been caught doing what he and his buddies were accused of doing, he would have made sure I paid a heavy price for my actions." Chris replaced the mike before heading down the aisle.

Gary signaled a thumbs-up.

Watson's campaign manager folded her arms tight across her chest.

Keith took a step toward the audience. "My father used the law to protect three sixteen-year-olds whose foolish actions led to accidentally burning down an abandoned barn. Lest you think we got off without punishment—" He moved closer to the front row. "A judge privately sentenced each of us to one hundred hours of community service. Cleaning out gutters. Picking up trash along the roads. Helping repair fences damaged in a storm. Following that incident, I never smoked another cigarette and didn't take another drink until my twenty-first birthday."

Keith paused. "Some of you in this room have been Armstrong Law Firm clients who trusted us to represent you. As your district attorney, I assure you and everyone else that I would never use my position to violate minor children's right to privacy, or to pursue a case for personal revenge. Ask yourselves if my opponent could make the same claim."

Corbin stood. "District Attorney Watson is the only candidate who doesn't have a criminal record."

"Thank you, Mr. Corbin." Nancy's tone made it clear the man's outburst was inappropriate. "Would you like to comment, Mr. Watson?"

He shook his head. "I'll wait."

"All right. Does anyone else have a question for either of the candidates?"

Silence.

"Mr. Watson, you have one minute for a closing statement, sir."

"Thank you, Ms. Campbell." Watson moved close to the front row, grinning. "And thank y'all for coming out tonight." His exaggerated Southern accent came across as insincere. "For the past sixteen years, I've served this district with honor, putting criminals behind bars to protect all you fine citizens."

He rattled off a half-dozen cases while moving along the front row as if addressing a jury. "The single most important question you need to consider. Should you vote for a former juvenile delinquent who has spent his career defending lawbreakers?" Watson paused as if waiting for the question to sink in. "Or an attorney who has the experience and the knowledge to continue serving as your district attorney? There is only one choice." Watson lowered his mike then ambled back to his stool.

"Thank you, Mr. Watson." Nancy turned toward Keith. "Mr. Armstrong, you have one minute, sir."

Squaring his shoulders, Keith moved to the aisle. "Tonight you have witnessed firsthand the reason I elected to take a significant cut in salary to run as your candidate. In your hearts and minds, you know that a district attorney who crosses the line to win a case or defeat an opponent is not worthy to hold the office."

Keith peered around the room. "Thirty years of experience and deep respect for our community more than qualifies me for the position. Which is why I'm asking for your vote to return integrity to the district attorney's office." He lowered his microphone.

Nancy raised her microphone. "Thank you, ladies and gentlemen, for attending tonight's event. Our candidates will remain for a few minutes to answer any questions you wish to ask either in person."

Following applause, a dozen voters headed straight to Keith, five to Watson.

Amanda nudged Gary. "This isn't over, is it?"

"No. Corrupt men whose authority is challenged don't give up without a fight."

Chapter 24

Wendy secured Ryan in his car seat before sliding behind the wheel, backing up, and turning around. At the end of the driveway, she climbed out and transferred the stack of envelopes from the mailbox to the front passenger seat. Ten minutes later she parked behind Abby's car. After setting the brake, Wendy stepped onto the pavement. With the diaper bag slung over her shoulder, she carried her little guy through the ranch-house kitchen to the den. "Are you ready to see your grandson's new accomplishment?"

"More than ready." Amanda lifted off her dining room chair, then dropped to one knee.

Wendy lowered her son to the floor four feet away from his honorary grandmother.

Amanda held her arms out. "Come give Nana a big hug." The moment Wendy released him, Ryan toddled straight into Amanda's arms. "I believe we have a future running back in our family, just like your daddy."

"Speaking of Chris." Wendy hung the diaper bag on the back of the chair. "I hear my brilliant husband put our crooked DA in his place last night."

"You'd have been proud of the way he defended his dad." Amanda carried Ryan to the crate of toys beside the fireplace.

Wendy propped her hip on the sofa arm. "Chris believes Watson will pull more stunts."

"Men who are desperate to hang onto power don't give up easily."

"After Keith announced he was running for district attorney, I thought Chris should one day throw his hat in the ring and run for judge. Not anymore."

Amanda settled on a club chair beside Ryan. "Politics is a tough business."

"You're handling the pressure like a pro, especially since this is your first political campaign."

"Thanks to dealing with Gunter Benson's crimes against us, I'm tough enough to handle men like Richard Watson." Amanda laced her fingers in her lap. "At least we haven't heard from Gunter in a while."

Wendy diverted her eyes to Ryan playing with a toy telephone. Other than her husband, no one knew about Gunter's latest letter.

"Uh-oh. Something's going on in your pretty head?"

Wendy blinked. Had she been that obvious? "Nothing important." Assuming Amanda believed her, she moved close to Ryan. "Nana will keep you company while Mommy goes next door to welcome Hilltop's new guests." Wendy leaned down to kiss her son's cheek then strode to the kitchen, flicking a wave over her shoulder. "I'll see you two later."

After pocketing the inn's key, Wendy stepped out to the carport. Grateful she had something to keep her busy until the first guest arrived, she grabbed the stack of mail from her car before making her way across the side yard and driveway. A warm sensation flowed over her as memories bubbled up from the first day Chris brought her, Amanda, and Erica to the property. Given the mansion's rundown condition, she'd failed to recognize its potential until she and her Awesam partners moved to Blue Ridge and transformed Eleanor Harrington's vacation home into a first-class inn.

Wendy climbed onto the front porch. Breathing in the warm summer air, she settled on a rocking chair with the mail on her lap. Her eyes drifted to the first envelope. Junk. Number two, more junk. Number three, a credit card statement she had already paid. She slid the statement on the bottom of the stack revealing envelope number four.

Cold fingers of dread sent a shiver racing up her spine. The postmark. The familiar handwriting. Wendy squeezed her eyes shut. If she ripped the envelope to shreds and tossed it in the trash, no one would know it existed.

Startled by Hilltop's cat brushing against her leg, Wendy's eyes popped open. Curiosity enticed her to turn the envelope over and slide her finger under the flap. Her hand froze. Not this time. Wendy bolted off the rocker then raced to her car. Gripping the mail in her left hand, she yanked the back door open. She hesitated, staring at her name scrawled on the dreaded envelope. If she opened the envelope now, at least she'd know what to expect. No. She'd failed to heed Chris's advice too many times. Not anymore. Wendy tossed the mail on the floor behind the passenger seat before slamming the door shut. Drawing in a deep breath, Wendy spun toward Hilltop the moment a high-end sportscar eased up the driveway. Time to assume the role of gracious innkeeper.

An hour after walking away from her car, Wendy escorted the last of the arriving couples to the door beside the den fireplace. "The Rainbow Suite served as the original owner's private retreat." She opened the door, strode to the French doors, and drew back the curtains. "There's a lovely view of our English country garden."

The woman smiled. "The view as well as not having to deal with stairs is why we reserved this room."

"Excellent choice. Please let us know if there's anything we can do to make your stay extra special." Wendy handed the woman's husband the key before walking out and returning to the foyer. After closing the guest book, she returned to the ranch house and tossed the key in the bowl on the kitchen counter.

"How'd everything go?" Amanda peered up from the dining room table.

"The new guests are all checked in. Where's Ryan?"

Amanda nodded toward her grandson curled up on the den floor beside Dusty. "He drifted off to dreamland a few minutes ago."

Wendy smiled while settling on a chair beside her partner. "Cuddling up with Dusty or Duke is Ryan's favorite napping spot. Where's Sierra?"

"In her room. She's been spending a lot of time alone the last few days, hopefully studying." Amanda pushed her laptop aside. "Other than visits from your mother and stepmother, anything exciting happening in the Armstrong household?"

Wendy blinked, her bottom lip caught between her teeth. Why was she asking?

"I recognize that look. Something's bothering you big time."

Denying would raise all sorts of questions. Besides, she'd claimed Amanda as her substitute mother, so why not trust her with the truth. "It's Gunter." Wendy relayed the story beginning with opening his letter, ending with typing a response.

"How'd Chris react when you confessed you'd mailed your letter?"

"The look in his eyes...he turned away without saying a word and headed straight to the basement." Wendy fingered her wedding rings. "That night, for the first time since our wedding, he slept in the guest room."

"Can't say I blame him." Amanda leaned back, her eyes locked on Wendy. "I don't understand why you continue holding out false hope that Gunter will somehow turn into a decent human being."

"Yeah, well, those days are over. From now on, I'm letting Chris deal with the bum."

"About time. Maybe Gunter will finally get the message and stop sending you letters. What do you say we indulge in slices of the apple pie Millie brought over last night while we wait for our little guy to wake up?"

"Perfect. Except I might need two slices."

Ninety minutes after swallowing her last bite, Wendy pulled into the garage beside Chris's car. Her breathing accelerated the moment he stepped out from the kitchen. She climbed out. "How long have you been home?"

"A couple of minutes." Chris kissed her cheek. "Anything exciting happen at Hilltop?"

"Nothing out of the ordinary. How about you?"

"Same." He opened the rear passenger door, released Ryan from his car seat, and carried him inside.

Wendy hesitated. How long should she wait before breaking the news? Drawing in a deep breath, she retrieved the diaper bag and mail from the back seat. Inside the kitchen, a bag from a local restaurant and a bottle of nonalcoholic wine sat on the counter. "You brought home dinner?"

"Caesar salad and your favorite summer pasta." Chris peered over his shoulder from the sofa. "Just needs warming up."

"Thank you, darling." Wendy set the diaper bag on the floor. Time for a little Wendy charm to pave the way for the big reveal. After pocketing the dreaded letter, she pulled a bottle of beer from the fridge and poured herself a glass of pregnant-lady beverage, then ambled to the sofa. "You're the best husband and daddy ever." Wendy handed Chris the beer.

"Thanks, for the brew and the compliment." Chris grinned while tapping his bottle to her glass. "Coming home is the best part of my day." He took a long swallow while propping his feet on the coffee table.

Wendy tucked her ankle under her knee then sipped the fake wine.

"How's it taste?"

"Not as good as the real thing." She patted her baby bulge. "But safe for our little gal." Should she tell him now or when he finished his beer? If she waited until after dinner, would he think she was avoiding the issue, or that she didn't consider the letter a big deal?

"Did you pick up the mail?"

Waiting was no longer an option. "I almost forgot. No I didn't." Wendy set her wine glass on the end table before pulling the letter from her pocket. "I didn't open it." She handed it to him.

Chris's eyes shifted from Wendy to the dreaded envelope. "How long were you planning to wait?"

"As long as possible, I suppose."

"At least you're honest. Do you want to hear what he wrote?"

"I don't know." Wendy picked at her fingernail. "What do you think?"

"As your attorney or your husband?"

"Both."

His eyes met hers. "Listen, then as I've requested more than once, leave the response and any further communication in my hands."

Wendy traced an X across her chest. "I promise."

"Wise decision." Chris ripped the envelope open and unfolded the single sheet of lined paper. "Are you ready?"

"No, but go ahead anyway."

"Here goes. *Dearest Darling Wendy. Your response to my letter told me everything I need to know. You still have feelings for the father of our son.*"

Wendy's cheeks burned. "How can he possibly believe I still give a hoot about him?"

"What do you expect when you respond to a narcissist?"

"I know I should have listened to you." Wendy broke eye contact. "But I didn't, so keep reading."

Chris shifted his attention back to the letter. "*Therefore, you'll be happy to know that I've identified an attorney who can prove my innocence.*"

"That scumbag is as guilty as sin." Shocked by her bitter tone, Wendy gasped.

"Are you going to keep interrupting?"

"Sorry. I won't say another word until you finish reading."

Chris eyed her then continued. "*I'm sure you're aware that lawyers don't come cheap. My guy needs ten grand to begin the process. When you find it in your heart to help me, transfer the money into my prison account. I'll forward the payment to the attorney. If you don't mind, would you send me an updated picture of my son? Thank you in advance for understanding. Love, Gunter.*"

"That man's delusional if he believes for one second that I'd give him a dime." Wendy's eyes narrowed. "Do you believe he wants money for a lawyer?"

"Are you serious?" Chris stared at her. "The man believed he was smart enough to act as his own attorney in his murder trial."

Sensing her cheeks were seconds from turning bright pink, Wendy reached for her wine glass. "Do you suppose he's trying to pull some sort of jailhouse con?"

"You can bet on it." Chris folded the letter then stuffed it back into the envelope.

Wendy swallowed a sip. "How do you plan to respond?"

"With a stern warning. I'll show you my response before I send it." Chris tossed the envelope on the coffee table before taking another swig of his beer.

Wendy planted both feet on the floor. "Are you gonna sleep in the guest room again?"

Chris stood then pulled her into his arms. "And miss out on sleeping with my beautiful wife who looks for the best in people? Not a chance."

Wendy wrapped her fingers around his neck. "After we put our little guy to bed, I'll reward my brilliant lawyer with Wendy-style gratitude."

Chris winked, his lips curving into a smile. "My favorite dessert."

Chapter 25

Following a late afternoon massage, Erica returned to the ranch house. She laid the spa key on the counter then pulled a bottle of water from the fridge and ambled to the den. Sierra sat at the dining room table with an open textbook and the baby monitor in front of her. "How's your studying coming along?"

"Okay, I guess. I called Mom while you were gone."

Erica pulled out a chair. "I imagine she was happy to hear from you."

"Not really. She told me that the day I first showed up at Grandma's house, she'd called Mom to let her know where I was." Sierra pushed her book aside." The whole time I lived in Morganton, Mom never once called to talk to me or even asked how I was doing. I suppose with me gone, she's relieved to have one less mouth to feed."

Erica gaped at Sierra's blank expression. Was she keeping her feelings bottled up? "When you talked to her today, did you tell her about Theo?"

"Yeah. Mom figured I ran off because I'd gotten myself pregnant. She asked if I'd applied for my monthly check from Uncle Sam."

"Do you understand what she meant?"

Sierra shrugged. "That I should go on welfare. Except I don't want to live like her in a broken-down trailer raising a bunch of kids. Instead, I wanna be like you and Amanda and Abby. You know, earn my own money to take care of me and Theo."

"You're an amazing young woman. I'm proud of you."

Sierra's chin quivered. "I wish you were my mother."

The girl was desperate for compassion. Erica placed her hand on Sierra's arm. "Even though I can't replace your mother—who I'm confident loves you—you can count on me and Amanda to be your honorary mothers."

Sierra's pleading eyes met Erica's. "Do you really think my mother loves me?" Her voice was barely above a whisper.

"I do." Erica's heart ached for her. "Mothers love their children in the best way they know how, but it's not always perfect."

Sierra averted her eyes. "Thank you for letting me move into your house."

"You're part of our family now, which means you're welcome to live here until you're ready to move out on your own." Erica pulled her hand away from Sierra's arm before removing her phone from her pocket. "Speaking of family, Brad's on his way to take me to our new house."

Sierra's eyes widened. "Are you gonna move out?"

"At some point. Until then, I'm here for you." Erica glanced at her phone. "Abby should be home any minute now."

Sierra's shoulders curled inward. "She doesn't much like me living here, does she?"

Erica stared at Sierra's downcast eyes. Denying wouldn't help; nor would admitting the truth. "Abby's been through a lot of changes during the past year and a half. Sometimes it takes her awhile to adjust to new situations." *Not exactly the truth but hopefully a satisfactory explanation.* "Besides, she wouldn't have stepped up to tutor you if she didn't care about you."

"I want Abby and Tommy to be my friends."

"Why don't you tell them?"

"They might laugh at me."

"I promise they won't."

A whimper sounded on the monitor. "My baby needs me." Sierra pushed her chair away from the table.

Erica's eyes followed the troubled young woman as she hastened to her room and closed the door. Should she or shouldn't she tell Abby what had just happened? Maybe Brad could help her decide.

Thirty minutes after receiving her fiancé's text, Erica held his hand while climbing onto their future home's deck. She set her laptop on the sofa. "We need to talk before our contractor shows up."

"About the project?"

"Not exactly." Erica ambled to the railing. "Something happened with Sierra before you picked me up." She relayed the entire conversation. "If I share everything with Abby, she's likely to resent her even more. If I don't, will I be disloyal to my daughter?"

"You're an incredible mother." Brad slid his arm around her shoulders. "What are your heart and mind telling you to do?"

Erica ran her finger along the railing. "To trust Abby and Sierra to work everything out on their own."

"There's your answer."

"It won't be easy."

"Parenting never is." Brad nodded toward his friend heading their way. "Time for two more important decisions. Erica, meet Jim, one of the best contractors in Blue Ridge."

Erica offered her hand. "We met when you contracted to work on Mildred Cunningham's fire-damaged house."

"You were her voice of reason." Jim smiled while accepting and then releasing her hand. "Brad told me you're a decorating expert, so I suspect you already have an idea in mind."

"Actually—" Erica moved away from the railing then lifted her laptop off the sofa. "I have pictures to show you."

Brad nudged his friend's arm while unlocking the French doors. "I told you she's a woman who knows what she wants."

An involuntary smile curled Erica's lips while she followed the guys into the great room. After setting her laptop on the island, she tapped the keypad. Little did Brad know she'd spent hours surfing the web, mulling over which style to choose. "What do you think about this kitchen?" Erica turned the screen toward Brad.

He studied the photo. "Looks perfect."

"About the bathroom." Erica revealed two side-by-side photos. "Which do you prefer?"

"Do you have a favorite?"

"The final choice is yours." Would he pick the one she hoped he'd pick?

After studying the photos, Brad tapped the one on the right. "You prefer that one, don't you?"

"How'd you know?"

"Lucky guess." He turned toward Jim. "We'll go with that look."

"Good choices. Email me the pictures, and I'll have a quote ready by the end of next week. Do you have a deadline in mind?"

Brad shot a quick glance at Erica. "We haven't nailed down a move-in date, so anytime in the next couple of months."

"Assuming the materials are readily available, I should have both projects finished by mid-September."

"Good timing. I'll coordinate with the floor guy tomorrow."

Erica emailed the photos to Jim, then closed her laptop. How would Brad react if she told him Sierra might need her longer than she'd first anticipated? Better to save that conversation for another day.

Abby maneuvered her wheelchair into the foyer then pushed the front door closed. Dusty bounded over, her backside in motion. "Hey, girl. You missed me, didn't you?" She patted her canine companion's head.

Sierra wandered from her room with Theo in her arms. "Where's Tommy?"

"His dad needs him on a construction site, so it's just you and me. Unless you want to skip tonight's study session."

Sierra shrugged. "What do you want to do?"

Begging off until Tommy could join them would send the wrong message. Besides, the sooner Sierra was ready to take her test, the sooner the tutoring sessions would end. "We'll go ahead with the lesson."

"I've already fed Theo, so I'm ready." Sierra carried him to his swing then settled on a chair beside him. "I made us sandwiches."

Abby wheeled her chair close to the table, across from her student. "What subject do you want to work on first? Hopefully not math since Tommy's not here."

"Actually um…" Sierra picked at her fingernail. "Is it okay if we talk about something else for a little while?"

"Like what?"

"I've been wondering—" Sierra hesitated for a moment. "—if you were one of the popular kids in high school?"

Why was she asking? Abby shrugged. "I guess so."

"Did you have a lot of friends?"

Abby tilted her head. "What do you mean by 'a lot'?"

"I dunno, like maybe five?"

"Then yeah, I had a lot of friends. What about you?"

Sierra turned her head away from Abby. "The popular kids don't hang out with girls like me."

"What do you mean, 'like you'?"

"You know." Sierra shrugged. "Kids who live in rundown trailer parks and wear second-hand clothes instead of living in big fancy houses with rich parents."

A twinge of guilt accosted Abby. Had she been one of *those* girls? "In some schools, being rich isn't all that important." Sierra's expression made it clear she didn't believe her. "When Mom and I moved from Asheville to Blue Ridge halfway through my senior year, we barely had enough money to buy groceries. Being the new kid in town, I didn't expect to make a single friend. Until Hannah, one of the most popular girls in school, introduced me to her friends. We've been close ever since."

"How come none of them ever come over here?"

"They're all away at college. Tommy and I get together with them every time they come home." Abby paused. "Truth is, real friends don't care where you live or what you wear. They like you for who you are."

"You're lucky Erica's your mom."

Abby stared at her. What was she really trying to say? "Yeah, I know."

"The thing is…" Sierra paused for a long moment, as if deciding what to say next. "I don't blame you for not wanting me to live here."

So that's where this was going. Well, two could play this game. "What's the real reason you suddenly showed up after dumping Theo on the crisis center stoop?" Abby's eyes narrowed. "Just like Dereck, you're after the GoFundMe money, aren't you?"

"I thought maybe you were different." Sierra's eyes turned cold. "But you're the same as all those snooty mean girls who laughed at me and called me names. Well, you'd better get used to me, 'cause I ain't moving out 'til I can take Theo with me." She bolted from her chair, sending it crashing to the floor, then dashed to her room slamming the door behind her.

The sting of shame weighing heavy on her shoulders, Abby gazed at Theo still sleeping peacefully in his swing. "Your mother deserves better."

She backed her wheelchair away from the table then maneuvered to the hall and tapped on Sierra's door. "Can I come in?"

Silence.

"Please?"

The door inched open. "What do you want to accuse me of now? Trying to steal money from your mom or Amanda?"

Abby peered up at her. "I'm sorry for the way I've treated you."

Sierra hesitated before pulling the door open. She dropped onto the side of the bed. Her eyes reddened. "All I wanted was for you and Tommy to be my friends."

Abby swallowed against the thickness in her throat. "Back in Asheville, Carrie was my best friend. She was one of the country club kids I hung out with. Until everyone found out about our house going into foreclosure and two of our cars being repossessed. Turned out dating one of the most popular guys in school was way more important to her than our friendship." Abby wheeled closer. "If you give me another chance, I want us to become friends."

Sierra stared at her for a long moment. "Even when I prove to you and everyone else that I'm capable of raising Theo on my own?"

Abby's mouth fell open. "You know, don't you?"

"That you want Theo to be your baby? Yeah, I know."

Reality struck as if a lightning bolt had penetrated the walls. God was giving Sierra a second chance to become the mother Theo deserved. "Truth is, he's not my baby. He's yours." Abby stretched her hand toward Sierra. "Sometimes friends end up like sisters, which means I'd be Theo's Aunt Abby?"

Sierra grasped Abby's hand while dabbing at tears spilling down her cheeks. "I'd like that."

"So would I."

Chapter 26

Following his afternoon nap, Wendy carried her little guy downstairs to the play area outside her and Chris's home office. Duke followed, sprawling on the floor beside him. "Mommy's class begins in five minutes."

"Mama." Ryan grabbed a handful of fur. "Doggie."

Wendy giggled while uncurling his fingers. "Smart boy, pausing between those two words." While he crawled to the basket of toys, Wendy slipped into the office, leaving the double doors open. She set her phone on her desk, booted her laptop, and logged onto the course. A few more months and she'd earn a business associate's degree—an accomplishment she hadn't imagined happening until Morgan challenged her.

Tuning out her little guy's babble, Wendy turned her attention to the screen. She remained focused on the professor for the full hour. When the session ended, she stood and stretched.

Still a bit unsteady on his feet, Ryan crawled in, grabbed her pant leg, and pulled up to a standing position.

"Hey, there." Wendy lifted him onto her lap. "Before long you'll have a baby sister to play with." Ryan reached for her mouse. She gently pulled his hand away. "Why don't we go upstairs and wait for your daddy to come home."

"Dada."

"Who loves you so much he chose you to be his son." Wendy pocketed her phone then carried Ryan to the bottom of the stairs. "Are you ready to practice big-boy stairs?"

Duke padded up the stairs ahead of them.

Ryan pointed. "Doggie."

Wendy lowered her little guy to the floor then held his hand while he climbed up to the landing. "By winter you'll walk up holding onto the railing all by yourself." Wendy lifted Ryan and carried him the rest of the way. After securing the baby gate, she pulled her ringing phone from her pocket then activated FaceTime. "Hey." Wendy held her phone in front of Ryan. "Say hi to Aunt Kayla." He jabbered while fingering the screen.

"He's obviously happy to see you." Wendy wiped away the smudge he left behind while settling on the sofa. "How's your summer job going?"

"Okay, I guess. Except I had more fun working at the crisis center than babysitting two spoiled little kids. At least their mother's paying me good money." Kayla paused for a long moment. "I think maybe Mom's getting a whole lot better."

Was her sister clinging to false hope? "Really?"

"She kinda seems to have a little more energy."

Definitely clinging.

"Last night after me and Riley helped her fix supper, we played Monopoly. Zach worked a late shift, so it was just the three of us."

"I'm glad you're spending time with her."

"Mom told us stories about growing up in Biloxi. Her mother wasn't a nice lady."

Wendy squeezed her eyes closed as a memory fought its way to the surface. Waiting for the bus with her mother outside their apartment building. Riding one then changing to another before arriving at their destination. The tubes in her grandmother's nose. The way she smelled funny and coughed a lot from smoking too many cigarettes. Worse than everything else, her grandmother's coldhearted comments that always brought Cynthia to tears.

"Me and Riley agree that compared to the grandmother we never met, our mom's like Mother of the Year."

"Believe me." Wendy opened her eyes. "Growing up in an abusive household takes a toll."

"I kinda figured out that I was wrong about Mom not feeling love for us. She just never learned how to show it. Now that she's better, she'll have lots more time to spend with us."

Wendy swallowed the lump rising in her throat. "Treasure every moment."

"I will."

Triggered by the garage door opening, Duke bolted to the back door.

Chris ambled in. "I'm home."

Wendy peered over her shoulder. "Come say hi to Kayla." She held the phone out.

Chris gripped the phone, smiling at his sister-in-law while he laid a folder on the coffee table. "How's your summer going?"

"I'm writing words for a song about Mom. Dad's gonna write the music."

"Can't wait to hear it." Chris settled beside Wendy.

"Maybe next time you and Wendy come to Nashville...Hold on. Got a text from my friend Harper. I'll talk to y'all later."

Chris set the phone on the coffee table beside the folder. "Did Kayla say anything about your mother?"

Wendy crossed her arms. "She believes against all odds that Cynthia's recovering."

"Sounds as if your sister needs a little hope to help her make it through the next few months."

"I suppose we all do."

Gripping the coffee table, Ryan pulled up and toddled to his daddy. Chris lifted him onto his lap. "How's my boy?"

The way he responded to their son's gibbering with a two-way conversation warmed Wendy's heart. Her focus drifted to the coffee table. If Chris's response to Gunter was inside the folder, it could wait. "I'll fix us dinner while my two favorite guys solve the world's problems." Wendy strode across the great room to the kitchen. Responding to a kick, she smiled while pressing her hand to her belly. In a few months, she and Chris would welcome their baby girl into the world.

Still smiling, Wendy pulled the refrigerator door open. "How does a chef salad sound?"

"What do you say, Ryan?"

He gibbered.

"Our guy approves."

"Two chef salads coming up."

During dinner and the two hours that followed, Chris didn't say a word about Gunter leading Wendy to believe the folder held something other than a letter. At eight thirty, she carried her son to his room while Chris remained in the den. "Sleepy time's here." After changing him into pajamas, she laid Ryan in his crib. "Good night, sweet boy." He yawned as his eyes closed.

Wendy slipped out, leaving the door open. Chris and the folder had disappeared. She peeked in the bedroom. No sign of him. Maybe he'd gone to their office. While heading toward the stairs, movement caught her eye. Wendy stepped out to the deck.

Chris leaned on the railing, facing the wooded backyard. He stared at her with longing eyes. "The first day I brought you here I had already fallen in love with you."

"For a long time, I believed my feelings for you were for all the wrong reasons. Until that night in Hilton Head when you proposed. Now I can't imagine living my life without you."

"Neither can I." Chris stroked her cheek then spun away from the railing before settling on a chair beside the glass-top table. He tapped his fingers on the folder. "I wrote a response."

Wendy sat across from him exhaling slowly. "I'm sorry I've put you in the middle of this ongoing drama."

"You're my wife and the mother of my son and my daughter." Their eyes met. "Everything that happens to you is important to me."

"From now on, I promise to let you handle everything related to Gunter."

"I know. Are you ready to hear what I wrote?"

"I'm ready."

"All right. Here goes. *Dear Mr. Benson. I am writing on behalf of Wendy Armstrong regarding your recent letters. First, be advised that under no circumstances now or in the future will my client send you money. Second, she wishes to cease all further communication with you. Should you ignore her request, as Mrs. Armstrong's attorney, I'm advising her to forward any letters from you unopened to my office for review and response. As her husband, I remind you that you have relinquished your rights and therefore no longer play any role in her life or my son's. Regards, Christopher Armstrong, Attorney at Law.*

Chris slid the letter back into the folder. "What do you think?"

"Sounds a lot like the last letter you wrote to him. Except for the last sentence. Maybe this time he'll get the message."

"Whether he does or he doesn't, at least he's behind bars more than halfway across the country."

"Hopefully for the rest of his miserable life." Wendy reached across the table to touch Chris's arm. "Thank you for loving me despite the baggage I brought into our relationship, darling."

"You're the most amazing woman I've ever met." Chris scooped the folder off the table then stood and pulled Wendy to her feet. He held her hand while they walked inside. After tossing the folder on an end table, he lifted Wendy into his arms. "Tonight it's my turn to show you how much I love you."

She wrapped her fingers around his neck while he carried her into the bedroom and closed the door before Duke could follow.

Chapter 27

Forty-eight hours after Keith learned of Richard Watson's ploy to accuse him of jury tampering, Amanda turned onto Armstrong Law Firm's parking space. She climbed out moments before Gary pulled up beside her. "Any idea why Keith called an emergency meeting?"

He met her on the sidewalk. "He's fighting back."

"That much I know."

Gary pushed the door open, then stood aside allowing Amanda to walk in.

Rosalie, the firm's plump, middle-aged receptionist, sat behind her desk with the phone pressed to her ear. She held up a finger while responding to the caller. "Yes, sir, I'll let Mr. Armstrong know…I'm sure he will." Her tone hinted of frustration.

"Who do you suppose she's talking to?" whispered Amanda.

"Based on her tone, an adversary."

Rosalie ended the call. "Mr. Armstrong's waiting in the conference room."

"Thanks." Gary gripped Amanda's elbow as they made their way down the hall then entered the small room awash in neutral colors.

Keith sat at the end of the table, his Bluetooth pressed into his ear. "They're here now. All right." He swiped his finger across his phone. "Vincent Adams, our private investigator, is on his way over."

Gary pulled a chair out for Amanda. "With an update?"

"Results."

Gary settled beside Amanda. "After two days? He's obviously a heck of a PI."

"One of the best. Vincent located Wendy's mother eighteen years after she abandoned her. You can run, but you can't hide from a determined private eye. On to the campaign." Keith leaned forward, eyeing Amanda. "Any polling results?"

"Based on the town hall exit survey, sixty percent of the attendees plan to vote for you. Twenty-eight percent are undecided, and twelve percent want to reelect Watson. We'll find out if those percentages translate to the rest of the population in two weeks when we initiate a public survey."

Gary twisted the cap off his water bottle. "We need to crush or at least counter Watson's latest sabotage attempt before then."

Keith's jaw tightened. "Our opponent won't stop the dirty tricks until he's either reelected or defeated."

"We knew going in that Watson would pull all sorts of dirty tricks to hold on to power." Chris stepped in carrying a briefcase. "Any word from Vincent?"

Keith nodded. "He'll arrive any minute with details."

"Wish I could stay." Chris glanced at his watch. "I'm due in court in ten minutes. I'll catch up later today."

Amanda's eyes drifted to the painting of downtown Blue Ridge on the wall behind Keith. How much scandal would Watson attempt to stir up before November? Would Keith and Linda continue to consider the fight worth the effort? Would she?

A distinguished-looking gentleman ambled in, befitting the image of a kind grandpa far more than a bulldog investigator. Settling across from

Keith, he laid down a folder. "I suspect you already know that you're fighting a corrupt candidate."

"Which is the only reason I'm running against him. What'd you find out?"

Vincent fingered his neatly trimmed white beard. "Ralph Gaines was a juror in the William Nickerson case."

Keith's brow pinched. "A young guy accused of selling drugs."

"Yeah. Anyway, Gaines was ready to cut you off at the knees until I told him I have proof he accepted a bribe."

Keith leaned forward, his arms crossed on the table. "Do you have proof?"

"I will when he shows up in ten minutes to spill his guts."

Keith chuckled. "The power of suggestion."

"Works every time." Vincent leaned back. "What's happening between your daughter-in-law and her mother?"

"They've reconnected. Unfortunately, Cynthia's battling late-stage cancer."

"Too bad. At least I found her while she's still alive."

Following a gentle tap, the door inched open. Rosalie stepped in. "Mr. Gaines is here."

Keith stood. "Show him in."

Rosalie stepped aside, allowing the red-faced, portly man sporting a scraggly beard to lumber in.

Keith motioned to his right. "Please have a seat."

Gaines hesitated before planting his bulk onto the chair beside Vincent, across from Amanda and Gary.

Keith returned to his seat while Vincent tapped his fingers on the folder he'd laid on the table. "Before I show Mr. Armstrong and his campaign managers the evidence, go ahead and tell them what landed you in this mess."

"First off—" Gaines cleared his throat. "My wife's the one who wanted me to take the money."

Amanda stared at the man. Two seconds and he'd already shifted the blame and confessed.

"Guess I can't blame her. A grand is a lot of money for poor folks like us." His focus darted from Keith to Vincent. "I ain't spent it yet, so if I give it back, will I stay out of jail?"

"Like I told you, that depends on what happens in the next few minutes. Beginning with you repeating what you told me an hour ago."

"Okay, here's exactly what happened. Couple days ago, a woman named Mrs. Dickerson showed up at our front door claiming she was investigating witness tampering."

Keith's brows raised. "Did she tell you she's DA Watson's campaign manager?"

"Nah. She said she worked for the government and wanted to know what I remembered about sitting on a jury. I told her not much after five years, especially since my memory ain't what it used to be. Then she told me and my wife that someone had seen me talking to the defendant's attorney at a restaurant during a lunch break." Gaines folded his arms across the table, staring at Keith. "You were that lawyer, weren't you?"

"I was."

"Is Watson doing you dirty, 'cause you're running against him?"

"So it seems."

"I figured a nice-looking lady who worked for the government knew what she was talking about, so I told her I'd probably seen you. Except I didn't, did I?"

Keith shook his head. "What did Ms. Dickerson want you to do?"

"After she set a stack of hundreds on the table, she asked me to write down that you'd talked to me about the trial, then tell a reporter. I told her I wasn't putting nothing in writing, but I was willing to talk. No reporter ever showed up. If I'd known she was lying, I would've told her to get lost." Gaines unfolded his arms and leaned back. "How much trouble have I gotten me and my wife into?"

Keith eyed Gaines for a long moment. "Are you willing to write and sign a statement claiming Ms. Dickerson attempted to coerce you into making false claims against DA Watson's opponent?"

"It's the truth, so I'll sign."

"All right." Keith removed a pad of paper and a pen off the credenza behind him then pushed it to Gaines.

"What do you want me to write?"

"Everything you just told us."

"I don't spell too good."

"Trust me, spelling doesn't count."

Amanda uncapped a bottle of water while watching Watson's latest victim. How many more would show up before the election?

Five minutes after writing the first word, Gaines looked up. "How do you spell coerce?" Keith responded. A minute later, Gaines laid down the pen. "You wanna read it to make sure it's okay before I sign?"

"Yes." Keith ran his finger down the single page. "Excellent job. After you add your signature, we'll all sign as witnesses."

"What's gonna happen to me?"

"Since you didn't sign or give any false statements, it means you're off the hook."

"Huh." Gaines's focus shifted from Keith to Vincent, then back to Keith. "Does that mean I can keep the money?"

"Why did you think she was giving you cash?"

Gaines shrugged. "To reward me for helping the government."

"Well then, the money's yours."

"That'll make my wife happy."

After Keith escorted Watson's would-be patsy out of the conference room, Gary turned toward Vincent. "How did you unravel Watson's plot so quickly?"

"I'm good at what I do, and Watson was sloppy."

Amanda pointed to the folder. "What's in there?"

Vincent opened it, a mischievous grin curling his lips.

Amanda laughed while staring at a blank sheet of paper. "Ah, the power of suggestion. Brilliant."

Keith returned. "Time to tell our adversary about our signed confession."

Vincent closed the folder. "You know what Watson will do, don't you?"

"Oh, yeah." Keith dropped onto his chair. "He'll claim he had no idea what his campaign manager was up to, then pay her off and fire her."

"Fortunately for us, we cut him off before he leaked his accusation to the public." Gary grabbed his water bottle. "Our timing might be off the next time he tries to pull a fast one."

"Another challenge for another day." Keith pulled his phone close to his chest then punched in a number and activated the speaker. The call went to voicemail. "Keith Armstrong, here. My team and I have wrapped up an informative meeting with a gentleman named Gaines. The result of our conversation will be of utmost interest to you. I suggest you call me directly at your earliest convenience." Keith ended the call. "Bets on how long before he responds?"

Vincent fingered his beard. "I'm guessing—" The phone buzzed. "Five seconds."

"You win." Keith swiped his finger across the screen, then activated the speaker. "Thanks for returning my call."

"Sorry I couldn't get to my phone in time. What's up?"

"I assume you've heard of Vincent Adams."

A moment of silence, then— "He's a private investigator."

"One of the best in Georgia, which is why he uncovered a plot to undermine my candidacy." Keith relayed the entire conversation with Watson's victim, ending with the signed confession.

Gary nudged Amanda, whispering. "Here comes the denial."

"I had no idea what Shirley was up to." Watson's over-the-top Southern accent failed to mask his anger over getting caught. "I guarantee she won't do it again." Watson abruptly ended the call.

A grin spread across Keith's face. "By this time next week, Watson will ensure the entire town knows he's hired a new campaign manager. For now, I'm treating us to a well-deserved celebration lunch."

Chapter 28

Millie stepped back from her dining room table to admire the formal dishes and stemware she had stored away more years ago than she could remember. The freshly cut flowers from Hilltop's garden created an elegant centerpiece. Eleanor would be proud of her. Smiling, Millie returned to her kitchen to finish preparing dinner. At least the lightning strike and fire that had destroyed her kitchen resulted in top-notch appliances suitable for a gourmet chef.

Ten minutes before her guests were due to arrive, the doorbell sent Millie scrambling to the foyer. She peeked through the peephole. Perfect timing. She pulled the door open.

Amanda held out a handful of envelopes. "I found your mail in Hilltop's box."

"Seems I need to have a talk with our mailman." Millie stepped aside while keeping a close eye on Amanda. "Thanks for checking."

"You're welcome." Amanda crossed the threshold. "Fancy outfit for a mystery club meeting."

Stifling a grin, Millie smoothed her new long-sleeve silk tunic over her white slacks. "What's the big deal?"

"I don't know. You tell me." Amanda sniffed. "What smells delicious?"

"Stuffed pork tenderloin and chocolate ganache cake."

"Hmm. I wonder what or who inspired you to evolve from appetizers and libations to gourmet meals?"

"We're celebrating."

"A club member's birthday?"

Millie shook her head. "Solving the Dereck Hackett mystery."

Amanda brushed past Millie then strode through the living room and into the dining room. She ran her fingers along the white tablecloth. "Why are there four instead of six place settings?"

Millie tossed the mail on the buffet. "Eileen has a cold, and Susan's babysitting her great granddaughter."

"Convenient." Amanda grinned. "Less competition."

Millie planted her right hand on her hip. "I have no idea what you're talking about."

"Don't you?" Amanda grinned while lifting a bottle off the buffet. "Expensive wine. Candles on the table. Makeup on your face." She leaned close. "Nice perfume. You might as well admit you're trying to win our first-to-land-a-man bet."

"Now you're being ridiculous."

"Am I? Think I'll hang around to personally thank the Polaris-riding ex-cop."

"Suit yourself." Millie turned away.

Amanda followed her to the kitchen. "Have you been checking out Victoria's Secret's catalogue?"

"Maybe I should ask you the same question." Millie removed a bowl of salad greens from her refrigerator.

"No need. I don't have the slightest intention of winning."

"Neither do I, so we might as well call the bet off."

"Not a chance." Amanda leaned back against the counter. "It's more fun watching you squirm."

"You're hopeless." Responding to the doorbell, Millie dashed to the foyer with Amanda following close behind. "Come on in. Stanley, Gordon, meet Amanda Smith, my most irritating Awesam partner."

Gordon chuckled, his eyes focused on Amanda. "You must have ticked Millie off big time."

"Somehow, I keep getting under her skin. Thank you both for helping dig up details about the Hackett brothers."

Stanley nudged his friend. "This guy did most of the work."

"Once a cop, always a cop." Gordon held up a bottle of wine, his eyes shifting to Millie. "I hope red's okay."

She nodded. "Perfect choice for our entrée."

Amanda gripped Millie's elbow. "Do you guys mind if I borrow your hostess for a minute?"

"Not at all."

Gordon followed Stanley into the living room while Amanda steered Millie to the porch.

She yanked her arm away from Amanda's grip. "Now what do you want?"

"Your special guest—"

"He's not special."

"Of course he isn't. You're wearing perfume to impress Bernie and Stanley. As I was about to say before you interrupted, for an old guy Gordon's good-looking. He's also charming." Amanda nodded toward the Polaris. "And adventurous."

Millie raised a brow. "What's your point?"

"I'm just saying he's a good catch."

"For someone who's fishing, which I'm not. Although—" Millie tapped her finger to her chin. "You'd end up embarrassed as all get-out if an old lady beat you in a catch-a-guy bet."

Amanda scoffed. "Based on everything I've observed during the past ten minutes, you're the one baiting the hook, not me."

Millie nodded toward the driveway. "Bernie just drove up, so you might as well go home and try to figure out how you're going to beat me."

"You're hopeless." Amanda rolled her eyes then stepped off the porch and onto the sidewalk. At the driveway, she stopped to talk to Bernie before heading toward the street.

Millie's eyes followed Amanda until Bernie joined her on the porch. "What did Awesam's president say to you?"

"She wanted to know if I was in on your scheme."

Millie's brows arched. "How'd you respond?"

"Like I had no idea what she was talking about." Bernie eyed Millie's outfit. "I've never seen you so gussied up."

"Big plans call for fancy moves."

"How confident are you that your scheme will work?"

"On a scale of one to ten, a solid eight."

Amanda strode past Hilltop Inn then up the ranch house driveway and into the den where Erica was tapping on her phone. "You won't believe what's going on at Millie's."

Erica turned toward her. "Try me."

Amanda settled on the sofa beside Erica while relaying the entire scene from the time she knocked on Millie's door. "She couldn't have been more obvious if she'd hung a sign around her neck."

"Strange. Especially since Millie claims chefs don't wear fragrance because the scent clashes with food aromas."

"One more dead giveaway."

"Perhaps. Unless..."

"What wild notion are you conjuring up?"

"Since you asked—" Erica stretched her arm across the back of the sofa. "What prompted you to head over to Millie's?"

"She called and asked if her mail had ended up in Hilltop's box."

"Her timing seems a bit too convenient, don't you think?"

Amanda's brows arched. "What are you suggesting, Sherlock?"

"Is it possible Millie set you up to spark your competitive nature?"

"Talk about a wild interpretation."

Erica tapped her fingers on the sofa back. "Or dead-on accurate."

"Hold on." Amanda stared wide-eyed at Erica. "Are you suggesting Millie staged the entire scene to provoke me into a romantic relationship with Gary?"

"If she considers snag-a-guy-for-Amanda too important to lose."

"Well, if you're right, and that's what our chief information officer is up to, it's likely to backfire big time."

Erica's head tilted. "How so?"

"If I'm not mistaken, Gordon had a twinkle in his eye when he smiled at Millie."

"Which could mean he's in on her plan."

"Or he's open to a late-in-life romance with a feisty chef who I have to admit looked sexy for an old gal."

"We could sneak over and peek in Millie's front window."

"Her guard cat would give us away." Amanda tapped a finger to her chin. "Maybe I'll show up in Hilltop's kitchen tomorrow morning for a little investigative work of my own."

"Good idea, and maybe I need to begin calling *you* Sherlock."

Following his last bite of pork, Gordon laid down his fork. "If my wife had half your cooking skills, I wouldn't have let her go."

Millie wiped her mouth with a napkin. "You're divorced?"

Gordon nodded. "Going on thirty years. I don't blame her for wanting out. Being married to a cop wasn't her idea of an ideal marriage. Especially when I took on dangerous undercover assignments."

Millie's eyes remained focused on Gordon. He was as different from her husband as sugar from salt. "Have you always been a bit reckless?"

He grinned. "Let's just say I've never shied away from challenges. What about you? Divorced? Widowed?"

"The latter. Rupert passed away a while back."

Stanley twisted his wedding ring. "My wife and I had seventy mostly good years together before she passed. I never expected I'd outlive her."

Bernie reached for her wine glass. "Staying busy helps cure loneliness, especially for folks our age."

"You've got that right." Stanley nodded. "To that end, what do you think about our mystery club meeting twice instead of once a month?"

Gordon nodded. "Especially if we come across new mysteries to solve."

"Considering Millie's busy schedule, if everyone agrees, we need to take turns hosting." Bernie faced Millie. "That is, if you don't mind us sharing the responsibility."

Millie stole a quick glance at Gordon. Visiting an ex-cop's home could be interesting. "I'll go along with whatever the group decides. For now, you guys relax while Bernie and I clear the table and serve dessert."

While indulging on chocolate ganache cake, they chatted about favorite foods. When they finished, they carried their wine glasses to the living room. Sitting on the sofa beside Bernie, Millie entertained her guests with stories about Hilltop.

An hour into the conversation, Stanley yawned prompting Gordon to help him to his feet. "Time for us old guys to call it a night."

Millie lifted off her sofa. "Before you leave—" She scurried to the kitchen, returning with two containers. "Cake for tomorrow's lunch."

"Believe me." Gordon grinned. "My slice will be gone way before lunchtime."

Bernie smiled. "If you're a sweets-for-breakfast kind of guy, you need to try Millie's cinnamon rolls. Hilltop's guests rave about them every morning."

"I'm a sweets-anytime kind of guy." Gordon handed Stanley his cane. "Are you ready for a wild ride home?"

"As ready as ever."

Millie escorted the guys through the foyer to the front porch. "Your fancy tricycle doesn't have a top, does it?"

"Nope."

"What do you do if you're caught in a sudden rainstorm?"

"Pull over and put on rain gear."

Millie tilted her head to the side. "Kind of inconvenient, don't you think?"

"Yeah, but worth the ride. Thanks for a delicious meal."

"You're welcome." Millie remained on the sidewalk with her eyes focused on the guys while they donned helmets then strapped themselves into the Polaris. The moment they backed down the driveway, she stepped onto the porch.

Bernie stood in the doorway, staring at her.

"What?"

"Your plan might end up delivering an added bonus."

"I have no idea what you're talking about."

"Sometime during the next couple of months, we'll find out if I'm right."

"Are you going to help me clean up the kitchen or stand here talking nonsense?" Millie brushed past her friend. What was Bernie up to?

Chapter 29

Following a mid-morning session with a client who had talked nonstop during the entire massage, Erica welcomed the solitude her office provided. She clicked on Hilltop's website then opened the reservation page. No scheduled massages until the day after tomorrow. Relieved, Erica pulled up the kitchen and bathroom photos she had shown their contractor. When she'd married Abby's father and years later Gunter, aka Brian Parker, she moved into their houses. Everything in the home she'd share with Brad would be of her choosing. Her style. Her forever home.

Erica peered around the narrow space off the massage room. The diploma from the Massage Institute of Cleveland caught her eye. Despite everything Gunter had stolen from her and Abby, in a convoluted way, his deception had unleashed their courage to pursue meaningful careers. As added bonuses, they'd each fallen in love with remarkable men.

Following a tap, the door opened. Amanda stepped inside. "How was today's client?"

"She barely stopped talking long enough to breathe. What'd you learn about last night's dinner party?"

"Nothing, other than the four of them decided to meet every two weeks. If Millie had some sort of ulterior motive, Bernie's either clueless or in on the scheme."

"Maybe Millie will give us some sort of clue during tomorrow afternoon's board meeting. For now, I need to get ready to meet Brad for lunch." Erica led the way through the massage room and reception area. Outside she breathed in the warm summer air as they headed across the side yard toward the ranch house.

"One of these days, you and Brad need to decide on a wedding date."

"We will when the time's right."

"For Brad or for you?" Amanda linked arms with Erica. "If you ask me, you need to stop worrying about Sierra."

"Not easy to do considering I'm the reason she moved in with us."

"Abby and I could have rejected your crazy idea, but we didn't because given the circumstances, we both understood it was the right thing to do."

"Which I appreciate. At the same time, leaving you two alone to take care of Sierra and Theo doesn't sit right with me."

"Neither should keeping Brad waiting indefinitely."

Doubt crept around the excuses racing across Erica's mind. Had she placed more importance on a wayward teenager than on the man who had captured her heart? "Speaking of Sierra, I've been meaning to ask if you've noticed a change in Abby's relationship with her during the past couple of days."

"Not really. Although…" Amanda paused. "Before I headed to the inn, they were sitting on the sofa chatting with each other."

"Which means Abby's spending her day off with her opposition."

"If they're still together, we'll know something's going on." Amanda released Erica's arm as they made their way through the carport and into the kitchen.

Erica set the spa keys on the counter before following voices drifting from the den. Her daughter and Sierra sat on the sofa facing each other with Theo propped up on the cushion between them.

Abby turned toward her, smiling. "Hey."

"Hi, sweetheart. Are you two studying?"

Abby shook her head. "Just talking. Tommy's coming over in a little while to take us out to lunch."

"You and Sierra?"

"And Theo."

Abby's focus returning to Sierra sparked a brow-raising glance with Amanda. Pressing her lips tight to prevent a myriad of questions from rolling off her tongue, Erica strode to the hall.

Amanda followed Erica into her bedroom, closing the door behind her. "Do you have any idea what happened to make those two suddenly act as if they're friends?"

"Not a clue. The next time I catch Abby alone, I'll find out."

"At the very least, it seems your daughter has given you permission to move forward with wedding plans."

"That's a stretch."

"Is it?" Amanda pulled her ringing phone from her pocket. "My daughter's calling. We'll talk later."

"Tell Morgan hi for me."

"Will do." Amanda waved over her shoulder while walking out.

Was her Awesam partner right? Erica held up her left hand and studied her engagement ring. Had she used Sierra and Theo as convenient excuses to delay setting a date? She lowered her hand to her side. A year and a half ago, her world had been thrown into chaos when she discovered her second marriage had been a sham. She'd been forced to sell nearly everything she had left to move to Blue Ridge to pay back taxes on a run-down mansion. Then moving into this house with two women she'd known for a little more than a month added to her anxiety.

Erica's phone pinged a text. "Change of plans. Meet me at school. Call when you arrive." She stared at Brad's message. Maybe the time had come to stop stalling. Erica slipped her phone into her purse then changed clothes and walked out of her room. "I'm on my way to meet Brad for lunch."

Abby peered over her shoulder. "Have fun, Mom."

"You too." Erica hastened to the kitchen and grabbed Abby's car keys then stepped out to the carport. Ten minutes later, she parked in the high school parking lot and called Brad. "I'm here."

"I'll let you in."

Erica climbed out and made her way to the entrance for the first time since attending a basketball game with Brad, Jimmy, and his girlfriend, Ashley. Today the front hall appeared empty.

Brad unlocked the door and pulled it open. "Sorry for the drama."

"When did you start locking the school down?"

"After the school shooting near Atlanta." Brad closed the door then kissed her cheek. "Forty minutes ago I expelled a kid from Ashley's class after he threatened another student."

"Are you expecting more trouble?"

"He's not a bad kid, so probably not." He released her. "Since our resource officer is off duty, I need to stay close in case I'm wrong."

"It's difficult to imagine anything terrible happening in a town as close-knit as Blue Ridge."

"The likelihood is minimal, but not nonexistent." Brad nodded toward the entrance. "Lunch is here." He opened the door to accept the delivery. "Sandwiches and cookies. Not as good as Millie's but sweet." Back in his office, Brad left the door ajar then removed two bottles of water from the mini fridge tucked in the corner. "Some days I regret not stocking my private stash with a couple of beers."

Erica smiled while unpacking their lunch. "Had I known, I would've snuck one in."

"Next time." He settled on the chair beside her. "Our floor guy called a half hour ago. They'll begin ripping out the old carpet and installing the new tomorrow." Brad unwrapped a sandwich. "He'll refinish the wood floors as soon as the kitchen remodel is finished. Which means we should be ready to pick out furniture early September."

"Sounds good." One more indication she was running out of excuses. Erica swallowed a bite of chicken salad sandwich. "Abby and Sierra seem to have worked out their differences." She explained.

"It appears my future stepdaughter is a peacemaker like her mom."

Erica stared wide-eyed at Brad.

"Don't look so surprised." He stretched his arm across the space between them and touched her knee. "I know you better than you realize."

Erica's heart drummed in her chest. The time had come. "I want to treat you to dinner at your house tomorrow night."

"To make up for missing out on lunch at a nice restaurant?"

Erica shook her head. "To begin planning an autumn wedding."

A grin spread across Brad's face. "I assume you mean this year."

"Definitely."

"We'll include a honeymoon in our plans."

Erica raised a brow. "Are you able to take time off during the school year?"

"If I was still coaching football—especially if we were in the running for playoffs—I'd be committing the unforgivable. As principal, I'll barely be missed." He kissed her temple. "About tomorrow night. I'll handle dessert."

A tap on the door. "Sorry for interrupting."

Brad turned toward Ashley. "Everything okay?"

"Yes, thanks to you diffusing the situation, class ended peacefully." Ashley eyed Erica. "How's Abby?"

"She's doing well. Let Jimmy know she is continuing to improve."

"He'll be glad to know. By the way, congratulations on your engagement."

"Thank you." Erica's eyes met Brad's. "In a few months, I'll change my name one last time and become Mrs. Erica Barkley."

Two hours after driving to town, Tommy pulled onto the ranch house driveway and parked beside the sidewalk. Abby released her seatbelt. "You were sweet to treat us to lunch."

Sierra leaned close to the front seat. "Thank you both for being my friend."

"You're welcome." Responding in unison with Tommy, Abby caught his eye. "Do you have time to come in?"

He shook his head. "I'm due back on the job." He popped the trunk before stepping onto the driveway.

Abby turned toward the back seat. The baby she had mistakenly believed belonged to her had drifted off to sleep during the drive home.

Sierra climbed out and rushed to the driver's side to release Theo's car seat then headed straight to the front door.

Abby pushed the passenger door open seconds before Tommy moved the wheelchair in place. After she maneuvered onto her ride, Tommy leaned down to kiss her cheek. "I'll come back after work for another tutoring session."

"See you then." Abby wheeled across the sidewalk to the front porch ramp.

Dusty and her mother greeted her in the foyer. "Based on Sierra's mood, I assume everyone had a good time."

"Yeah. Where is she?"

"In her room with the door closed. We need to talk. Privately."

Abby gripped her chair's push ring. "Is something wrong?"

"Not at all."

Relieved, Abby led the way down the hall to her bedroom. "Is this about Sierra?"

"Indirectly." Her mom closed the door before sitting on one of the twin beds. "This morning when I saw the two of you getting along, I realized the time had come for me to stop stalling."

"Oh my gosh." Abby's eyes widened. "You and Mr. Barkley...I mean Brad...picked a date, didn't you?"

"Not yet, but we will tomorrow night." Her mom paused. "I'm curious about what changed between you and Sierra during the past few days."

Abby broke eye contact. "Sierra was one of those girls popular kids made fun of." She explained. "The day after we left Asheville and checked into the Blue Ridge Inn, Hannah showed up when I most needed a friend. I did the same for Sierra." Tears pooled in Abby's eyes. "Even though it hurts like crazy, I've accepted the fact that Theo is her baby, not mine. Although, I did volunteer to be Theo's Aunt Abby."

Her mother grasped her hand. "I couldn't be prouder of you, sweetheart."

"I'm kinda proud of myself." Abby dabbed at the tears sliding down her cheeks. "Now about your wedding..."

Chapter 30

Wendy carried the newly delivered package to the nursery across the hall from their little guy's room with Ryan and Duke following close behind. Eight-inch-wide horizontal swaths of pale pink and white stripes accented the wall where the crib would stand. A crystal chandelier hung from the light blue ceiling featuring fluffy white clouds. "Your baby sister will sleep in a room fit for a princess."

Clutching Wendy's pant leg, Ryan pulled onto his feet. "Baby."

"Your fourth word. Before long you'll be talking a blue streak." Wendy opened the package and removed a pale green bumper pad and matching sheets. "Now all we need is the crib to put these in." She laid the new items on the rocking chair Chris had moved from Ryan's room. "In a few months, I'll rock your sister the same way I rocked you when you were a tiny baby."

Responding to Cynthia's ringtone, Wendy spun away from the playpen, then lifted her phone off the windowsill and pressed FaceTime. "Perfect timing to see the progress on your granddaughter's room. Chris finished painting last weekend." Wendy aimed her phone toward the newly painted wall then up toward the ceiling. "We ordered furniture yesterday."

"Fancy room. "If I hadn't been forced to work two jobs when you were a baby, maybe I could've bought pretty furniture for your room."

Even if I had to work three jobs, I would never abandon my babies. Relieved she hadn't uttered the comment aloud, Wendy turned the phone around. "I'm blessed to have a wonderful husband and an expanded family. How are you feeling?"

"A little weaker this week than last, but relatively pain free. Thank goodness I refused to subject my body to the ravages of chemotherapy to add a few more agonizing weeks to my time on this side of heaven. Enough talk about me. Is Ryan awake?"

"He's right here." Tamping down her emotions, Wendy aimed her phone at the playpen. "Glamma wants to say hi."

Ryan gripped the mesh sides then pulled up to his feet and fingered the phone.

"There's my handsome grandson. Your mommy needs to bring you to Nashville next week so Glamma can love on you."

Surprised by the request, Wendy turned the phone back toward her. "Are you inviting us?"

"I want to spend as much time as possible with you and my grandson. Kayla and Riley will also be happy to see you. If you're available."

Wendy mentally reviewed her schedule. With his father's campaign in full swing and a big trial scheduled to begin next week, Chris couldn't take time off. It didn't matter. She could manage the four-hour drive on her own. "I'll come Monday and stay a couple of days." The doorbell rang, sending Duke scrambling from the room. "Someone's at my front door. I'll call you when I'm on the way."

"I'll treasure every moment I spend with you and my grandbaby."

"Until Monday." She swallowed the lump attacking her throat, pocketed her phone, and rushed to open the door.

"Good morning, Mrs. Armstrong."

"Personal delivery to our door?" Wendy smiled at their mailman. "Must be for Chris."

"Actually, it's addressed to you—certified mail." He thrust a manila envelope and a pen toward her. "I need your John Henry, or better yet your Wendy Armstrong." He grinned, obviously tickled by his joke, and patted Duke's head while Wendy signed the receipt. "Have a good one."

She returned the pen. "You too."

Tentacles of fear crept through her brain the moment she read the return address—a law firm in Hilton Head, South Carolina. Her heart pounded against her ribs while she returned to the nursery and sat on the floor beside the playpen. Wendy peeled back the envelope's flap and pulled out the document, silently praying that nothing bad had happened to her stepmother or her half-brothers. A gasp escaped as she scanned the first page. She squeezed her eyes shut, hoping yet knowing what she'd read hadn't been an illusion.

Startled by her phone's ringtone, Wendy swiped her finger across the screen. "You know, don't you?"

"I can't believe he'd stooped to such a despicable level." Donna's tone screamed of anger. "Does Chris know?"

"Not yet." Wendy slid the document into the envelope. "He'll know what to do to make this go away."

"I hope you're right, for both our sakes."

"Try not to worry. I'll call you tonight with an update." Wendy ended the call then stood and lifted Ryan from the playpen. "We have to make an important stop on the way to the board meeting." She carried him out of the nursery, closing the door behind her. Fifteen minutes later Wendy released her little guy from his car seat and walked into the Armstrong Law Office reception area.

Rosalie looked up from her desk. "What a pleasant surprise."

"Is Chris in his office?"

"He's in the conference room prepping a client for next week's trial. Is everything okay?"

Wendy laid the dreaded envelope on Rosalie's desk. "This was delivered to our house a few minutes ago. Will you make sure Chris gets it before he leaves?"

Rosalie eyed the envelope. "Absolutely."

"Thank you, and tell him I've talked to Donna." Wendy returned to her SUV and secured Ryan in his seat. She slid onto the driver's seat, gripped the steering wheel, and backed onto the street. By the time she parked in the ranch house driveway and opened the rear passenger door, her anxiety had given way to seething anger.

Millie rushed across the side yard and handed Wendy a foil-wrapped plate. "Do you mind if I carry Ryan in?"

"Suit yourself." Wendy scowled while grabbing the diaper bag off the floor.

"Grammy will take good care of you." After Wendy released Ryan, Millie carried him to the carport. She jerked her head around the second Wendy slammed the door closed. "You're mommy's in a mood. Did she have a fight with your daddy?"

Wendy caught up with Millie at the kitchen door. "Chris and I don't fight."

"Something happened to make you madder than a ticked-off polecat." Millie headed straight to the dining room table and sat across from Erica. "Awesam's chief financial officer is having some sort of hissy fit."

Wendy dropped the diaper bag on the floor before setting the plate on the table. "For good reason."

Amanda leaned forward. "What's going on?"

"I'll tell you what's going on." Disgust laced her voice. "After cheating on his wife for years, my poor excuse for a father is suing me and Donna for colluding to destroy his reputation and marriage." Wendy dropped onto a chair. "He claims the collusion began when Chris and I showed up at his house last year claiming I was his daughter."

Erica's eyes widened. "Talk about twisting reality."

"Sounds like a ridiculous lawsuit." Responding to Ryan pulling away from her grasp, Millie lowered him to the floor.

Wendy's eyes followed her little guy while he crawled to the toys stashed in the corner. "Douglas Hewitt is a disgusting human being. The timing couldn't be worse for Chris, with Keith's campaign in full swing and finding the right attorney to take his dad's place."

"Hmm." Millie scooted her chair closer to the table. "Sounds as if your husband could use a little investigative help from the Blue Ridge Mystery Club."

"Don't be ridiculous." Wendy glared at Millie. "You're a book club, not some sort of FBI team."

Millie scoffed. "Like I've explained more than once, the word *book* isn't in our title. Besides, we're likely to turn up enough dirt to help him win the case."

"You know doggone good and well that my husband's firm has their own investigator."

"Who's most likely paid hefty fees for his work." Millie lifted her chin. "A former police officer working the case won't cost Chris a dime."

"Since you brought the subject up—" Amanda folded her arms across the table. "What's really going on between you and Gordon Davenport?"

A mischievous smile curled Millie's lips. "You're worried about losing our bet, aren't you?"

"Answering a question with a question. Clever diversion." Amanda mirrored Millie's expression. "Also revealing."

Millie scoffed. "You're not nearly as smart as you think you are, Ms. President."

"Enough already." Wendy peeled the foil off the plate releasing the sweet scent of oatmeal raisin cookies. "I don't have time to listen to you two carry on over nonsense. So let's get this meeting going."

"Good idea." Amanda opened her laptop. "We'll start with a financial update."

After sharing details about their bottom line, Wendy's brain swirled in expanding circles of thought. What was Douglas Hewitt's real motivation? Would Chris have to fight him in court? Gripping her pant leg, Ryan stood. Wendy lifted him onto her lap then gave him a cookie while eyeing Hilltop's chef's smug expression. Maybe Millie's little band of amateur sleuths digging into her father's life wasn't such a bad idea after all.

Rain clouds had darkened the late afternoon sky by the time Wendy parked in her garage and carried Ryan to the great room. "Your daddy's mood will likely match the weather when he comes home. Which means we need to do a little prep work." She turned on Chris's favorite music then returned to the kitchen, closed her eyes, and pressed her fingers to the pain attacking her temples. Hadn't she endured enough humiliation when forced to admit the truth about Gunter?

Duke's bark announced a car pulling into the garage. forcing Wendy's eyes open. She grabbed a beer from the fridge then pried off the cap and opened the back door. Chris climbed from behind the wheel. His expression made it clear he'd read Douglas Hewitt's accusations. "I figured you'd want something stronger than water."

"Good assumption." Chris swallowed a mouthful while heading to the great room.

Wendy followed him, settling on the sofa beside him as Ryan toddled over. His son's failure to bring a smile to Chris's face told her everything she needed to know. She summoned a breath. "I don't understand why Douglas is drawing attention to Donna filing for divorce. You'd think he'd sign the papers and move on."

"He's a narcissist who's incapable of accepting responsibility for his own failures." Chris lifted his son onto his lap. "Good news for his attorney, since he'll charge him a fortune to stretch this insanity out as long as possible to satisfy his client's inflated ego."

Wendy tucked her ankle under her knee while stretching her arm across the back of the sofa. "I'm sorry you're dragged into this mess."

Chris swallowed another sip of beer before facing Wendy. "By the time we finish, Douglas Hewitt will wish he'd never taken you and your stepmother on."

Chapter 31

Seconds after Erica parked in front of the open garage, Brad rushed from the kitchen then pulled the driver's door open. "Perfect timing." She stepped onto the pavement.

He wrapped his arms around her waist. "I figured the least I could do is help carry in the groceries."

"A team effort." Erica grinned. "Everything's behind my seat."

Brad kissed her before grabbing two bags and a bottle of red wine off the floor.

Erica followed him into the kitchen where Jan had prepared thousands of meals for her family. The dark wood cabinets and marble countertops were a stark contrast to the gray-green cabinets and granite counters Erica had chosen for the home she would share with Brad.

He set the bags on the island. "How'd your board meeting go?"

"You won't believe what's going on with Wendy." Erica detailed everything she knew about the lawsuit.

"The man cheats on his wife, she files for divorce, and now he expects to win a lawsuit against her and Wendy?" Brad uncorked the wine. "Some men don't have the brains God gave a goose."

Erica removed ingredients from the bags. "Douglas Hewitt has no idea that he unleashed a tornado called Millie Cunningham."

"He'll find out soon enough." Brad pulled a bottle of Erica's favorite chardonnay from the fridge and poured two glasses, handing one to Erica. "A toast to begin tonight's celebration."

She swallowed a sip. "What delicious dessert have you chosen for tonight?"

Brad's eyes met hers. "Dark chocolate brownies."

"One of my favorites."

"I know." Brad's grin widened. "I also know you make lists of tasks for the day, you're good at reading people, and you're not crazy about change."

Amazed, Erica gazed into his deep blue eyes. "How—"

"Do I know so much about you, my love?"

"The thought crossed my mind."

"When Jan died, I didn't believe I could ever fall in love again. Until the night I met you at Hilltop Inn's grand opening. From that moment on, everything about you intrigued me. Your beautiful smile. The way you greeted other guests. Your relationship with your daughter."

"The moment you took my hand in yours and introduced yourself as Brad, I had no idea who you were. Until Abby rushed in and called you Mr. Barkley." Erica swallowed another sip. "That's also when I understood why Millie had called you movie-star handsome."

Brad's eyes remained locked on hers while he set his glass on the island. "Is that why you were watching me when I walked away from you and Abby to talk to a friend?"

Erica's brows raised. "You noticed?"

"Only because I turned around to see your beautiful face again."

"Abby called you pretty hot for an old guy."

Brad laughed, his eyes twinkling. "To teenagers everyone over forty is old."

"She also called me a good catch." Erica grinned, her head tilted. "Turns out she was right on both counts."

"At least when it comes to the good-catch part." Brad stroked Erica's cheek, awakening every nerve ending in her body. "God brought you into my life to give me the chance to fall deeply in love for the second time in my life."

Erica set her glass beside Brad's before she laced her fingers around his neck. "You are the first and will be the last man I love with every fiber of my being."

He kissed her tenderly. When their lips parted, he gazed into her eyes as if peering deep into her soul. "We'll spend the rest of our lives making each other happy, my love."

"Yes, we will. Beginning tonight with me preparing you a celebration-worthy dinner." Erica unlaced her fingers. "Thanks to Millie's version of veal parmesan."

"What can I do to help?"

Erica handed him a sheet of paper. "I'll need all of these items."

Brad chuckled. "I was right about you making lists."

"Among other observations." Erica laid out the ingredients while Brad found everything on her list. "You and I are a good team, coach."

"Indeed we are."

An hour after Erica began preparations, she placed Caesar salads, roasted asparagus, and veal parmesan on the table. Satisfied, she slid onto the padded banquette built into the kitchen's bay window.

Brad sat across from her then held her hand while blessing their meal and thanking God for bringing her into his life. Neither Abby's father nor Gunter ever said grace—one more remarkable difference between her exes and Brad Barkley.

Brad gently squeezed her fingers before releasing her hand and pouring two glasses of red wine.

Erica clicked her glass to his. "Enjoy."

He cut a piece of veal and popped it into his mouth, obviously savoring the taste. "I don't know who deserves more accolades—you for preparing this, or Millie for providing the recipe."

"Definitely, Millie. She also had a hand in helping Wendy prepare her first meal for Chris."

"A professional chef in the family is a huge plus."

"Even one as cantankerous as ours." While enjoying their entrée, they talked about their jobs and plans for their new home. When finished, Brad cleared the table before serving the brownies. Erica dug her fork into the dense chocolate. "Delicious. Homemade?"

"That depends." Brad aimed his fork at her. "Does home baked qualify?"

Erica laughed. "Betty Crocker or Duncan Hines?"

"Ghirardelli."

"My new favorite brownie mix."

When he'd swallowed the last bite, Brad pushed away from the table. "As soon as we clean up, what do you say we talk about wedding plans while enjoying another glass of wine on the deck?"

"The perfect spot." Twenty minutes after carrying the dessert plates to the sink, Erica settled beside her fiancé on the cushioned sofa facing the outdoor fireplace. Swatches of pink and orange sky filtered through the trees in the wooded backyard. "I've been thinking about a venue."

Brad slid his arm around her shoulders. "You want an intimate wedding in Hilltop's gazebo, don't you?"

Erica leaned into him, breathing in the subtle scent of his cologne. "How'd you know?"

"The way you talked about Chris and Wendy's gazebo wedding."

"I assume you don't mind an outdoor wedding, even if the weather is a bit cool."

"I'd marry you in the middle of a basketball court if that's what made you happy."

"Under a goal post would make more sense for an ex-football coach." Erica snuggled closer. "Although I'll stick with the English country garden venue. Considering when the work on our home is scheduled to be finished, plus Wendy's October due date, I'm thinking the first Saturday in November is a good date, with Millie catering the reception at the inn."

"I'll mark my calendar."

Erica swirled her wine. "What do you think of Charleston for our honeymoon? It's close enough to drive. There's a ton of history and a lot of restaurants."

Brad squeezed her shoulder. "You've done your homework."

"I'm marrying a high school principal. Homework's required."

He chuckled. "I'll make reservations at the best hotel in South Carolina."

"The one thing that would make our wedding absolutely perfect would be Abby standing by my side as my maid of honor."

"What are the chances?"

"Last week her neurologist added spinal cord stimulation to her physical therapy. He told us the prospect of a full recovery has moved from well above average to—given enough time—highly probable."

"How did Abby respond to the news?"

"She wanted to know if he meant months or years, which he couldn't predict." Erica paused for a long moment. "I'm counting on her fierce determination to result in the former."

Amanda peered out the sliding glass door at light spilling onto the patio from the outdoor post lantern. Her mind drifted to the morning she and Wendy sat in Gunter's New Orleans house, making a list of what was left of their meager assets. Until Morgan asked what they each wanted to accomplish personally. Wendy had shared her dream of becoming a businesswoman whom people looked up to, and now she was a successful chief financial officer close to earning a college degree.

Amanda spun away from the glass. During the past eighteen months, she had achieved her goal to become financially independent and control her own destiny. More than a decade had passed since she'd lost the love of her life. Still, everything she'd accomplished since leaving New Orleans failed to fill the void Preston's death left in her heart.

Erica's footsteps followed the kitchen door opening and closing. "It's almost midnight. I'm surprised you're still awake."

"I couldn't sleep." Amanda moved away from the sliding glass door then leaned back against the sofa. "How'd dinner go?"

"Millie's recipe was a big hit."

"What about the wedding plans?"

"The first weekend in November." Erica ambled beside Amanda, facing the fireplace. "I still say two Awesam weddings in the gazebo is a pattern. Three and it becomes a tradition. By the way, when are you seeing Gary again?"

"He called a couple of hours ago. We're meeting tomorrow at two for lunch. In case you have some wacky idea rolling around in your head for another planning meeting."

"With or without your candidate?"

"Without." Amanda pushed off the back of the sofa. "Keith's tied up in court."

"Of course, he is."

Amanda huffed. "What's that comment supposed to mean?"

"Convenient for Gary." Erica turned toward the hall while flicking her hand over her shoulder. "I'm just saying."

Rolling her eyes, Amanda waited for Erica to leave before making her way to her bedroom and quietly closing the door. While she changed into her pajamas, Erica's comment resonated for a brief moment until common sense returned. She and Gary were campaign partners. Nothing more. Besides, she had given her heart away a long time ago.

Chapter 32

Counting on a brisk walk to clear her mind, Amanda parked two long blocks from the restaurant. Dreams of Preston had awakened her twice during the night. The first involved remodeling their shotgun house. Happy memories. The second depicted the phone call that had sent her racing to the hospital to hold his hand while he slipped into eternity.

Adjusting her sunglasses against the bright afternoon sun, Amanda stepped onto the sidewalk fronting the park and turned toward the train station. At least summers in North Georgia were far less humid than those of New Orleans. She crossed Depot Street then headed up East Main, passing by tourists meandering in and out of stores. Good news for the local economy and Hilltop Inn's occupancy rate.

A middle-aged couple holding hands walked past her. She and Preston had held hands numerous times while strolling along the Mississippi River. It had been months since she last dreamed of him. Why last night? Amanda stepped up her pace until she arrived at Harvest on Main. The dreams had likely been triggered by Erica's comment about today's meeting. Whatever the reason, she had to tuck the past away and focus on today.

Amanda pushed her sunglasses up while climbing onto the restaurant porch. The hostess escorted her inside to a table tucked in the corner.

Always the gentleman, Gary stood until she settled across from him.

"I hope I'm not late."

"You're right on time. Thanks for meeting me on such short notice."

"Life as a campaign manager." Amanda hung her purse over the back of the chair. "What's going on?"

"A couple of important issues have surfaced."

This is definitely not a date. "I'm listening."

"First, an anonymous donor infused Watson's campaign with enough money to pay for local television ads—a clear indication the donor considers Keith a threat."

"For good reason. Fortunately, we have a fundraising dinner scheduled next weekend. As of this morning, fifty-eight people have made reservations. I assume that's a good turnout for a small town."

"Better than good. One of my banking customers is a professional videographer. He'll help us create our own ads for a nominal fee."

Amanda wrapped her fingers around her water glass. "Good lawyer versus bad lawyer theme?"

"Something like that."

The waiter approached. "Are you folks ready to order?"

Amanda glanced at the menu. "I'll have the harvest salad."

"Make it two." Gary's eyes remained focused on Amanda while their waiter collected the menus and walked away.

"You said there are a couple of issues."

"Yesterday, Watson hired a new campaign manager." Gary paused. "Which could become a problem."

"Why? Is he some sort of criminal?"

"She. Her name's Melissa Grovner, a residential real estate agent."

Amanda raised a brow. "What sort of problem could a woman who sells houses give our candidate?"

"Not Keith. Me."

Amanda stared wide-eyed at Gary. "Do you have a history with this woman?"

"Big time." Gary leaned forward, his arms propped on the table. "Melissa and I dated all through our junior and senior years. When I left for college, she had it in her mind that we'd end up married after I graduated."

"Same issue Chris had with Britany Livingston before he met Wendy. Her mother and Linda are close friends, which complicated the issue. At some point Britany accepted the fact that Chris didn't love her. Now she's happily married to a guy who adores her."

"Too bad I can't claim the same outcome." Despite no one sitting close to them, Gary's voice was barely above a whisper. "My ex—"

"What's her name?"

"Brenda. Anyway, we began dating casually toward the end of our sophomore year. Being a dumb college kid, I continued to date Melissa during summer breaks." Gary paused for a long moment. "Until my junior year when the relationship with Brenda turned serious."

"Let me guess. When you came home between your junior and senior year, you told Melissa about your new girlfriend."

Gary nodded. "Needless to say, she was ticked off as well as humiliated."

"A dangerous combination for a scorned woman."

"As I soon discovered. A couple of days after I told Melissa about Brenda, she showed up at the sheriff's office with a nasty bruise on her arm and accused me of hitting her. She demanded a restraining order."

Amanda's brow wrinkled.

"In case you're wondering, Melissa lied."

Had he read her expression as doubt? "I can't imagine you hitting a woman."

"For good reason." Gary's eyes locked on hers. "I never have and I never will."

"I believe you. What happened after Melissa's false accusation?"

"Turned out the time she claimed I abused her, I'd been hiking with the sheriff's son. Unfortunately, Melissa had used the allegation to explain to her friends why she broke up with me. When the truth surfaced, she dug in, claiming the sheriff was prejudiced."

"That happened nearly three decades ago. You don't think she's still mad at you, do you?"

"She divorced her second husband last year. Based on rumors, her relationship with her two daughters is more than a little strained. The biggest irony? When news of Brenda's affair surfaced, she and my ex became friends."

"In other words—" Amanda tapped her finger on the table. "Melissa's a bitter woman who's still caught up in a small-town soap opera."

"Watson's attempt to disgrace Keith failed, so he's targeting his campaign team."

Amanda stopped tapping. "You're not quitting the campaign, are you?"

"And validate her lie? Not a chance."

"Thank goodness." Amanda's muscles relaxed. "Does Keith know what's going on?"

"I filled him in first thing this morning. He's counting on us to devise a plan to counter any false accusations Watson's new campaign manager might try to use against us."

Amanda leaned back. "If I ever have the slightest inclination to run for political office, I'll count on you to talk some sense into me."

"You've got it. Although with me as your partner, you couldn't lose."

Partner? Befuddled by Gary's comment and his smile, Amanda broke eye contact while absently running her finger along her jawline. He meant *campaign* partner, didn't he? Of course, he did. *Besides, I'm a forty-four-year-old woman, not a silly teenager on a date with the most popular guy in town.*

"Do you have a plan in mind?"

Sensing her cheeks were seconds from turning bright pink, Amanda blinked. "What?"

Gary leaned closer, still smiling. "Ideas to counter our opponent."

Had he noticed her reaction? "The truth works."

"For honest politicians."

"Good point." Amanda eyed their waiter approaching with their meal. Grateful for the well-timed disruption, Amanda shifted the conversation to the fundraising dinner and campaign strategies. When finished she insisted the waiter split the bill in half.

A bemused grin curled Gary's lips. "As Keith's finance manager, I have the authority to cover lunch as a campaign expense."

"Better to reserve the cash in the event our opponent pulls more dirty tricks."

After they each paid their share, Gary donned his sunglasses as they made their way to the front porch and down the ramp to the sidewalk. "Where did you park?"

Amanda nodded toward the right. "Past the train station. I might do a little shopping before heading home."

"Hopefully, Watson will behave himself for a couple of days."

Amanda lowered her sunglasses. "Before we're through with him, he'll rue the day he took us on."

Gary laughed. "I've always heard redheads are fiery. You're proving the rumor has merit. Until Saturday." He turned away, walking in the opposite direction from her truck. Three steps past the restaurant's entrance, he glanced back at her, smiling.

Surprisingly pleased, Amanda returned the smile. If she were fishing, Gary Redding would make a great catch. Even though she had no intention of baiting the hook now or maybe never, at least she would enjoy his company. She waited for him to disappear around the corner before walking away. A block from the restaurant, she stopped to peer into a boutique window. She could barely remember the last time she'd bought a new outfit. Two hours after giving in to temptation, Amanda pulled up into the ranch house driveway the same moment Erica returned from the spa.

"How was lunch?"

"Interesting." Amanda pulled three shopping bags off the truck's passenger seat before climbing out.

"Based on all those purchases, you either shopped to commiserate or to celebrate."

Amanda shrugged while walking into the kitchen. "The mood struck; I reacted." She set the bags on the counter then padded to the den sofa. "Our opponent is up to dirty tricks again."

Erica sat beside her, her eyes widening while Amanda relayed details about Watson's new campaign manager. "You have to admit Gary Redding is a fascinating man."

"Which makes him a good campaign partner." Amanda kicked off her shoes before propping her feet on the coffee table. "In case you're wondering, today was a business meeting, not a date."

"Then why did your eyes light up every time you mentioned Gary's name?"

Amanda rolled her eyes. "You're delusional."

"We've lived together for eighteen plus months. I know when you're in a good mood."

Amanda shrugged. "Why wouldn't I be after treating myself to a shopping spree for the first time in who knows how many years."

"That day at Blue Ridge Inn when you, Wendy, and I learned we were illegally married to Gunter, I swore I would never trust another man." Turning toward Amanda, Erica stretched her arm across the back of the sofa. "Then I met Brad and realized my heart had merely been damaged, not destroyed."

"You deserved a second chance—make that a third—to find true love." Amanda stared straight ahead. "As for me, I had my chance years ago when I met Preston. Now I'm perfectly content living as an independent, single woman."

"Perhaps. However, I can't help but wonder if Preston would want you to spend the rest of your life alone."

"He'd want me to do whatever makes me happy." Amanda closed her eyes, hoping to summon her soulmate's image, as she had hundreds of times before. She waited. An image emerged, but it wasn't Preston's. Her pulse accelerated. The face filling her mind's eye belonged to Gary Redding.

Chapter 33

Monday morning before dawn, Wendy tiptoed from the bedroom to the den with Duke padding behind her. She breathed in the rich aroma of dark roast coffee brewing for Chris while popping a decaf pod in the Keurig, her go-to coffee maker during pregnancy. After adding creamer and sweetener, she carried her mug to the French doors. A gas lantern cast a warm glow on the deck overlooking their heavily wooded backyard.

Chris eased behind her and wrapped his arms around her chest.

Wendy leaned against him. "I hope I didn't wake you."

"You didn't. Are you any less anxious about your trip now than you were last night?"

"Not really. All those wasted years, and now that we've reconnected…" Wendy pressed her hand to her baby bulge. "Losing my mother a second time feels far more painful than the first."

"During the next few days, you'll have a chance to create new memories to replace the old."

"All good, I hope."

Duke scrambling from the great room to the bedroom hall made it clear Ryan had awakened.

Chris released Wendy. "I'll take care of our boy."

She turned, her eyes meeting his. "While I prepare his daddy's standard pre-trial breakfast."

"Lucky me, marrying the sexiest short-order cook in town."

Wendy tilted her head. "You always know how to make a pregnant lady smile."

Chris stroked her cheek then headed straight to their son's room.

Spending the next three nights two hundred miles away from the man she loved with all her heart tugged at Wendy's heartstrings. Hopefully, the time would pass quickly for her and for Chris. She traipsed to the kitchen and removed a carton of eggs from the fridge. Humming to calm her nerves, Wendy focused on finishing the task at hand.

"Our little guy is ready for breakfast." Chris ambled in and lowered Ryan into his high chair.

"Breakfast number one is served." Wendy set a plate of two over-easy eggs and dry toast along with a mug of black coffee on the counter in front of Chris's stool. "Time to take an order for number two." She poured orange juice into a sippy cup and placed it on the high-chair tray. "Would you like scrambled eggs and toast before our big trip?"

Ryan giggled while lifting his cup to his mouth.

"I'll take your response as a yes." After preparing her baby's food, Wendy refreshed Chris's coffee then settled on the stool beside him. "Has your dad said much about DA Watson's latest gimmick?"

"Only that he's more determined than ever to defeat him."

"At some point after Keith replaces him, you two will end up on opposite sides in a courtroom."

"Something I'm definitely not looking forward to. Not only because he's my father, but he's also a darn good attorney." Chris sipped his coffee. "Which makes hiring his replacement a big deal."

"Are you any closer to a decision?"

"We've narrowed candidates to a young man who graduated law school four years ago and a fifty-three-year-old woman who wants to leave public service and go into private practice."

"Do you have a preference?"

"I'm leaning toward experience." Chris glanced at his watch. "Time to get ready for today's trial. Thanks for breakfast, angel." He carried his mug to their bedroom. Twenty minutes later he returned and kissed Wendy's cheek. "Text me when you arrive, and tell the Gilmore family hi for me."

"I will."

Chris hugged his son before grabbing his briefcase and heading to the garage.

Wendy released a long sigh while lifting Ryan into her arms. "I don't know who will miss your daddy more, you or your mommy. Now it's time for us to figure out what to pack."

At eight o'clock Wendy stashed two suitcases, Ryan's overstuffed diaper bag, and his stroller in the back of her SUV before returning to the great room. Their black Lab sprawling on the floor beside Ryan peered up at her. She stooped to pat his head. "You know we're going away, don't you?" His tail brushed the floor one time before he laid his head on his front paws. Wendy gathered her little guy into her arms. "Tell Duke bye-bye."

Ryan tapped his fingers to his palm. "Doggie. Bye-bye."

"You're the smartest one-year-old on the planet." Wendy carried Ryan to the garage and secured him in his car seat facing an interactive toy. "Hopefully this will keep you busy until the motion lulls you to sleep." She patted her little guy's cheek then closed the door and slid behind the steering wheel. After entering the Gilmores' address into her phone app, Wendy pressed Cynthia's number.

She answered at the second ring. "Are you on the way?"

"We're leaving now."

"Drive carefully. You're carrying precious cargo."

"I will." Wendy ended the call then peered over the back seat. "In four hours we'll be in Nashville visiting the family I had no idea existed until a year ago."

A fluttering sensation assailed Wendy's chest the moment she turned onto the familiar driveway. "We're here." Having awakened a half hour earlier, Ryan babbled a response while she climbed out and opened the back door. "Glamma Cynthia will be happy to see you." Wendy released her little guy from his seat.

When they were halfway to the porch, the front door flew open. Riley scurried toward them. "Can my little nephew walk by himself?"

"Yes, especially if someone holds his hand."

Riley peered up at Wendy, her eyes pleading. "Can I, please?"

"Of course." Wendy lowered her son to the sidewalk and placed his hand in Riley's. "Aunt Riley's gonna walk with you."

"Me and Mommy bought you some toys."

Wendy controlled her conflicting emotions as best she could while following her sister and son into the Gilmores' foyer. The first time she had walked into the Gilmores' house, she had never expected to return. Now here she was for the third time. Would it be the last before—

"Look at our big boy." Cynthia emerged from the back of the house. "I believe he's grown an inch or two since I last saw him." She stooped to pat Ryan's cheek, then straightened. "I'm glad you're here safe and sound." She embraced Wendy.

"So am I."

"How's my granddaughter?" The moment Cynthia pressed her hand to Wendy's belly, the baby kicked as if reacting to her grandmother's touch. "Oh my." Cynthia's face beamed. "She's an active little gal. Maybe she knows it's lunchtime. I hope you like mac and cheese, Riley's favorite lunch. I added a salad for us grown-ups."

"Sounds delicious."

Cynthia led the way to the kitchen. "We brought Riley's high chair down from the attic. I figured Ryan's too active to sit on my lap during an entire meal. Same as Zach when he was that age." Cynthia continued to talk a blue streak about random topics until they finished eating. "It's such a lovely day. Do you mind sitting out back?"

"Great idea. After I bring my bags in and change Ryan."

"Riley, honey, you go help your big sister, then join me in the backyard."

"Okay." Riley grasped Wendy's hand while they headed through the foyer and out the front door. "Kayla says Mommy's getting better. Zach says she's gonna die soon. I think Kayla's right."

At a loss for words, Wendy swallowed the fist-sized lump erupting in her throat.

"I'll race you." Riley pulled her hand away from Wendy's before dashing to the driveway.

Relieved the nine-year-old didn't expect a response, Wendy stepped up her pace.

"I won."

Catching up with Riley at her SUV, Wendy opened the back hatch. "You're a fast runner."

"Not as fast as Zach. Is the little bag Ryan's?"

"Uh-huh." After Wendy set both suitcases on the driveway and released the handles, Riley pulled the smaller bag up the driveway to the front sidewalk. Wendy shouldered the diaper bag then followed her little sister to the combination kitchen and den. Riley sprinted out the French doors.

Grateful for a few minutes alone, Wendy changed her little guy's diaper. After covering them both with sunscreen, she donned a visor and sunglasses then stepped out to the back deck. Riley raced over. "Can I carry him?"

Wendy hesitated.

"I'm strong, and I promise I won't drop him."

"All right." After transferring Ryan to his aunt's arms, Wendy's focus remained glued on the pair until Riley reached the elaborate playset tucked in the corner beside a wooden fence. Relieved, she settled on a white rocking chair beside her mother then eyed the array of pots displaying colorful plants.

"Yesterday, we reattached the baby swing for Ryan." Cynthia leaned back on a blue pillow.

"It's fun watching Riley play with her nephew."

"My youngest has always had a special place in her heart for babies. Can't say the same thing about Zach. Over the past few months, he's been angry most all the time. Brent says he's going through a phase. In my opinion, he's having a hard time dealing with the inevitable."

"At least Riley seems unaffected."

"Other than you, Riley's my most optimistic child. Kayla's somewhere in between her brother and little sister. She's hopeful, but not in total denial."

"Kayla's a perceptive girl."

"So I've noticed." Cynthia set her rocking chair in motion. "Sometimes when I watched you play on our apartment building's tiny front lawn, I dreamed of living in a fancy house with a big backyard. By the time my dream came true, I was too self-absorbed to be a proper mother to my children." Cynthia paused, adjusting her sunglasses. "At least I wasn't as bad as my mother."

Wendy glanced at her mother's clenched jaw. "I remember riding the bus to visit her, but I have no memories about ever seeing your father."

"For good reason." Cynthia remained silent for a long moment, as if debating whether or not to explain. "My mother killed him."

Wendy gasped. "How? Why?"

"With a pair of scissors. I suppose because she finally got fed up with him beating her up. I was nine when they locked her behind bars. Thirteen when they let her out. She came home sick and enraged at her attorney's failure to convince a jury she wasn't guilty. I expect her lousy attitude did more to sway them than her lawyer's incompetence." Cynthia adjusted her sunglasses. "I always knew she was happy when she called me her sweet Cindy Marie."

"I didn't know you had a middle name."

"There's a lot you don't know about me. Most of it not so good." Cynthia fell silent for a long moment. "I suppose you wouldn't be surprised to learn I cheated on my husband."

That she cheated? No. That her mother trusted her with the news? Definitely.

"It happened a year after Riley was born—with a man I'd met at the gym. I convinced myself Brent was to blame for spending so much time building our business. Truth was, I finally came to terms with the painful fact that I would never be a famous singer."

Ironic. My father cheated on his wife and my mother cheated on her husband. "Does Brent know?"

"About the affair?" Cynthia nodded. "It took a while, but he eventually forgave me. Turned out he's a much better person than I am."

Hesitant to face her mother, Wendy focused on Ryan giggling while his aunt pushed him in the baby swing. When it came, her voice was soft. "Forgiveness is good for the soul."

Cynthia's gentle rocking came to a halt. Silence hung for a beat before she spoke, her voice hoarse. "I've committed two offenses I believed could never be forgiven."

"I—"

"Let me finish," Cynthia whispered, her hand trembling in her lap. "Please. I don't know if I'll be strong enough to say it again." She paused, drawing a shaky breath. "When I met Brent, I thought he was my way out. My chance to start over. To chase the life I thought I deserved. And I was terrified that if he found out I had a child, he'd leave. So, I made the most cowardly choice imaginable." Her voice cracked. "I walked away from you."

A hush settled between them, thick with unsaid pain. Wendy's throat tightened, but she stayed quiet, sensing there was more—something heavier still to come.

Cynthia's jaw clenched as if holding back a flood. Then she turned, her eyes shadowed behind her sunglasses. "My second offense..." Her voice faltered. "I told him you had died. I'm so, so sorry, Wendy. For all the years, for all the silence, for every birthday and Christmas and scraped knee I wasn't there for you. For not being the mother you deserved."

Tears slipped from beneath Wendy's sunglasses. She reached up and slowly pulled them off, meeting her mother's eyes. "I forgive you, Mom." Her voice thick with emotion, she continued, "Because the only thing that matters now is the relationship we build from this moment forward."

Cynthia's breath caught, her face crumpling with a mix of relief and sorrow. She stood and held out her hand. "Come with me. There's something I want you to see."

Wendy hesitated, glancing back toward the laughter.

"Please, it will only take a couple of minutes."

Wendy looked at her mother's outstretched hand—fragile, trembling, hopeful. "Okay," she whispered. She took her mother's hand, the warmth reassuring her as they walked inside together.

In the quiet of the house, Cynthia led her into the living room. "There." She nodded toward the piano.

Wendy turned—and gasped.

Among the framed family photographs, one new picture had been carefully placed as if it had always belonged there. A photo of her, Chris, and Ryan, all smiling, full of life and love. Wendy pressed a hand to her chest. "Oh, Mom..." Tears streamed freely now, unashamed, cleansing.

She turned to Cynthia, her voice barely audible through her tears. "This is the most beautiful gift you could ever give me."

"You are my daughter." Cynthia's voice trembled. "Along with you, your wonderful husband, your son, and my future granddaughter. You are now and will always be part of this family. Forever."

Wendy reached out and clasped both of her mother's hands.

"My darling Wendy," Cynthia whispered, tears spilling down her cheeks, "I don't deserve your grace. But I thank God every day that He's given me a second chance. I only pray He lets me live long enough to hold my granddaughter in my arms."

Wendy nodded, unable to speak. She pulled her mother into a hug, holding her tightly as if trying to make up for every year lost. When she finally found her voice, it came out in a whisper of fierce, unwavering love. "I pray the same prayer with all my heart, Mom."

PAT NICHOLS

Thank you for continuing to follow the Awesam partners as they experience new challenges and adventures. This series will continue with new books every year. Whispers of Hope, book seven, will publish in October 2025. You preorder the eBook now.

Acknowledgements

When I retired from the corporate world in 2005, I had planned to relax, sleep late, and complete our travel bucket list; until the loss of a close family friend inspired me to write *Jenny's Grace*, a fictional story loosely based on her life. That experience led me to come out of retirement, follow my dream to write, and launch a new career as a novelist. I am grateful for the amazing people who are traveling on this journey with me.

My editor, Sherri Stewart is a wonderful partner who overcomes my punctuation challenges and inspires me to take my work to new levels. Elaina Lee, my cover designer, has created all of my covers. Both women are a joy to work with.

My beta readers, Pat Davis, Bev Feldkamp, Carlene Dunn, Kitty Metzger, Kathy Warner, CJ Bruce, Zanase Duncan, and Lynn Worley provided excellent feedback and suggestions for *Summer of Second Chances* before I sent the manuscript to my editor. My dedicated launch team members are always the first to post reviews, which help new readers discover my series. My newsletter friends and readers' loyalty always make my heart sing.

A special thanks to my high-school-sweetheart husband for smiling when I talk about my characters as if they were on the way over for dinner. I'm grateful to my family whose encouragement helps me prove it's never too late to follow your dreams.

Above all I'm grateful to God for His amazing grace, his Son, and the gift of eternal life.

www.ingramcontent.com/pod-product-compliance
Lightning Source LLC
LaVergne TN
LVHW041913070526
838199LV00051BA/2602